MARVEL

AVENGERS ASSEMBLE™

TIME WILL TELL

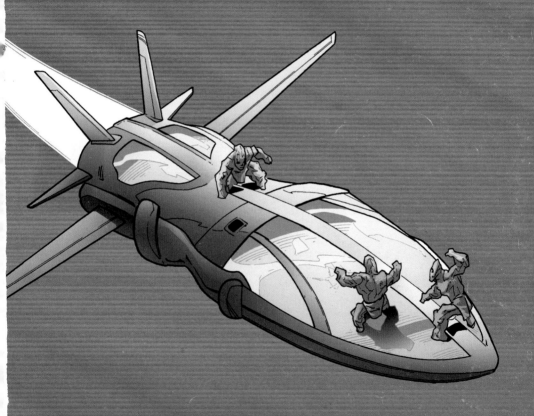

MARVEL

AVENGERS ASSEMBLE™

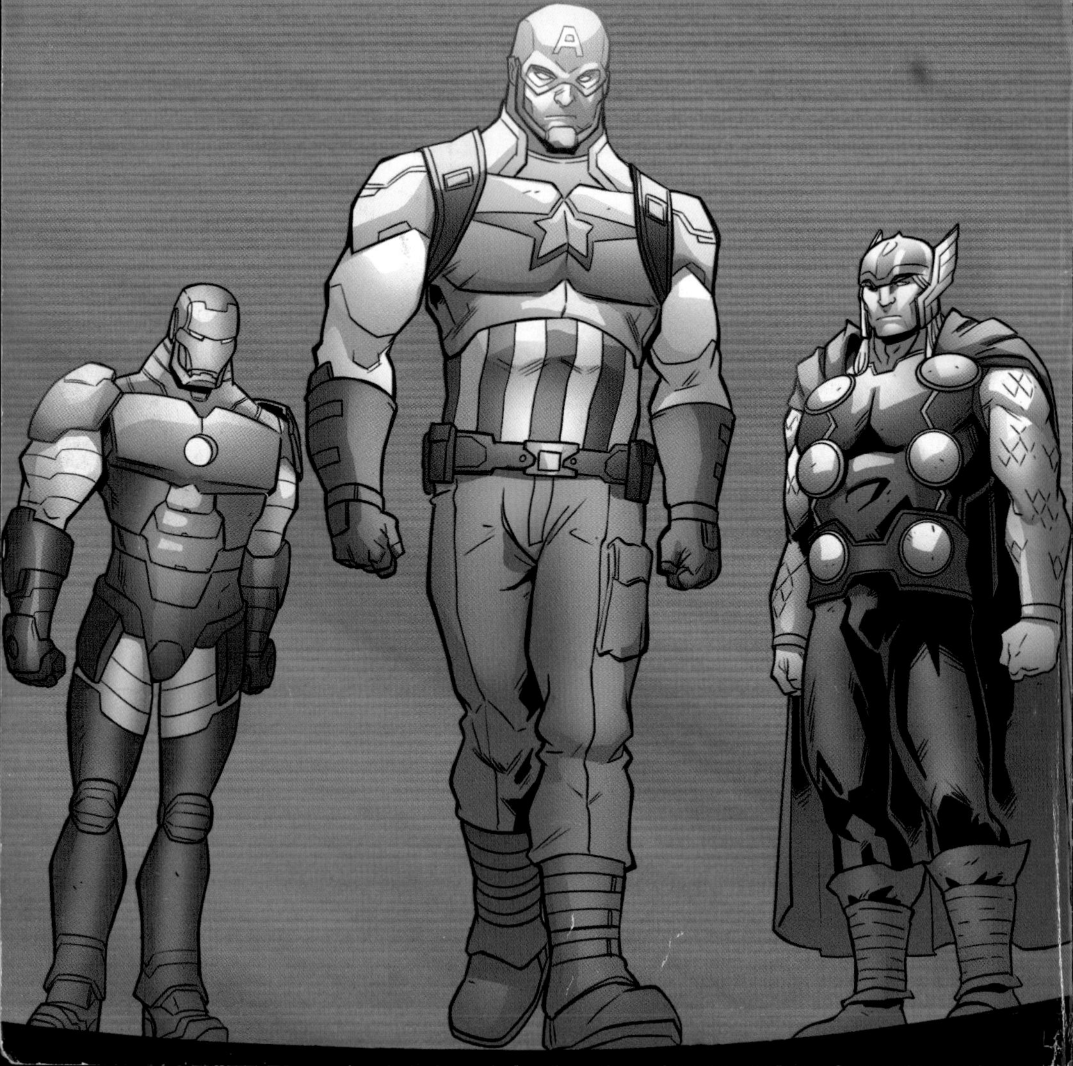

TIME WILL TELL

Buddy Scalera, Joe Caramagna & Ralph Macchio
WRITERS

Ron Lim, Mario Del Pennino, Craig Rousseau & Scott Hanna
PENCILERS

Chris Sotomayor, Guru-eFX & Carlos Lopez
COLORISTS

VC's Joe Sabino & Joe Caramagna
LETTERERS

Katherine Brown
PROJECT MANAGER

Darren Sanchez
EDITOR

Avengers created by Stan Lee & Jack Kirby

COLLECTION EDITOR: **JENNIFER GRÜNWALD**
ASSISTANT EDITOR: **CAITLIN O'CONNELL**
ASSOCIATE MANAGING EDITOR: **KATERI WOODY**
EDITOR, SPECIAL PROJECTS: **MARK D. BEAZLEY**

VP PRODUCTION & SPECIAL PROJECTS: **JEFF YOUNGQUIST**
SVP PRINT, SALES & MARKETING: **DAVID GABRIEL**
BOOK DESIGNER: **ADAM DEL RE**

EDITOR IN CHIEF: **C.B. CEBULSKI**
CHIEF CREATIVE OFFICER: **JOE QUESADA**
PRESIDENT: **DAN BUCKLEY**
EXECUTIVE PRODUCER: **ALAN FINE**

AVENGERS ASSEMBLE: TIME WILL TELL. First printing 2018. ISBN 978-1-302-91276-5. Published by MARVEL WORLDWIDE, INC., a subsidiary of MARVEL ENTERTAINMENT, LLC. OFFICE OF PUBLICATION: 135 West 50th Street, New York, NY 10020. **Printed in the U.S.A.** DAN BUCKLEY, President, Marvel Entertainment; JOHN NEE, Publisher; JOE QUESADA, Chief Creative Officer; TOM BREVOORT, SVP of Publishing; DAVID BOGART, SVP of Business Affairs & Operations, Publishing & Partnership; DAVID GABRIEL, SVP of Sales & Marketing, Publishing; JEFF YOUNGQUIST, VP of Production & Special Projects; DAN CARR, Executive Director of Publishing Technology; ALEX MORALES, Director of Publishing Operations; DAN EDINGTON, Managing Editor; SUSAN CRESPI, Production Manager; STAN LEE, Chairman Emeritus. For information regarding advertising in Marvel Comics or on Marvel.com, please contact Vit DeBellis, Custom Solutions & Integrated Advertising Manager, at vdebellis@marvel.com. For Marvel subscription inquiries, please call 888-511-5480. **Manufactured between 9/28/2018 and 10/30/2018 by SHERIDAN, CHELSEA, MI, USA.**

10 9 8 7 6 5 4 3 2 1

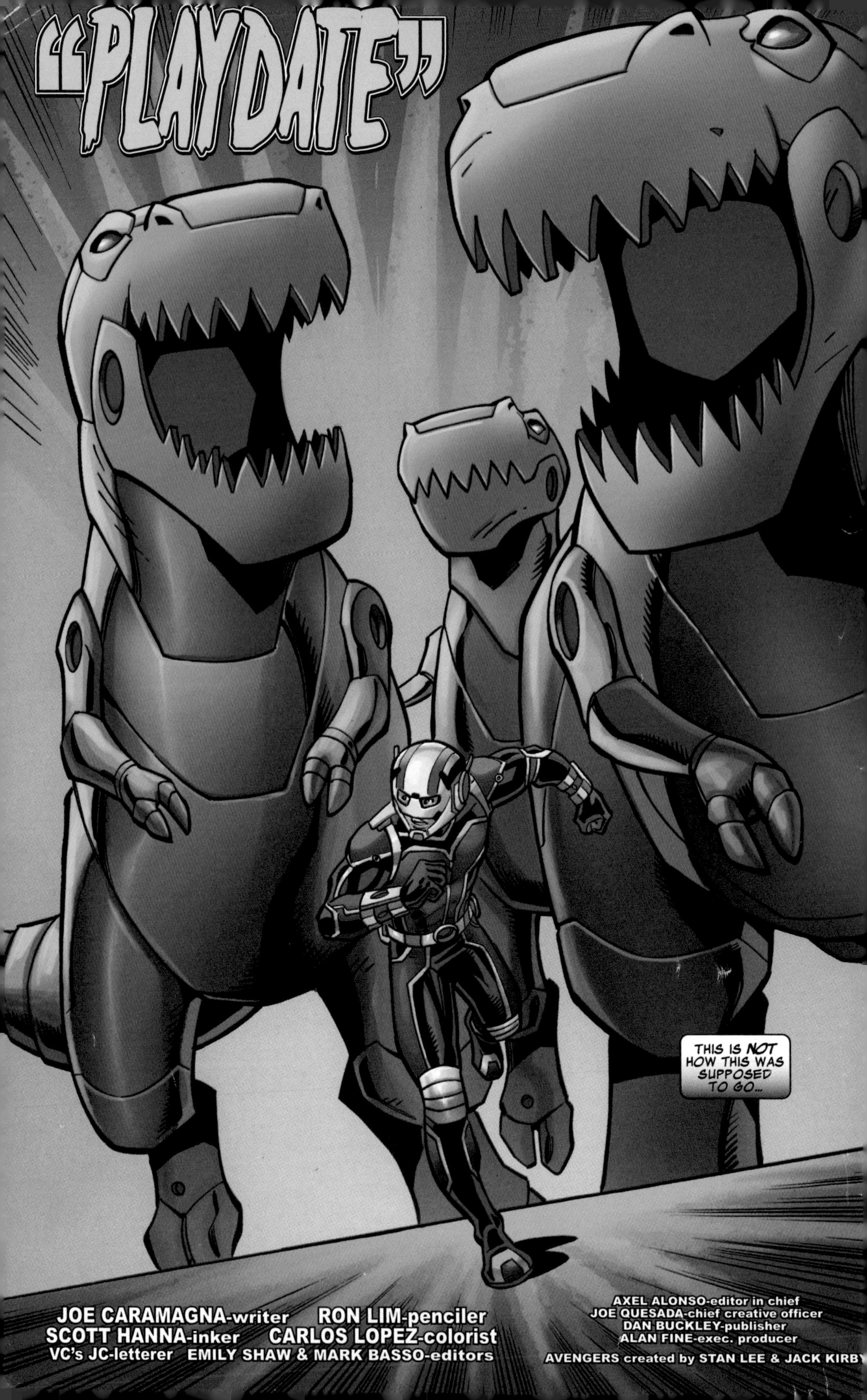
"PLAYDATE"
THIS IS NOT HOW THIS WAS SUPPOSED TO GO...
JOE CARAMAGNA-writer RON LIM-penciler
SCOTT HANNA-inker CARLOS LOPEZ-colorist
VC's JC-letterer EMILY SHAW & MARK BASSO-editors
AXEL ALONSO-editor in chief
JOE QUESADA-chief creative officer
DAN BUCKLEY-publisher
ALAN FINE-exec. producer
AVENGERS created by STAN LEE & JACK KIRBY

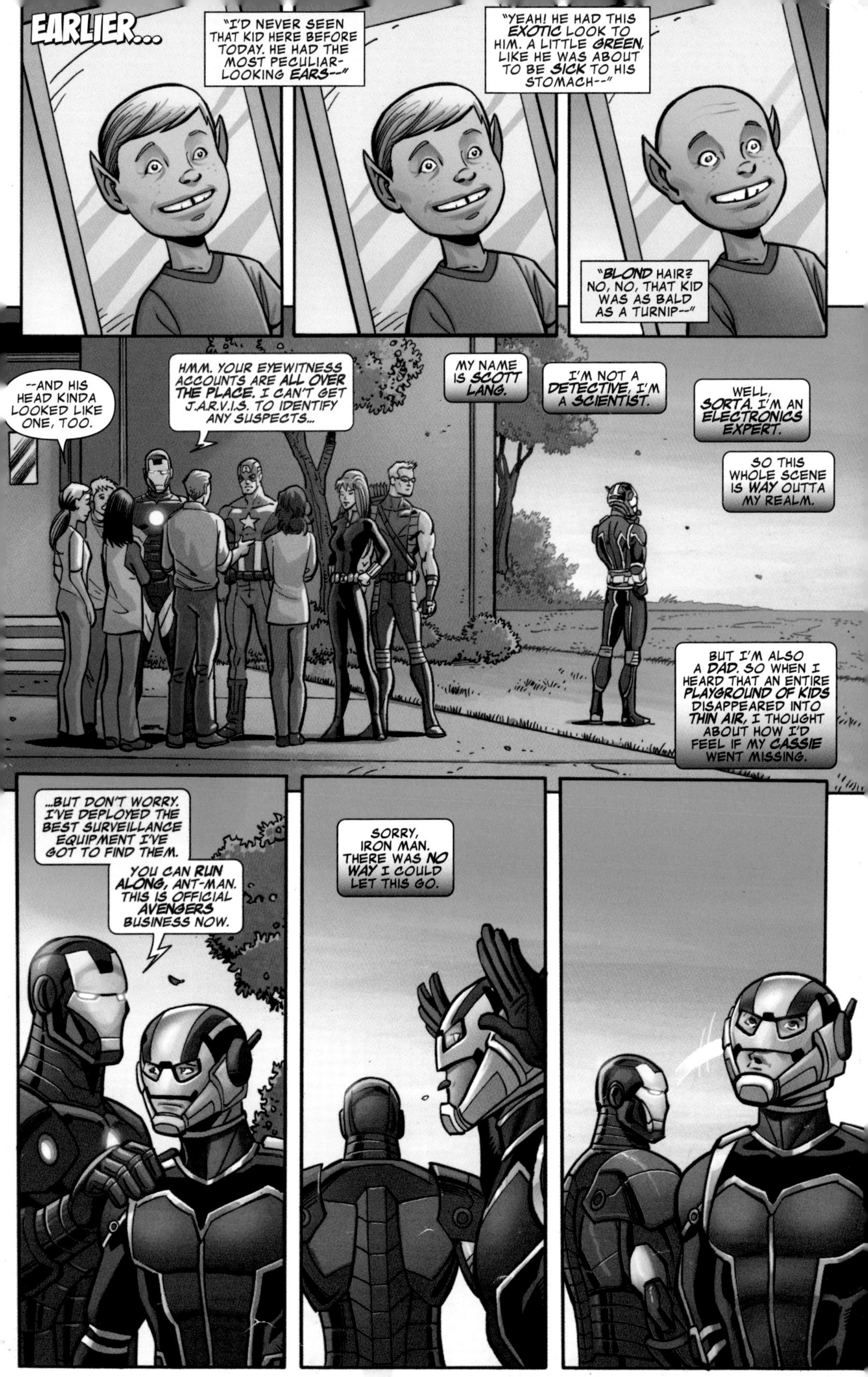
EARLIER...
"I'D NEVER SEEN THAT KID HERE BEFORE TODAY. HE HAD THE MOST PECULIAR-LOOKING EARS--"
"YEAH! HE HAD THIS EXOTIC LOOK TO HIM. A LITTLE GREEN, LIKE HE WAS ABOUT TO BE SICK TO HIS STOMACH--"
"BLOND HAIR? NO, NO, THAT KID WAS AS BALD AS A TURNIP--"
--AND HIS HEAD KINDA LOOKED LIKE ONE, TOO.
HMM. YOUR EYEWITNESS ACCOUNTS ARE ALL OVER THE PLACE. I CAN'T GET J.A.R.V.I.S. TO IDENTIFY ANY SUSPECTS...
MY NAME IS SCOTT LANG.
I'M NOT A DETECTIVE, I'M A SCIENTIST.
WELL, SORTA. I'M AN ELECTRONICS EXPERT.
SO THIS WHOLE SCENE IS WAY OUTTA MY REALM.
BUT I'M ALSO A DAD. SO WHEN I HEARD THAT AN ENTIRE PLAYGROUND OF KIDS DISAPPEARED INTO THIN AIR, I THOUGHT ABOUT HOW I'D FEEL IF MY CASSIE WENT MISSING.
...BUT DON'T WORRY. I'VE DEPLOYED THE BEST SURVEILLANCE EQUIPMENT I'VE GOT TO FIND THEM.
YOU CAN RUN ALONG, ANT-MAN. THIS IS OFFICIAL AVENGERS BUSINESS NOW.
SORRY, IRON MAN. THERE WAS NO WAY I COULD LET THIS GO.

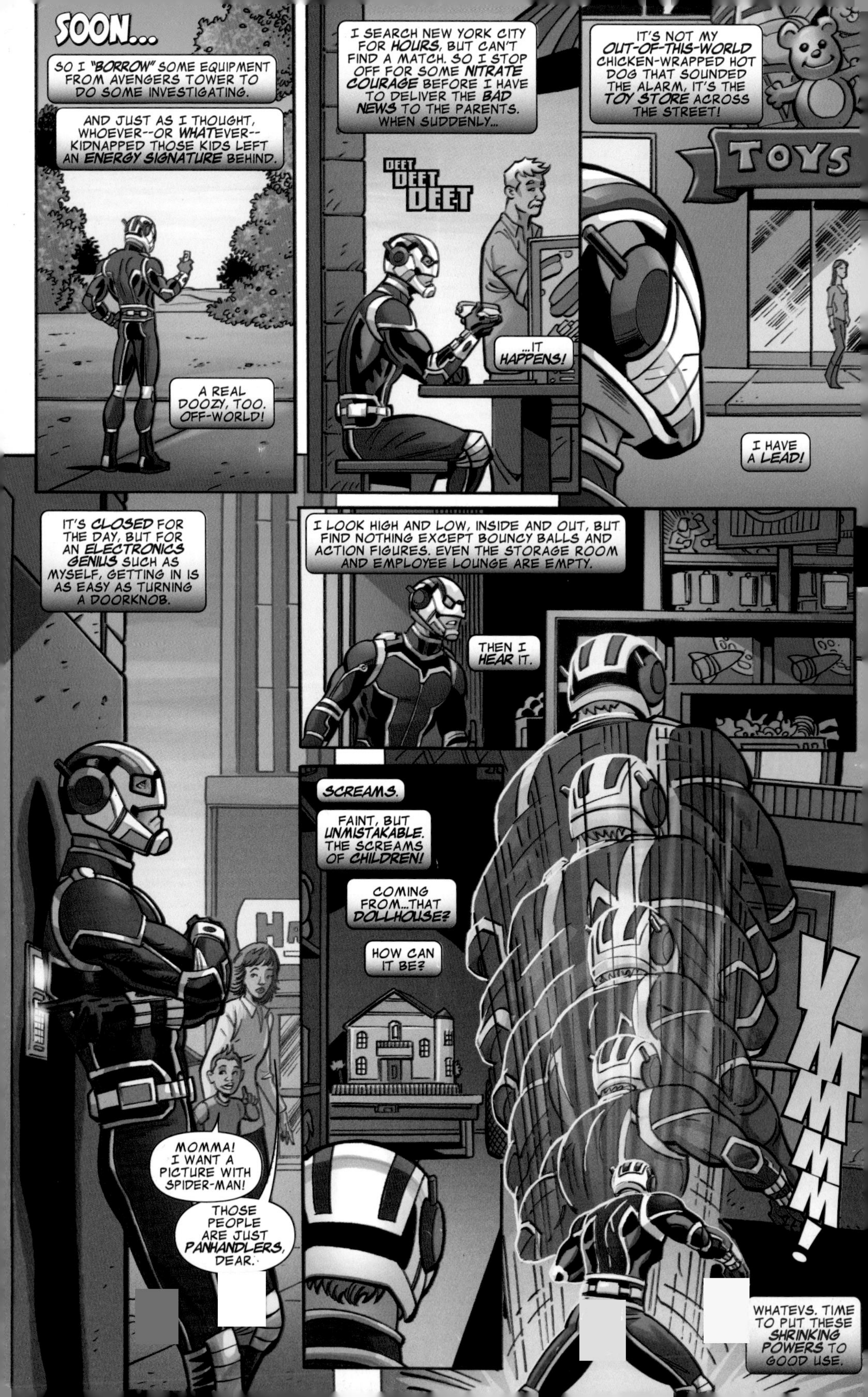
SOON...
SO I "BORROW" SOME EQUIPMENT FROM AVENGERS TOWER TO DO SOME INVESTIGATING.
AND JUST AS I THOUGHT, WHOEVER--OR WHATEVER--KIDNAPPED THOSE KIDS LEFT AN ENERGY SIGNATURE BEHIND.
A REAL DOOZY, TOO. OFF-WORLD!
I SEARCH NEW YORK CITY FOR HOURS, BUT CAN'T FIND A MATCH. SO I STOP OFF FOR SOME NITRATE COURAGE BEFORE I HAVE TO DELIVER THE BAD NEWS TO THE PARENTS. WHEN SUDDENLY...
DEET DEET DEET
...IT HAPPENS!
IT'S NOT MY OUT-OF-THIS-WORLD CHICKEN-WRAPPED HOT DOG THAT SOUNDED THE ALARM, IT'S THE TOY STORE ACROSS THE STREET!
TOYS
I HAVE A LEAD!
IT'S CLOSED FOR THE DAY, BUT FOR AN ELECTRONICS GENIUS SUCH AS MYSELF, GETTING IN IS AS EASY AS TURNING A DOORKNOB.
MOMMA! I WANT A PICTURE WITH SPIDER-MAN!
THOSE PEOPLE ARE JUST PANHANDLERS, DEAR.
I LOOK HIGH AND LOW, INSIDE AND OUT, BUT FIND NOTHING EXCEPT BOUNCY BALLS AND ACTION FIGURES. EVEN THE STORAGE ROOM AND EMPLOYEE LOUNGE ARE EMPTY.
THEN I HEAR IT.
SCREAMS.
FAINT, BUT UNMISTAKABLE. THE SCREAMS OF CHILDREN!
COMING FROM...THAT DOLLHOUSE?
HOW CAN IT BE?
VMMMM!
WHATEVS. TIME TO PUT THESE SHRINKING POWERS TO GOOD USE.

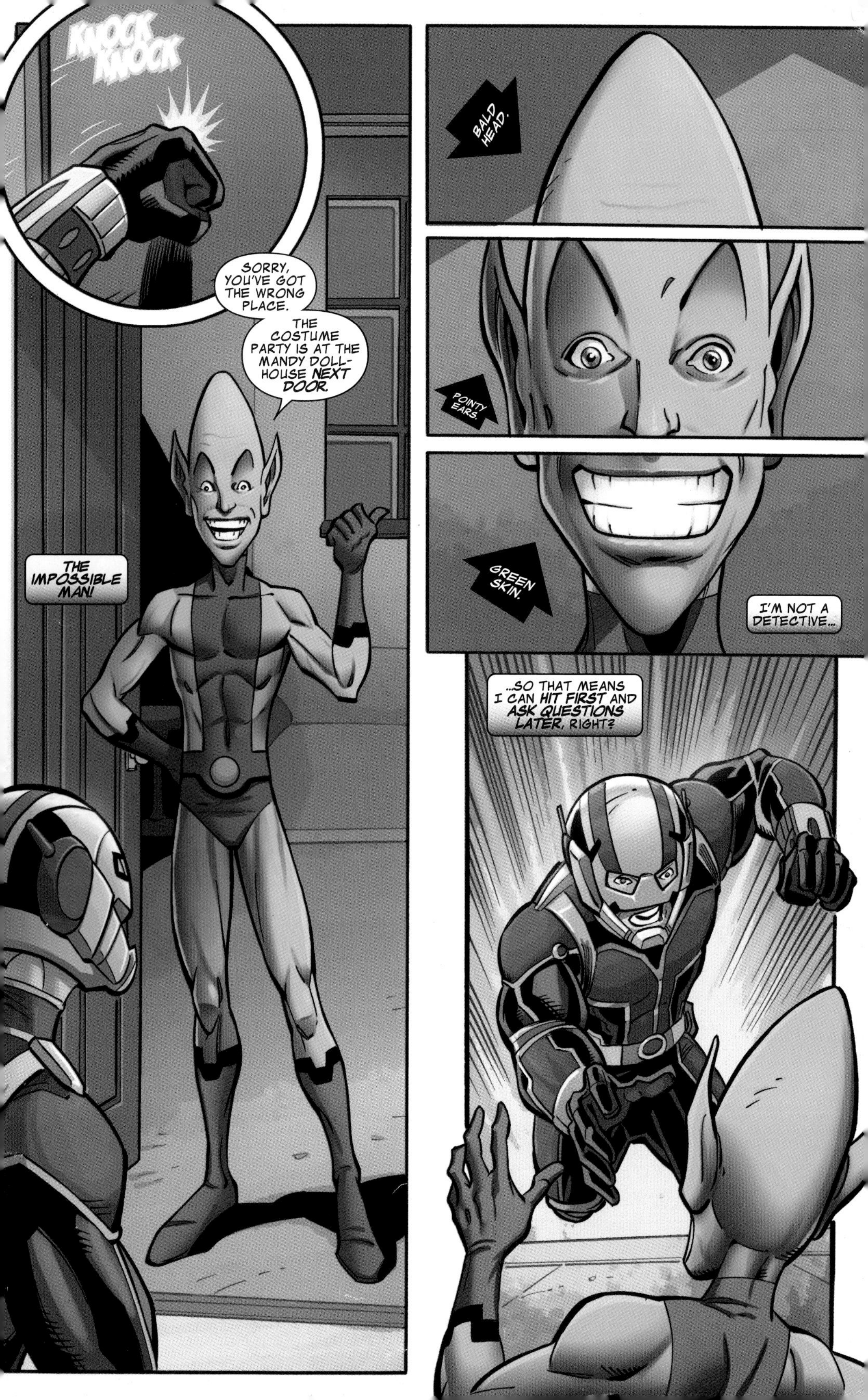
KNOCK KNOCK
SORRY, YOU'VE GOT THE WRONG PLACE.
THE COSTUME PARTY IS AT THE MANDY DOLL-HOUSE NEXT DOOR.
THE IMPOSSIBLE MAN!
BALD HEAD.
POINTY EARS.
GREEN SKIN.
I'M NOT A DETECTIVE...
...SO THAT MEANS I CAN HIT FIRST AND ASK QUESTIONS LATER, RIGHT?

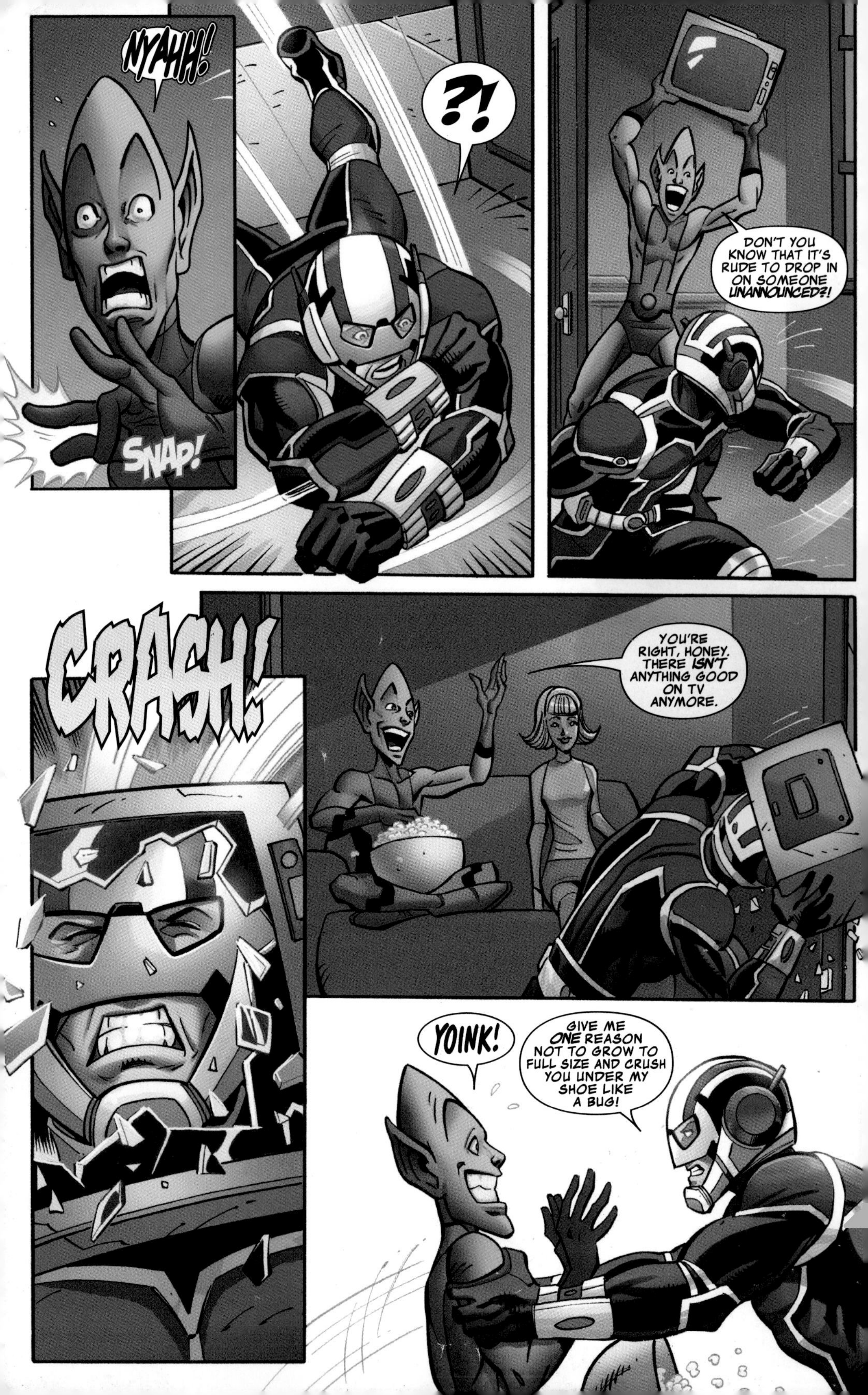
NYAHH!
SNAP!
?!
DON'T YOU KNOW THAT IT'S RUDE TO DROP IN ON SOMEONE UNANNOUNCED?!
CRASH!
YOU'RE RIGHT, HONEY. THERE ISN'T ANYTHING GOOD ON TV ANYMORE.
YOINK!
GIVE ME ONE REASON NOT TO GROW TO FULL SIZE AND CRUSH YOU UNDER MY SHOE LIKE A BUG!

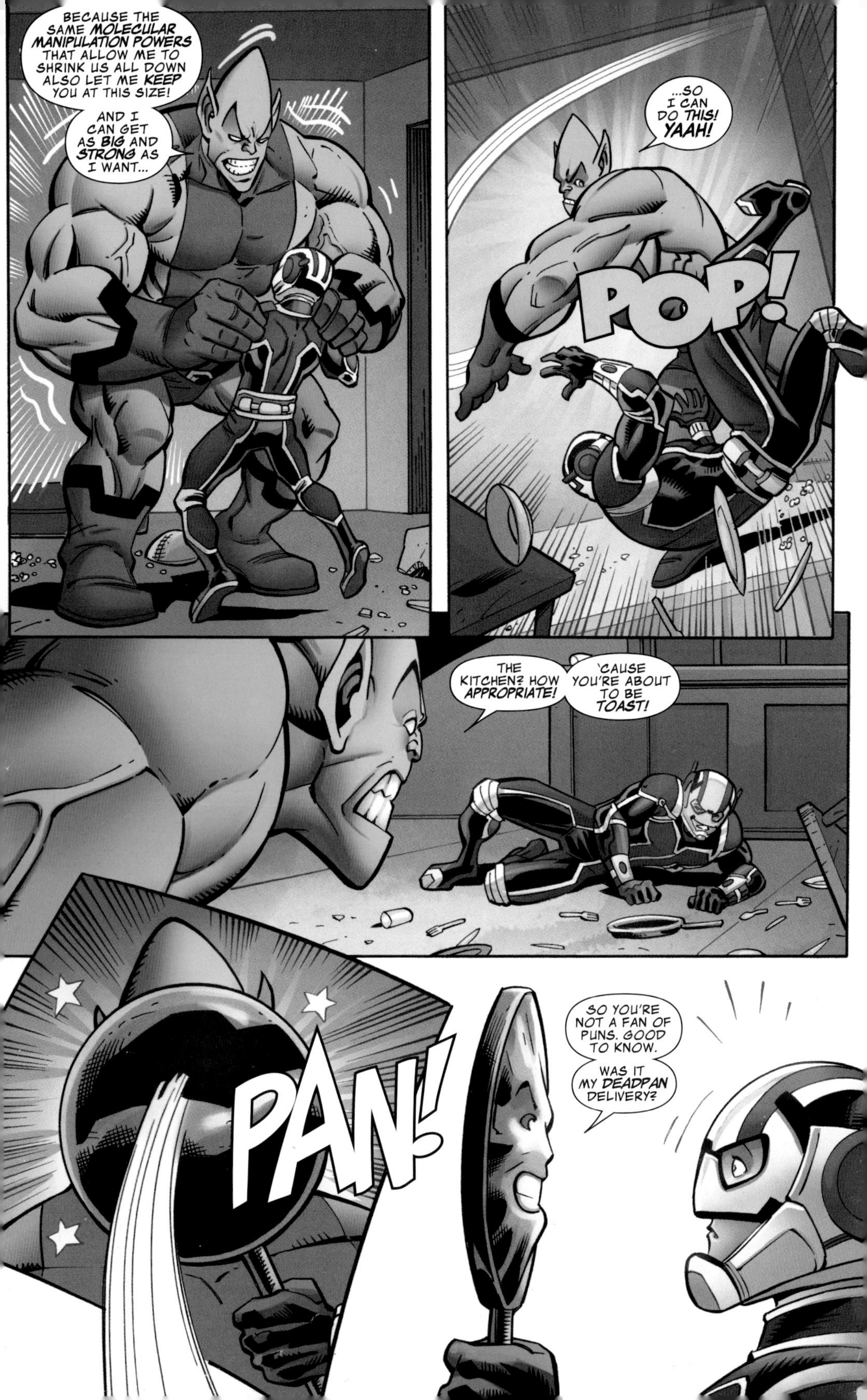
BECAUSE THE SAME MOLECULAR MANIPULATION POWERS THAT ALLOW ME TO SHRINK US ALL DOWN ALSO LET ME KEEP YOU AT THIS SIZE!
AND I CAN GET AS BIG AND STRONG AS I WANT...
...SO I CAN DO THIS! YAAH!
POP!
THE KITCHEN? HOW APPROPRIATE!
'CAUSE YOU'RE ABOUT TO BE TOAST!
PAN!
SO YOU'RE NOT A FAN OF PUNS. GOOD TO KNOW.
WAS IT MY DEADPAN DELIVERY?

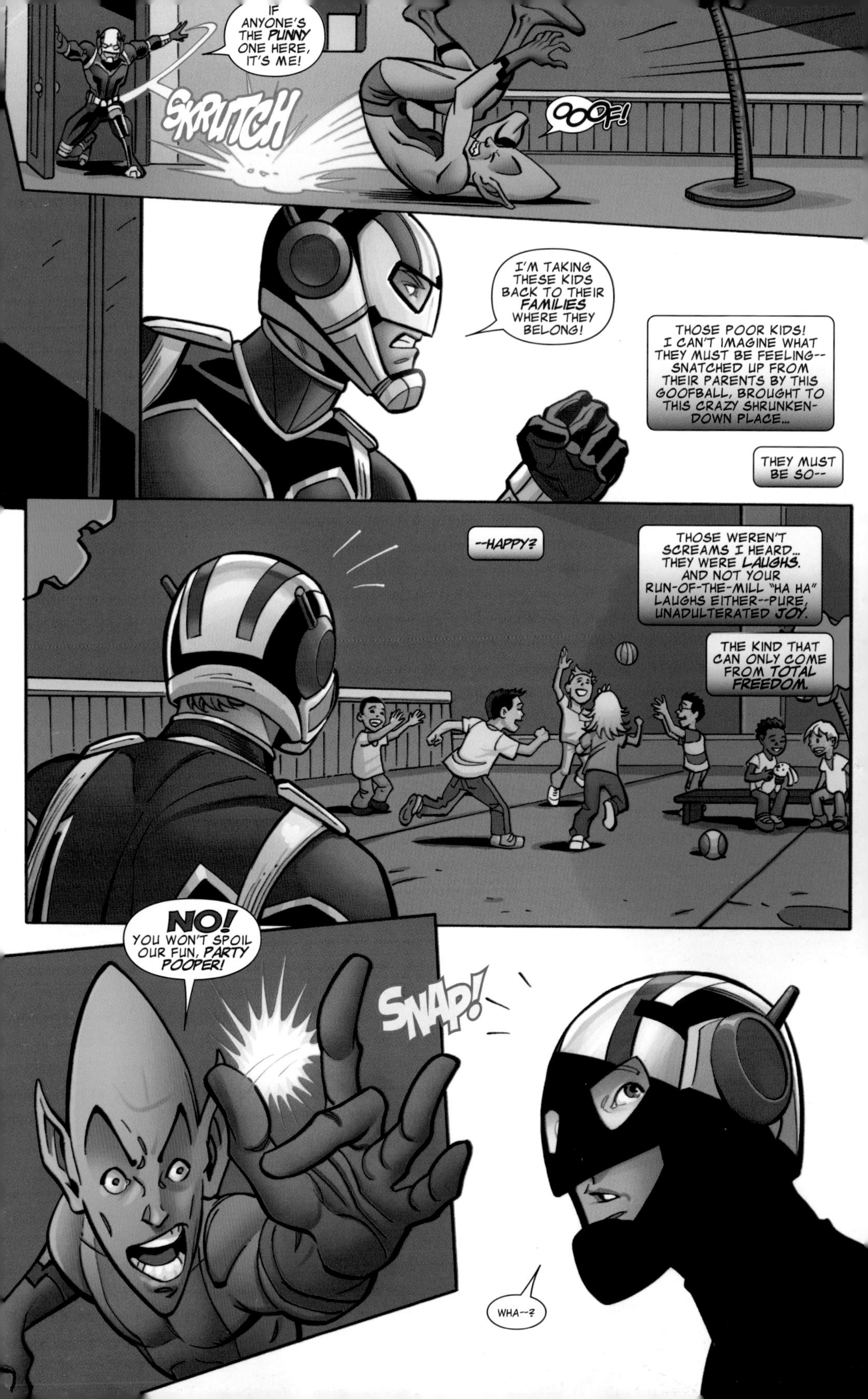
IF ANYONE'S THE PUNNY ONE HERE, IT'S ME!
SKRUTCH
OOOF!
I'M TAKING THESE KIDS BACK TO THEIR FAMILIES WHERE THEY BELONG!
THOSE POOR KIDS! I CAN'T IMAGINE WHAT THEY MUST BE FEELING-- SNATCHED UP FROM THEIR PARENTS BY THIS GOOFBALL, BROUGHT TO THIS CRAZY SHRUNKEN-DOWN PLACE...
THEY MUST BE SO--
--HAPPY?
THOSE WEREN'T SCREAMS I HEARD... THEY WERE LAUGHS. AND NOT YOUR RUN-OF-THE-MILL "HA HA" LAUGHS EITHER--PURE, UNADULTERATED JOY.
THE KIND THAT CAN ONLY COME FROM TOTAL FREEDOM.
NO! YOU WON'T SPOIL OUR FUN, PARTY POOPER!
SNAP!
WHA--?

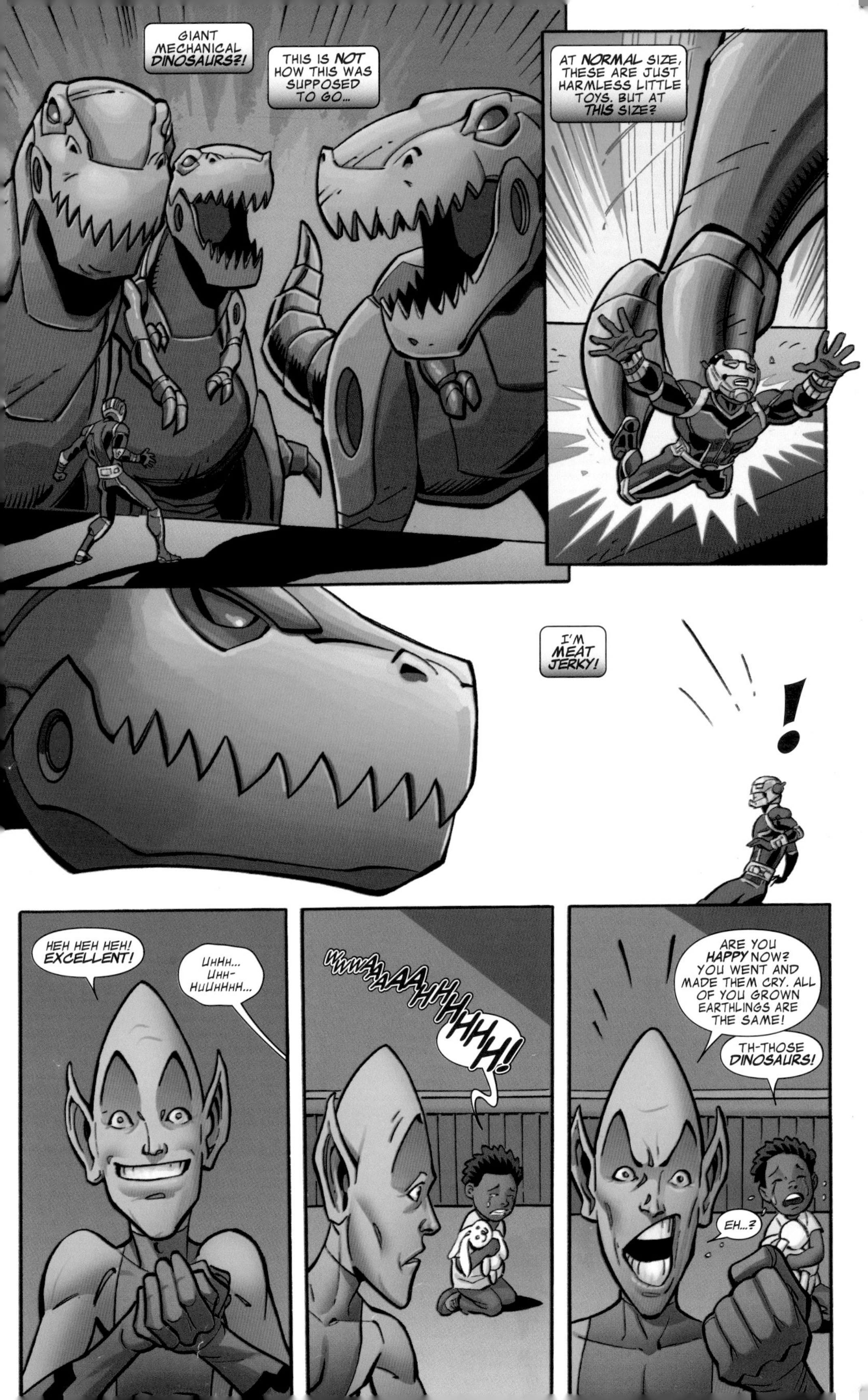
GIANT MECHANICAL DINOSAURS?!
THIS IS NOT HOW THIS WAS SUPPOSED TO GO...
AT NORMAL SIZE, THESE ARE JUST HARMLESS LITTLE TOYS. BUT AT THIS SIZE?
I'M MEAT JERKY!
!
HEH HEH HEH! EXCELLENT!
UHHH... UHH-HUUHHHH...
WWWAAAAAHHHHHH!
ARE YOU HAPPY NOW? YOU WENT AND MADE THEM CRY. ALL OF YOU GROWN EARTHLINGS ARE THE SAME!
TH-THOSE DINOSAURS!
EH...?

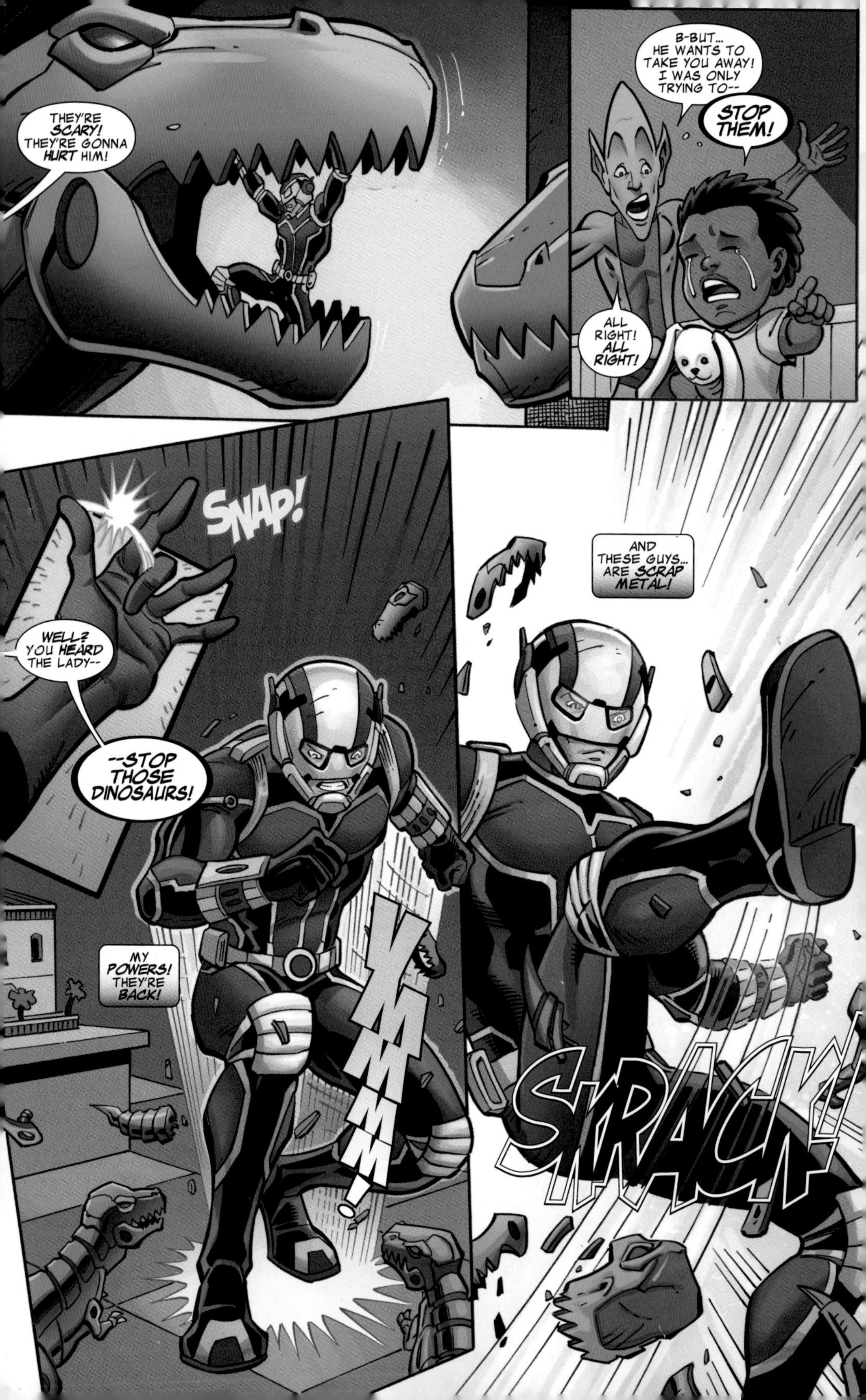
THEY'RE SCARY! THEY'RE GONNA HURT HIM!
B-BUT... HE WANTS TO TAKE YOU AWAY! I WAS ONLY TRYING TO--
STOP THEM!
ALL RIGHT! ALL RIGHT!
SNAP!
AND THESE GUYS... ARE SCRAP METAL!
WELL? YOU HEARD THE LADY--
--STOP THOSE DINOSAURS!
MY POWERS! THEY'RE BACK!
SKRACK!

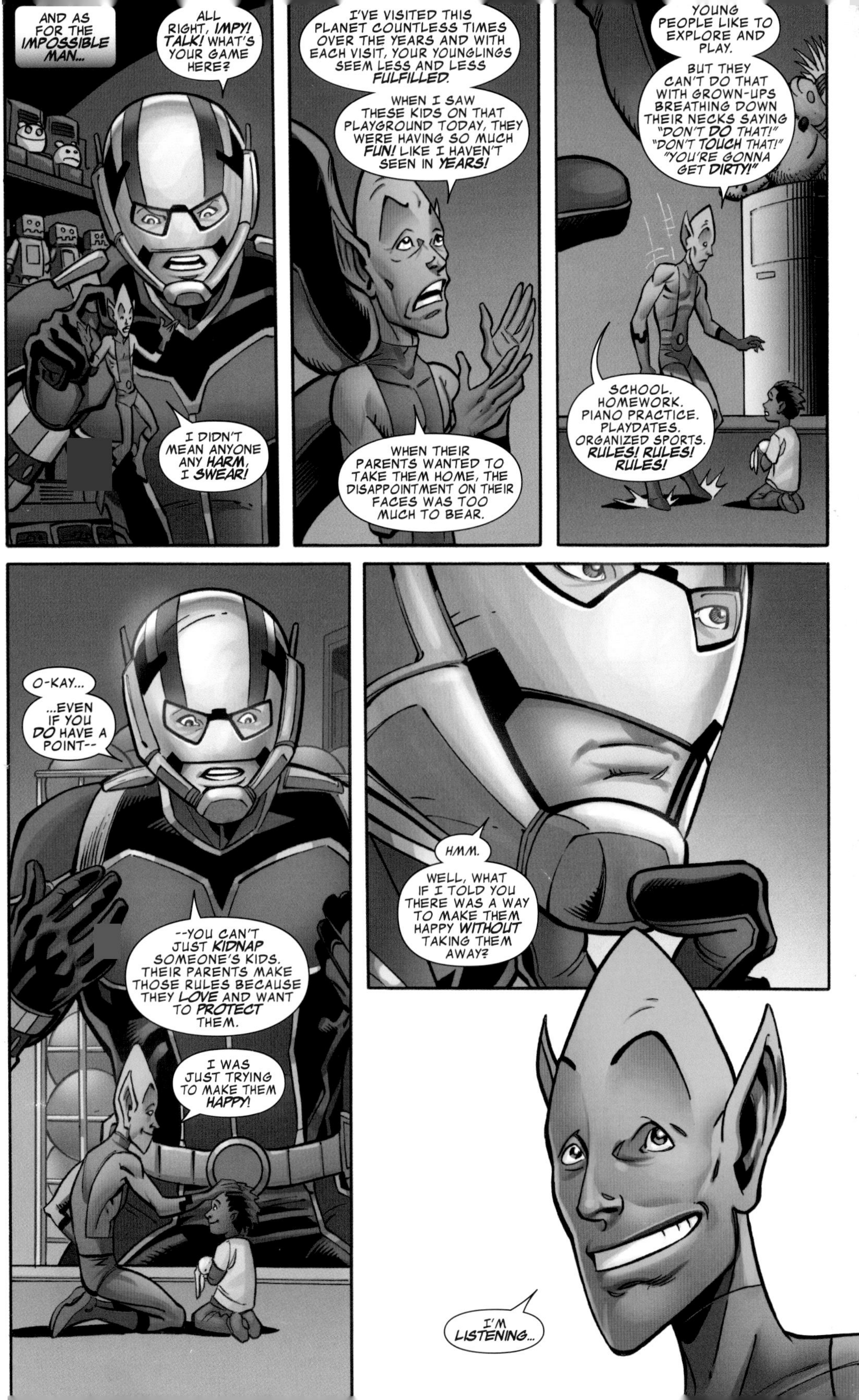
AND AS FOR THE IMPOSSIBLE MAN...
ALL RIGHT, IMPY! TALK! WHAT'S YOUR GAME HERE?
I DIDN'T MEAN ANYONE ANY HARM, I SWEAR!
I'VE VISITED THIS PLANET COUNTLESS TIMES OVER THE YEARS AND WITH EACH VISIT, YOUR YOUNGLINGS SEEM LESS AND LESS FULFILLED.
WHEN I SAW THESE KIDS ON THAT PLAYGROUND TODAY, THEY WERE HAVING SO MUCH FUN! LIKE I HAVEN'T SEEN IN YEARS!
WHEN THEIR PARENTS WANTED TO TAKE THEM HOME, THE DISAPPOINTMENT ON THEIR FACES WAS TOO MUCH TO BEAR.
YOUNG PEOPLE LIKE TO EXPLORE AND PLAY.
BUT THEY CAN'T DO THAT WITH GROWN-UPS BREATHING DOWN THEIR NECKS SAYING "DON'T DO THAT!" "DON'T TOUCH THAT!" "YOU'RE GONNA GET DIRTY!"
SCHOOL. HOMEWORK. PIANO PRACTICE. PLAYDATES. ORGANIZED SPORTS. RULES! RULES! RULES!
O-KAY...
...EVEN IF YOU DO HAVE A POINT--
--YOU CAN'T JUST KIDNAP SOMEONE'S KIDS. THEIR PARENTS MAKE THOSE RULES BECAUSE THEY LOVE AND WANT TO PROTECT THEM.
I WAS JUST TRYING TO MAKE THEM HAPPY!
HMM.
WELL, WHAT IF I TOLD YOU THERE WAS A WAY TO MAKE THEM HAPPY WITHOUT TAKING THEM AWAY?
I'M LISTENING...

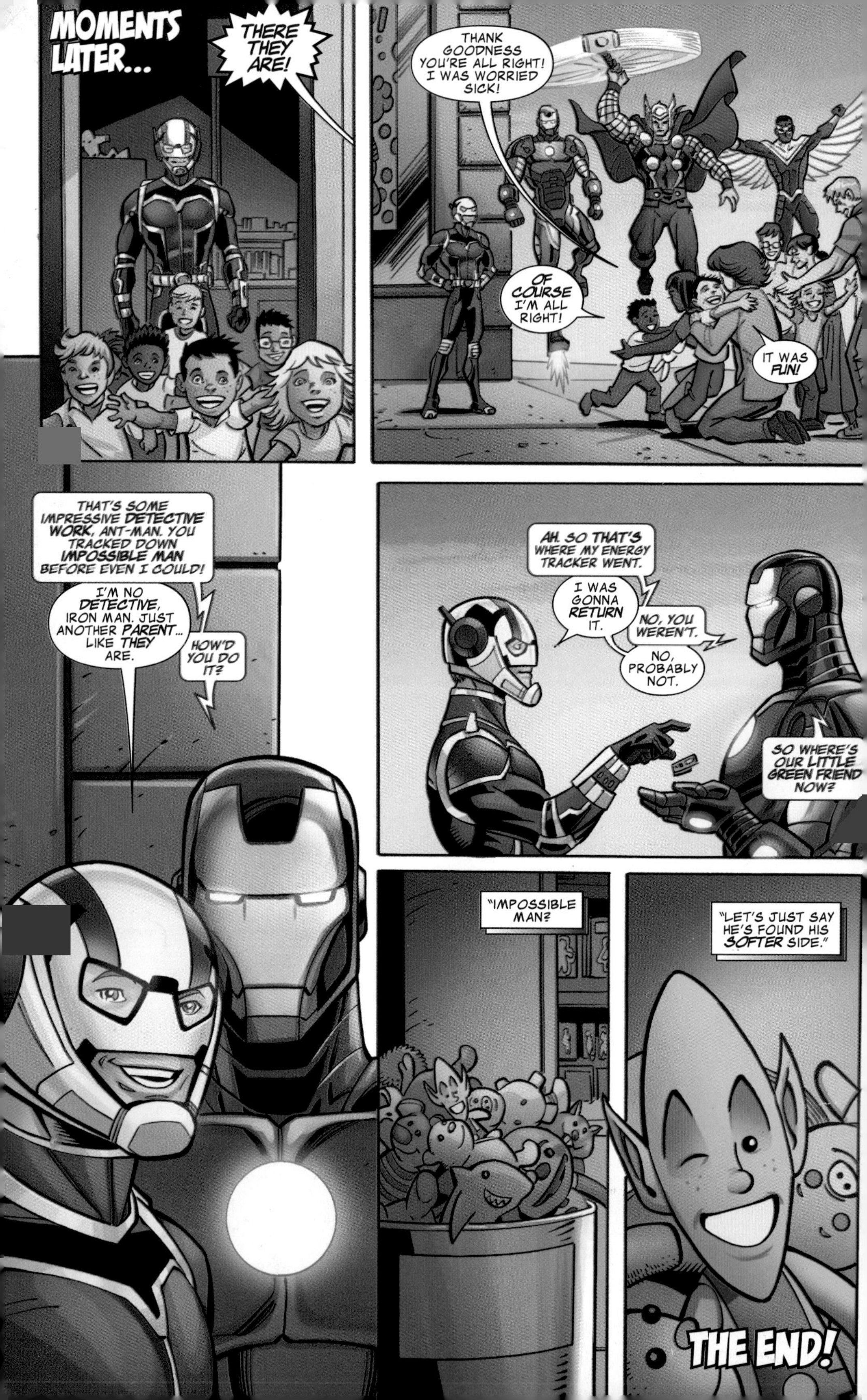
MOMENTS LATER...
THERE THEY ARE!
THANK GOODNESS YOU'RE ALL RIGHT! I WAS WORRIED SICK!
OF COURSE I'M ALL RIGHT!
IT WAS FUN!
THAT'S SOME IMPRESSIVE DETECTIVE WORK, ANT-MAN. YOU TRACKED DOWN IMPOSSIBLE MAN BEFORE EVEN I COULD!
I'M NO DETECTIVE, IRON MAN. JUST ANOTHER PARENT... LIKE THEY ARE.
HOW'D YOU DO IT?
AH. SO THAT'S WHERE MY ENERGY TRACKER WENT.
I WAS GONNA RETURN IT.
NO, YOU WEREN'T.
NO, PROBABLY NOT.
SO WHERE'S OUR LITTLE GREEN FRIEND NOW?
"IMPOSSIBLE MAN?
"LET'S JUST SAY HE'S FOUND HIS SOFTER SIDE."
THE END!

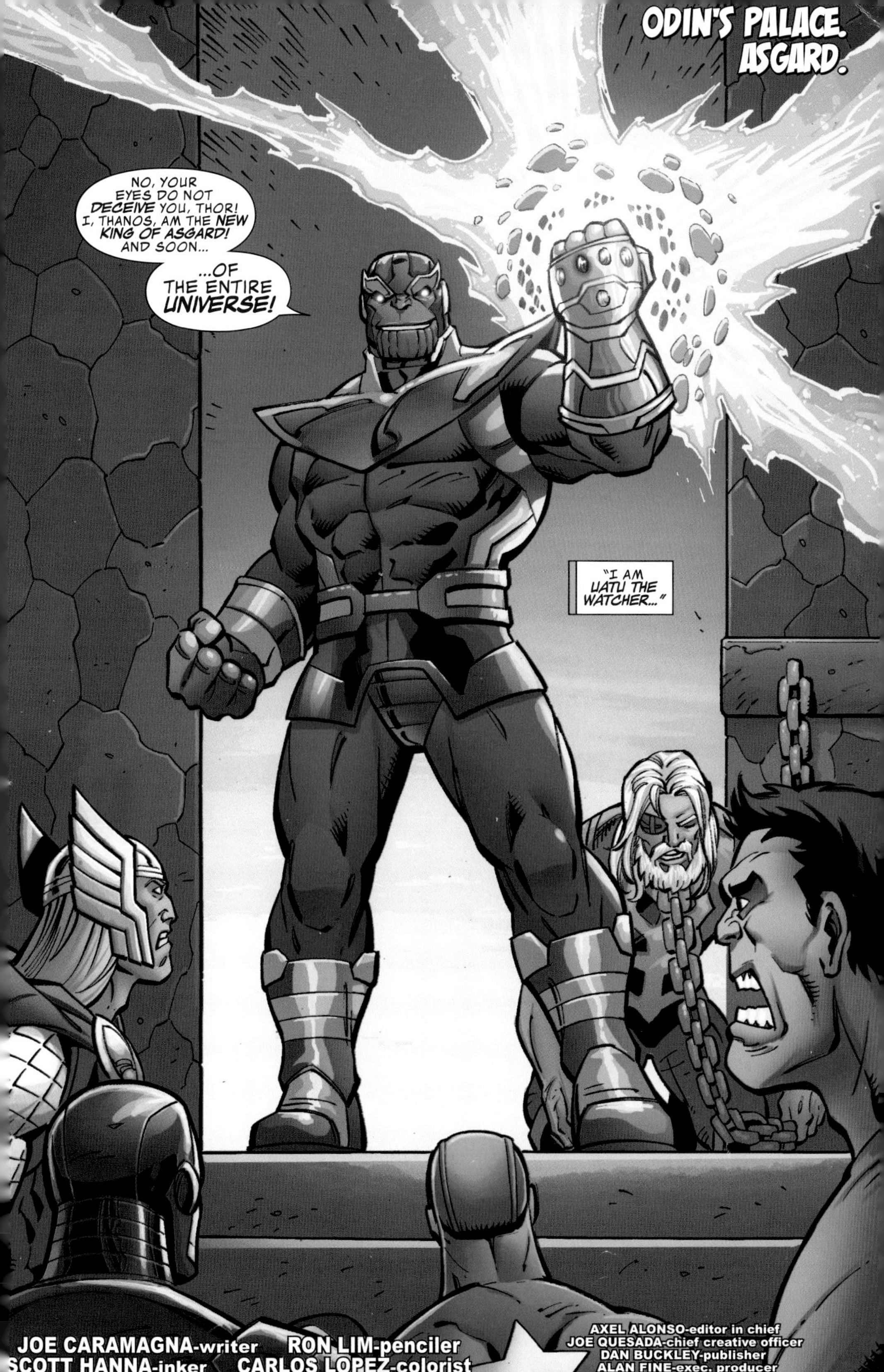
ODIN'S PALACE. ASGARD.
NO, YOUR EYES DO NOT DECEIVE YOU, THOR! I, THANOS, AM THE NEW KING OF ASGARD! AND SOON...
...OF THE ENTIRE UNIVERSE!
"I AM UATU THE WATCHER..."

JOE CARAMAGNA-writer RON LIM-penciler
SCOTT HANNA-inker CARLOS LOPEZ-colorist
VC's JC-letterer EMILY SHAW & MARK BASSO-editors
AXEL ALONSO-editor in chief
JOE QUESADA-chief creative officer
DAN BUCKLEY-publisher
ALAN FINE-exec. producer
AVENGERS created by STAN LEE & JACK KIRBY

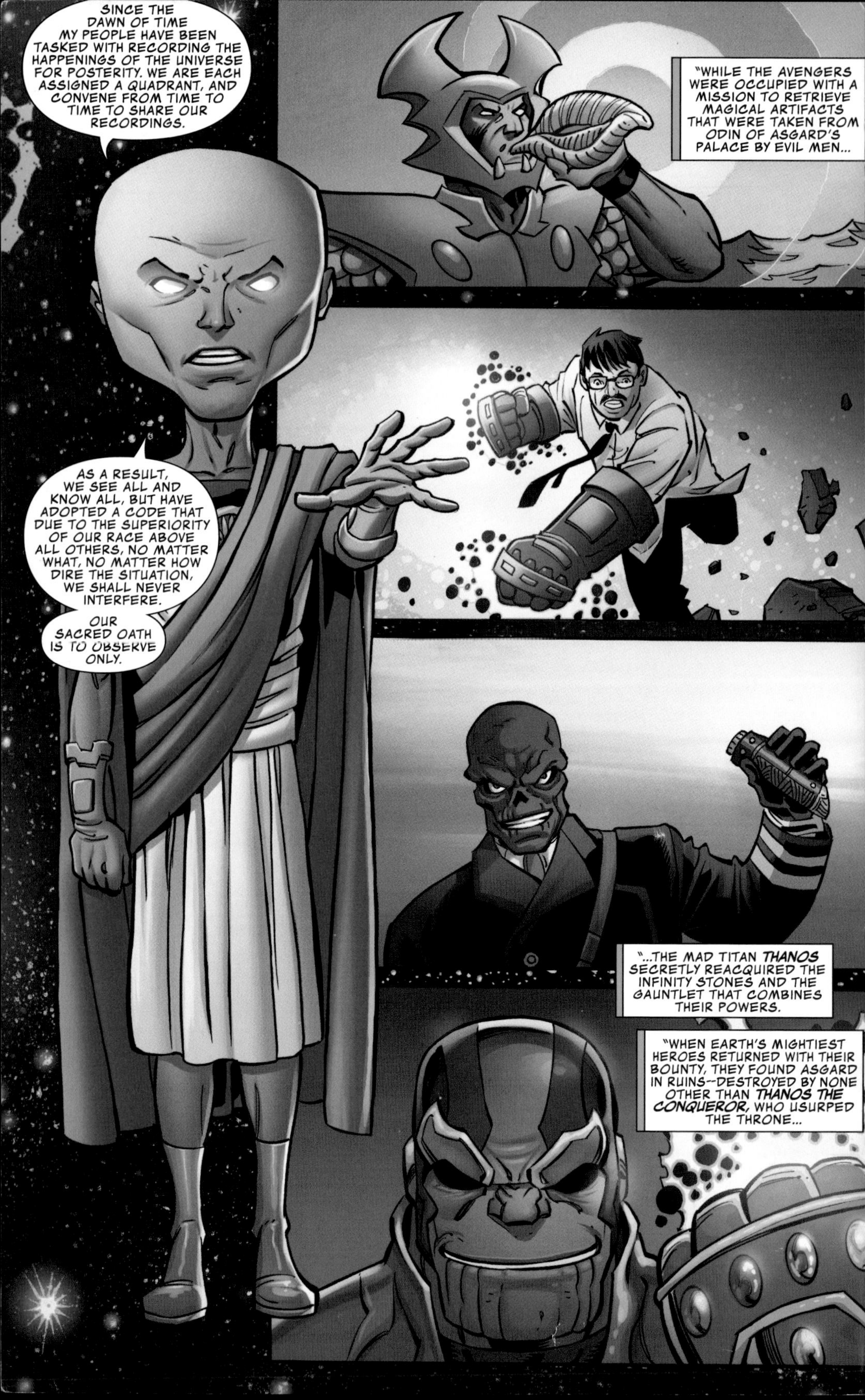
SINCE THE DAWN OF TIME MY PEOPLE HAVE BEEN TASKED WITH RECORDING THE HAPPENINGS OF THE UNIVERSE FOR POSTERITY. WE ARE EACH ASSIGNED A QUADRANT, AND CONVENE FROM TIME TO TIME TO SHARE OUR RECORDINGS.
"WHILE THE AVENGERS WERE OCCUPIED WITH A MISSION TO RETRIEVE MAGICAL ARTIFACTS THAT WERE TAKEN FROM ODIN OF ASGARD'S PALACE BY EVIL MEN...
AS A RESULT, WE SEE ALL AND KNOW ALL, BUT HAVE ADOPTED A CODE THAT DUE TO THE SUPERIORITY OF OUR RACE ABOVE ALL OTHERS, NO MATTER WHAT, NO MATTER HOW DIRE THE SITUATION, WE SHALL NEVER INTERFERE.
OUR SACRED OATH IS TO OBSERVE ONLY.
"...THE MAD TITAN THANOS SECRETLY REACQUIRED THE INFINITY STONES AND THE GAUNTLET THAT COMBINES THEIR POWERS.
"WHEN EARTH'S MIGHTIEST HEROES RETURNED WITH THEIR BOUNTY, THEY FOUND ASGARD IN RUINS--DESTROYED BY NONE OTHER THAN THANOS THE CONQUEROR, WHO USURPED THE THRONE...

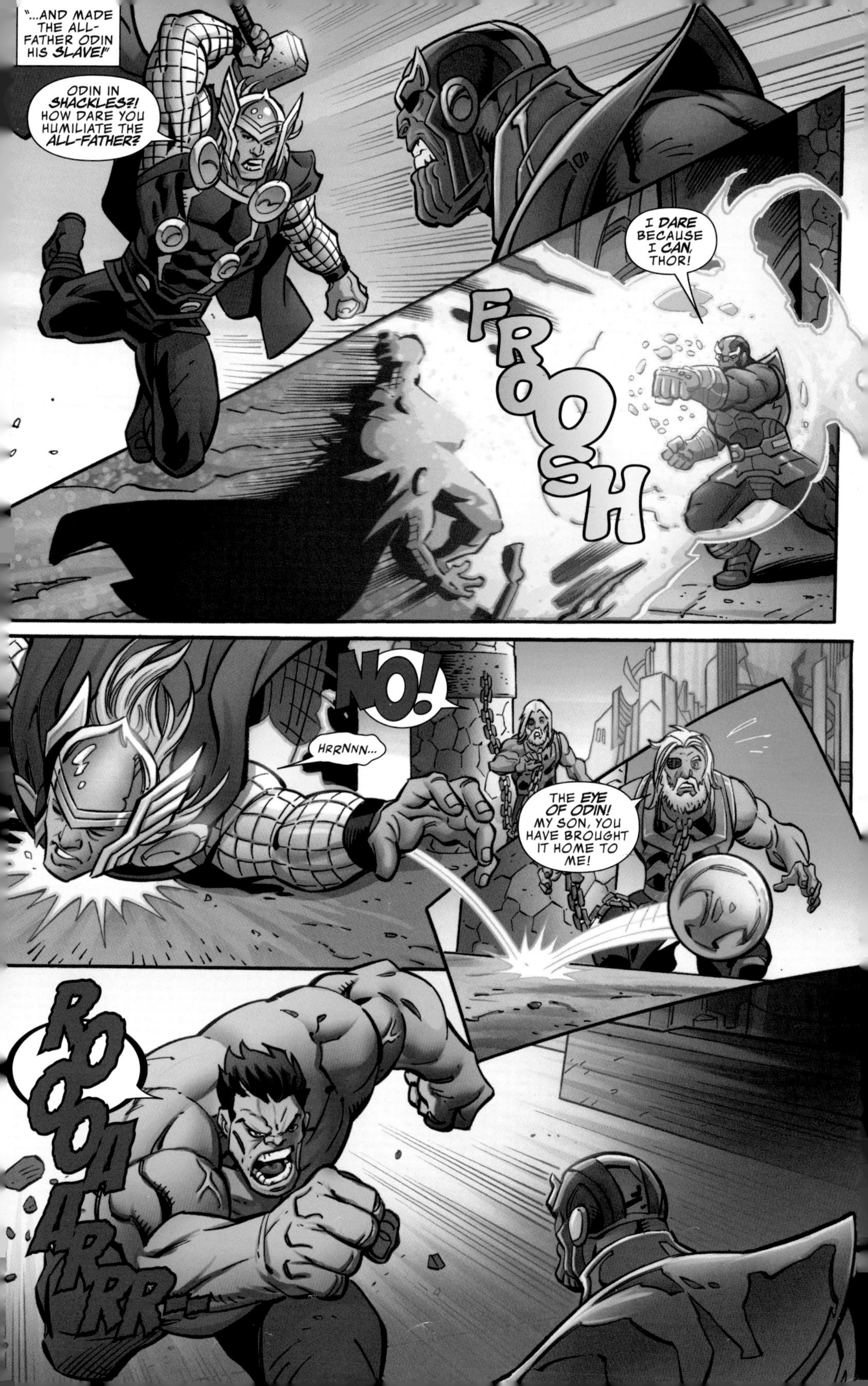
"...AND MADE THE ALL-FATHER ODIN HIS SLAVE!"
ODIN IN SHACKLES?! HOW DARE YOU HUMILIATE THE ALL-FATHER?
I DARE BECAUSE I CAN, THOR!
FROOSH
NO!
HRRNNN...
THE EYE OF ODIN! MY SON, YOU HAVE BROUGHT IT HOME TO ME!
ROOOOARRR

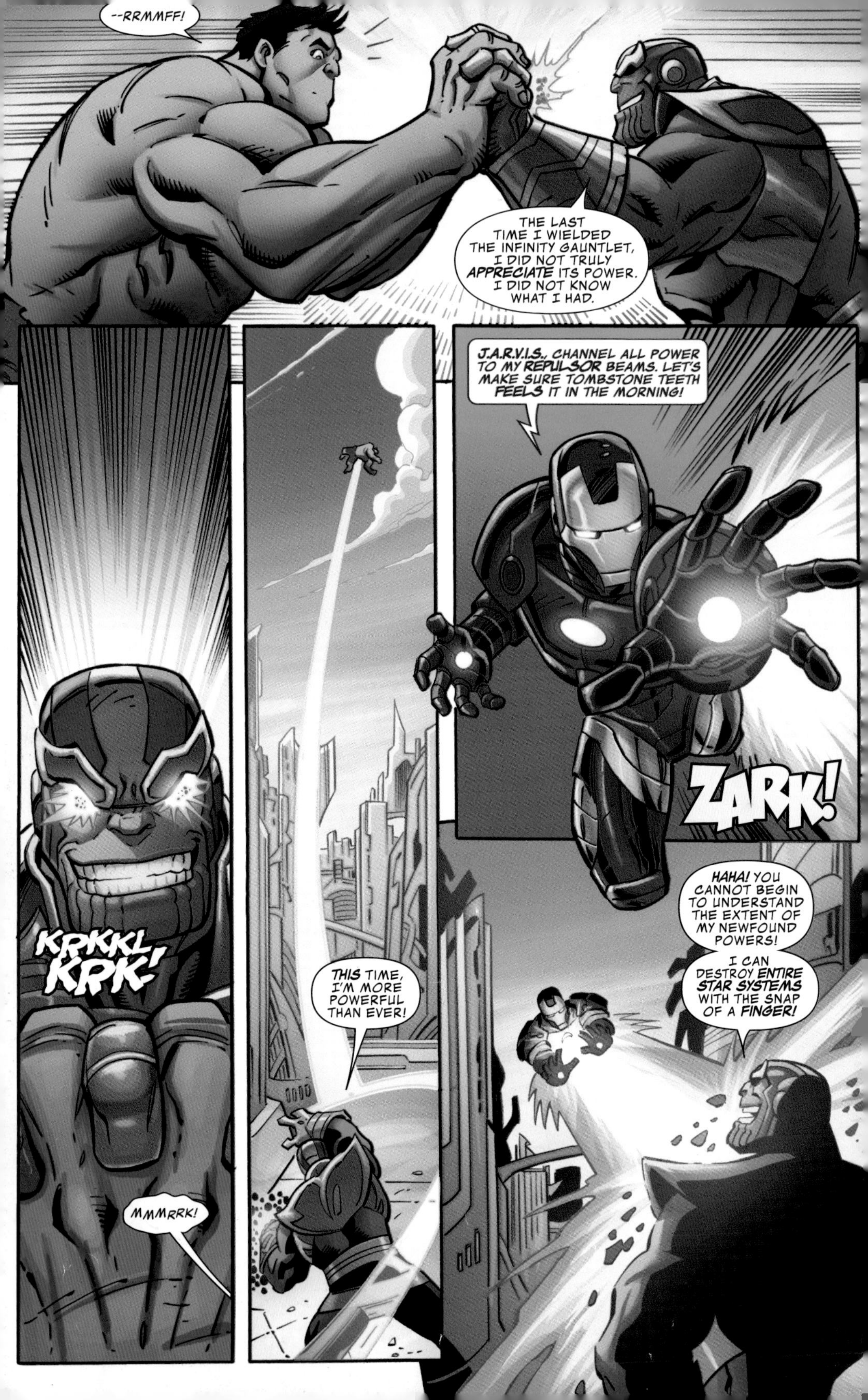
--RRMMFF!
THE LAST TIME I WIELDED THE INFINITY GAUNTLET, I DID NOT TRULY APPRECIATE ITS POWER. I DID NOT KNOW WHAT I HAD.
KRKKL KRK!
MMMRRK!
THIS TIME, I'M MORE POWERFUL THAN EVER!
J.A.R.V.I.S., CHANNEL ALL POWER TO MY REPULSOR BEAMS. LET'S MAKE SURE TOMBSTONE TEETH FEELS IT IN THE MORNING!
ZARK!
HAHA! YOU CANNOT BEGIN TO UNDERSTAND THE EXTENT OF MY NEWFOUND POWERS!
I CAN DESTROY ENTIRE STAR SYSTEMS WITH THE SNAP OF A FINGER!

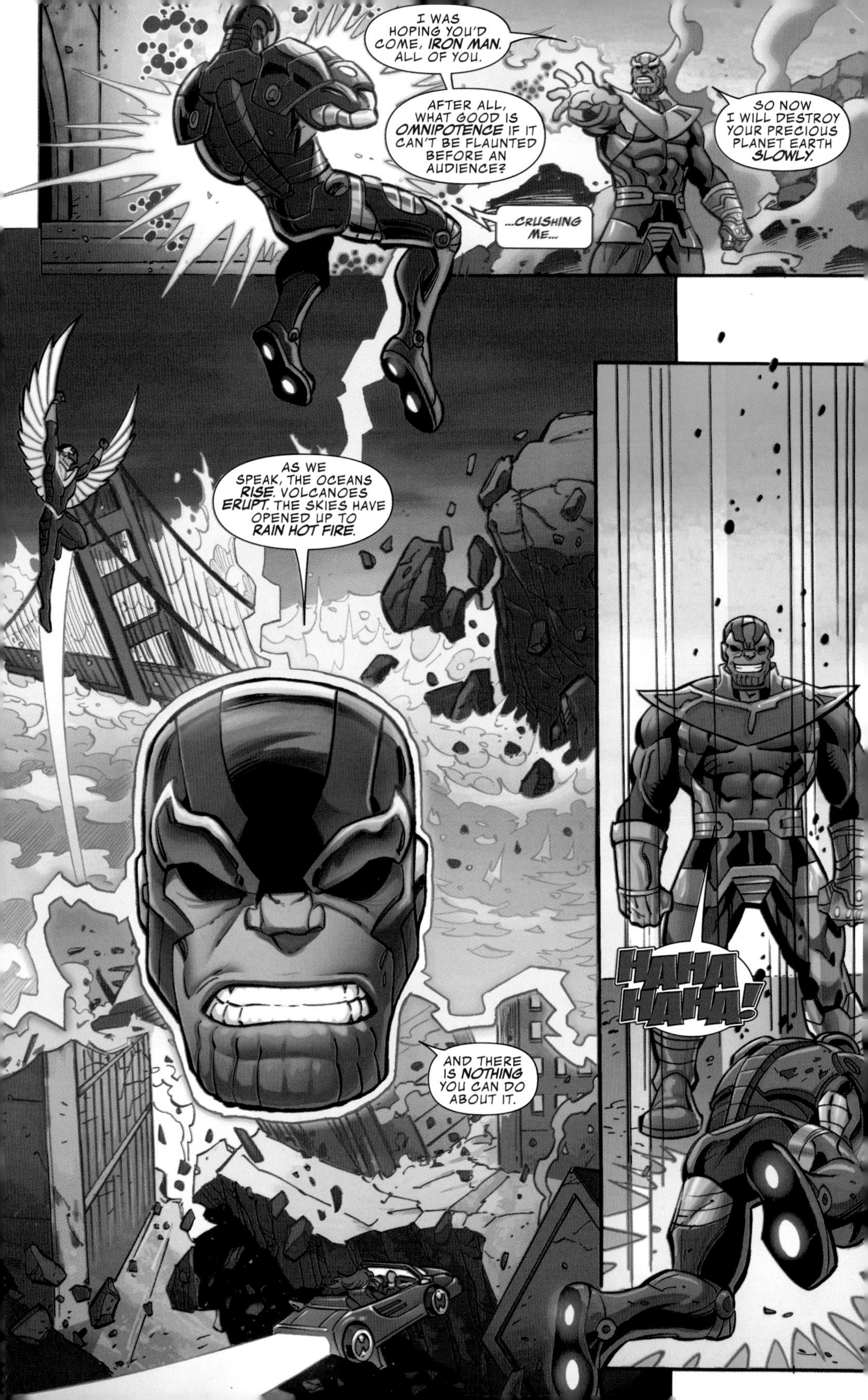
I WAS HOPING YOU'D COME, IRON MAN. ALL OF YOU.
AFTER ALL, WHAT GOOD IS OMNIPOTENCE IF IT CAN'T BE FLAUNTED BEFORE AN AUDIENCE?
SO NOW I WILL DESTROY YOUR PRECIOUS PLANET EARTH SLOWLY.
...CRUSHING ME...
AS WE SPEAK, THE OCEANS RISE. VOLCANOES ERUPT. THE SKIES HAVE OPENED UP TO RAIN HOT FIRE.
AND THERE IS NOTHING YOU CAN DO ABOUT IT.
HAHA HAHA!

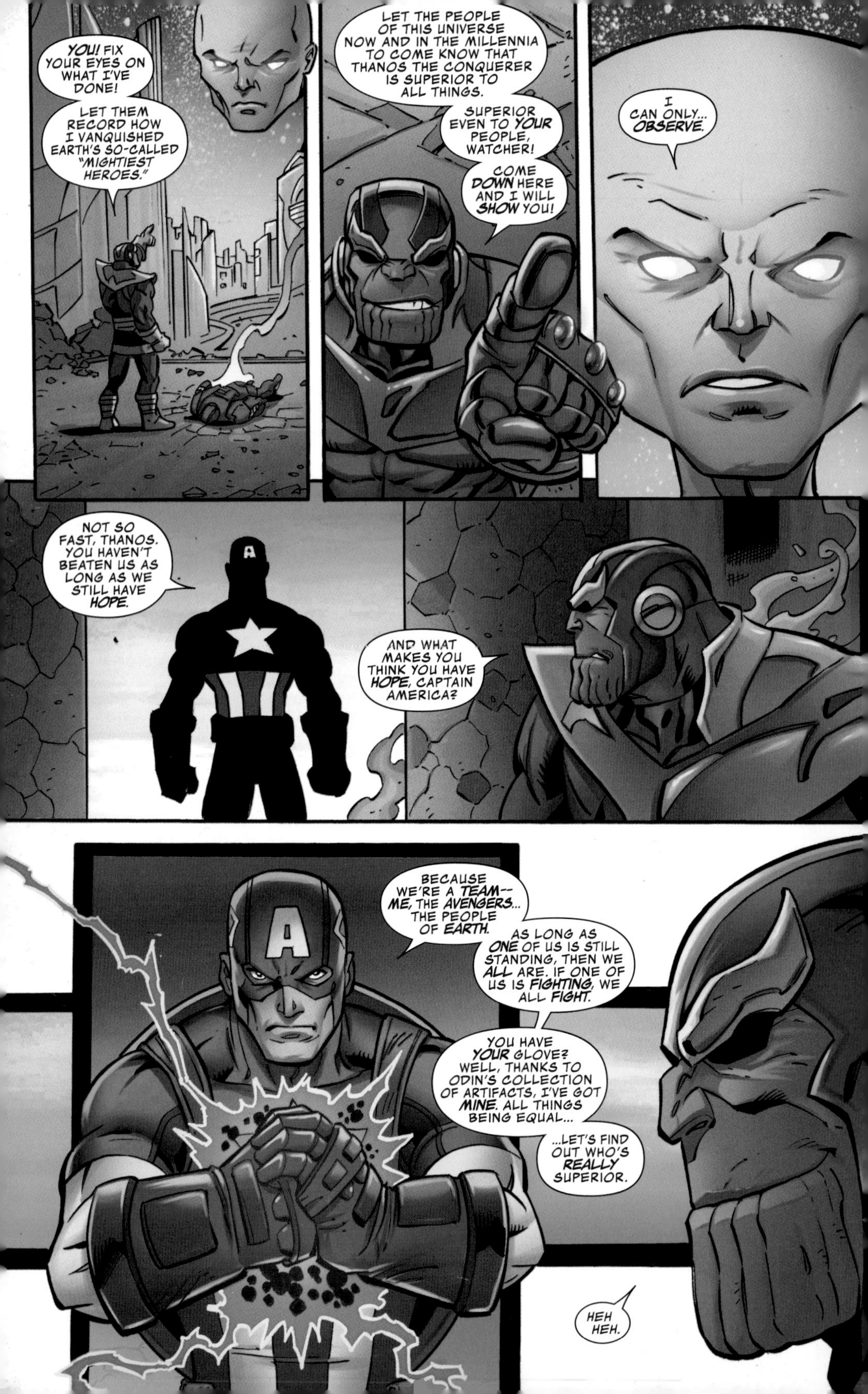
YOU! FIX YOUR EYES ON WHAT I'VE DONE!
LET THEM RECORD HOW I VANQUISHED EARTH'S SO-CALLED "MIGHTIEST HEROES."
LET THE PEOPLE OF THIS UNIVERSE NOW AND IN THE MILLENNIA TO COME KNOW THAT THANOS THE CONQUERER IS SUPERIOR TO ALL THINGS.
SUPERIOR EVEN TO YOUR PEOPLE, WATCHER!
COME DOWN HERE AND I WILL SHOW YOU!
I CAN ONLY... OBSERVE.
NOT SO FAST, THANOS. YOU HAVEN'T BEATEN US AS LONG AS WE STILL HAVE HOPE.
AND WHAT MAKES YOU THINK YOU HAVE HOPE, CAPTAIN AMERICA?
BECAUSE WE'RE A TEAM-- ME, THE AVENGERS... THE PEOPLE OF EARTH.
AS LONG AS ONE OF US IS STILL STANDING, THEN WE ALL ARE. IF ONE OF US IS FIGHTING, WE ALL FIGHT.
YOU HAVE YOUR GLOVE? WELL, THANKS TO ODIN'S COLLECTION OF ARTIFACTS, I'VE GOT MINE. ALL THINGS BEING EQUAL...
...LET'S FIND OUT WHO'S REALLY SUPERIOR.
HEH HEH.

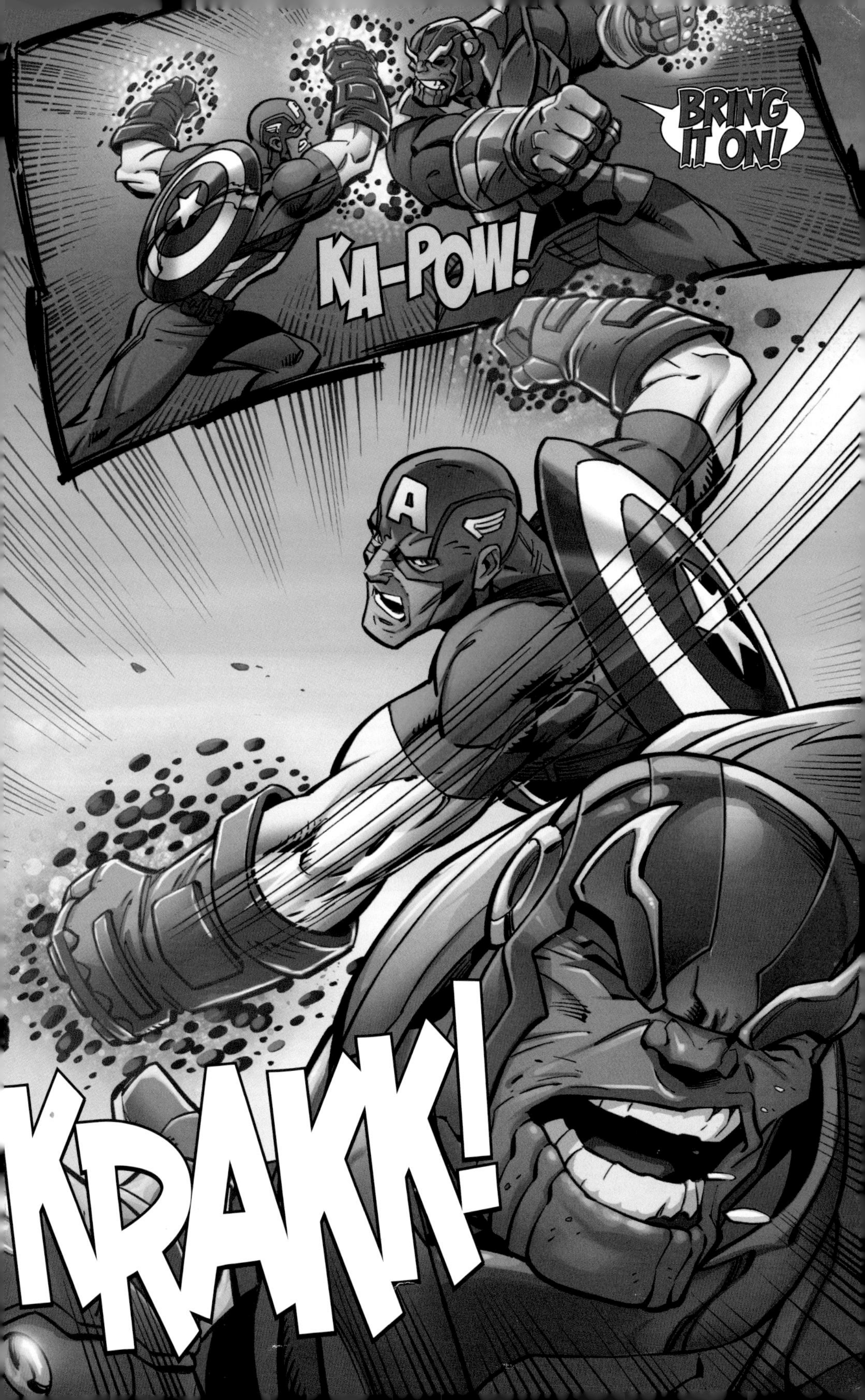
BRING IT ON!
KA-POW!
KRAKK!

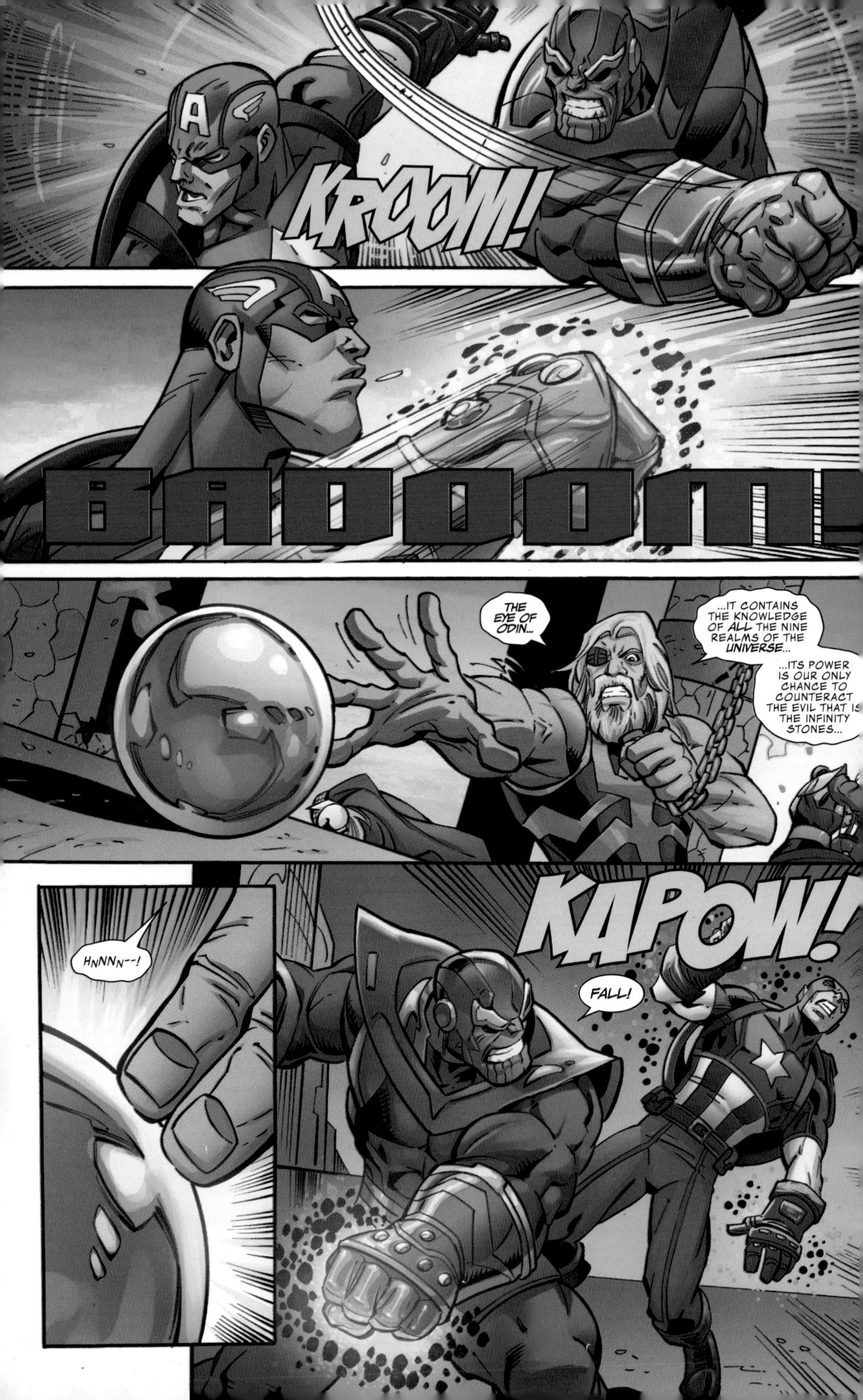
KROOM!
BADOOM!
THE EYE OF ODIN...
...IT CONTAINS THE KNOWLEDGE OF ALL THE NINE REALMS OF THE UNIVERSE...
...ITS POWER IS OUR ONLY CHANCE TO COUNTERACT THE EVIL THAT IS THE INFINITY STONES...
HNNNN--!
KAPOW!
FALL!

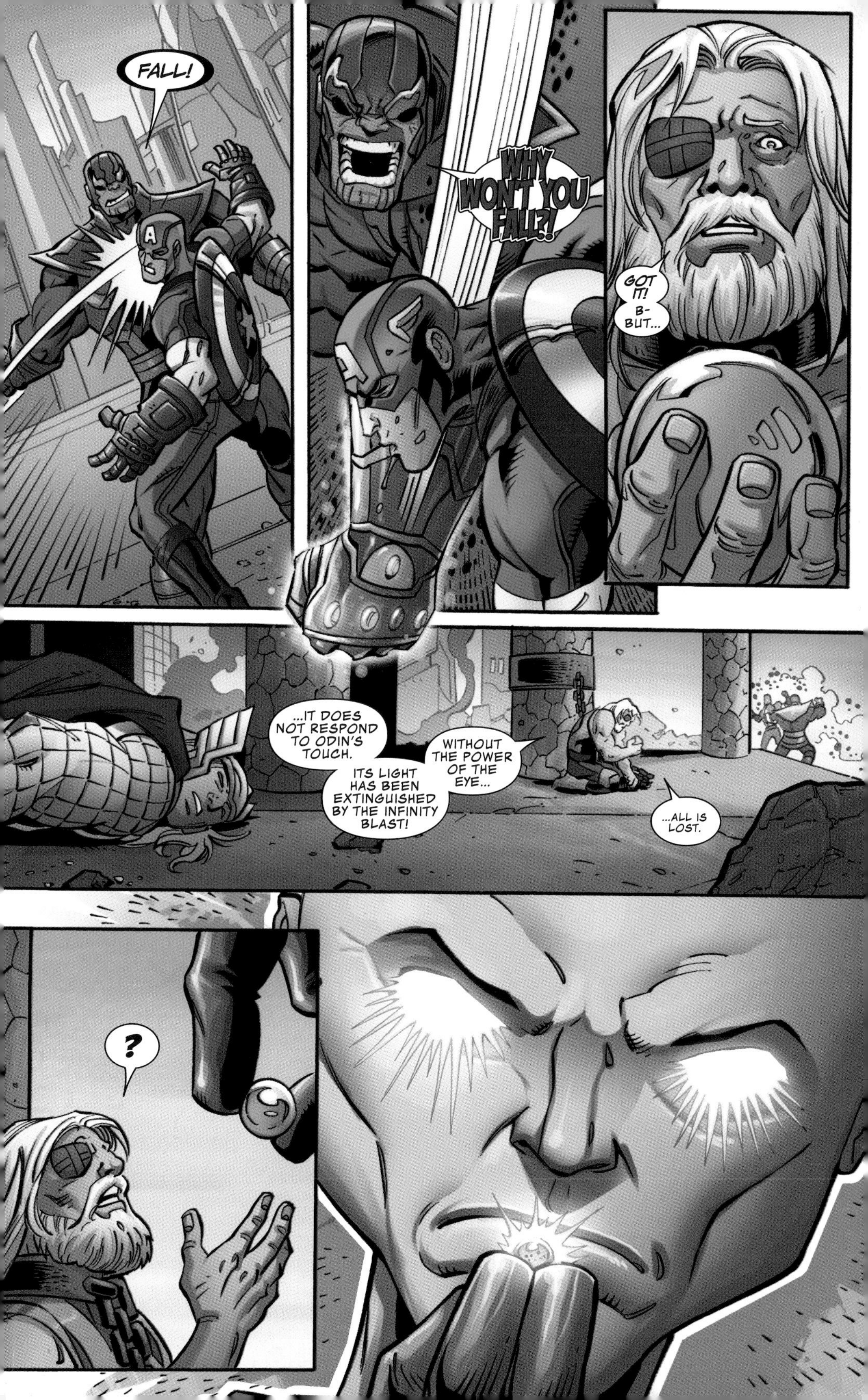
FALL!
WHY WON'T YOU FALL?!
GOT IT! B-BUT...
...IT DOES NOT RESPOND TO ODIN'S TOUCH.
ITS LIGHT HAS BEEN EXTINGUISHED BY THE INFINITY BLAST!
WITHOUT THE POWER OF THE EYE...
...ALL IS LOST.
?

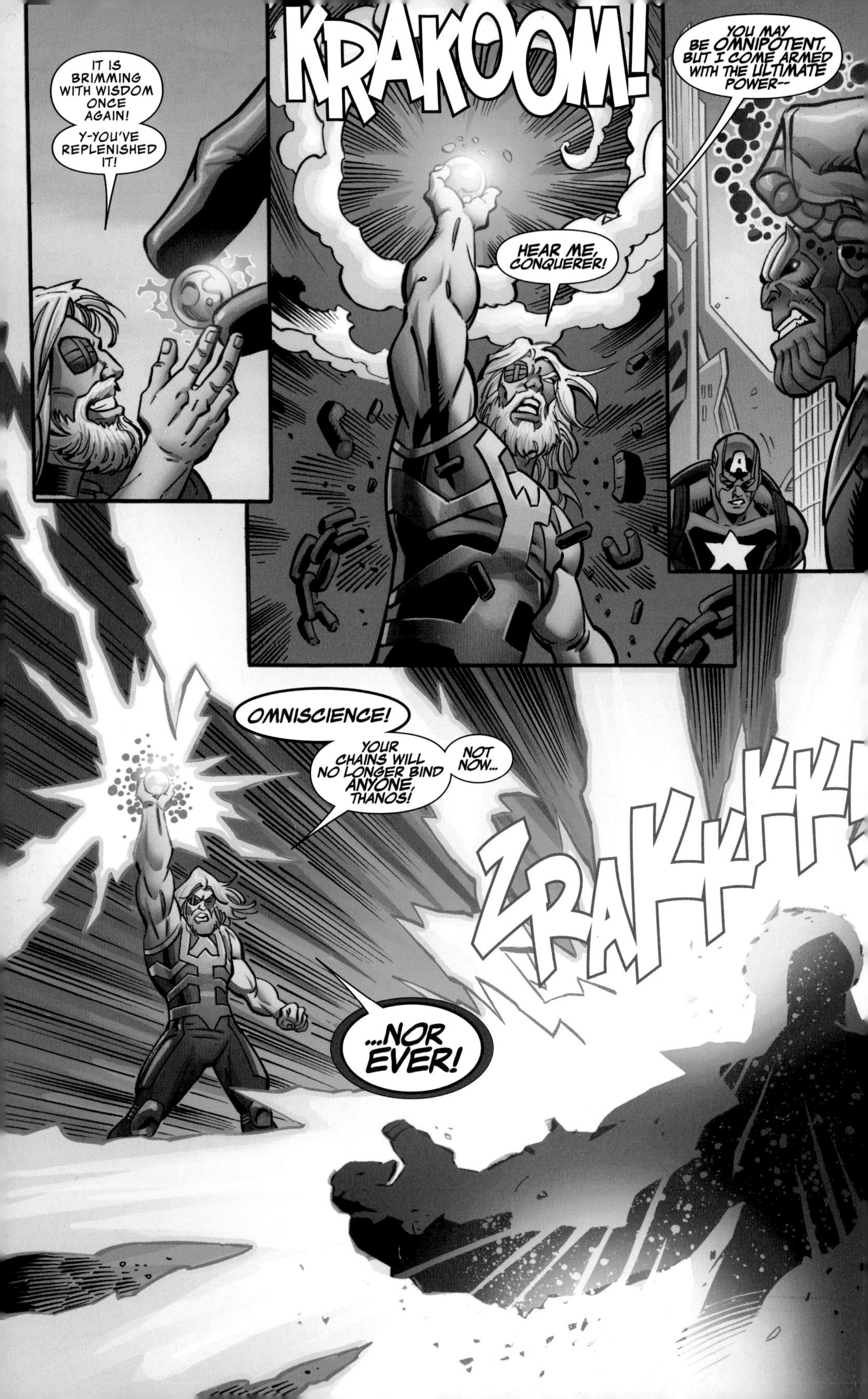
IT IS BRIMMING WITH WISDOM ONCE AGAIN!
Y-YOU'VE REPLENISHED IT!
KRAKOOM!
HEAR ME, CONQUERER!
YOU MAY BE OMNIPOTENT, BUT I COME ARMED WITH THE ULTIMATE POWER--
OMNISCIENCE!
YOUR CHAINS WILL NO LONGER BIND ANYONE, THANOS!
NOT NOW...
...NOR EVER!
ZRAKKKK!

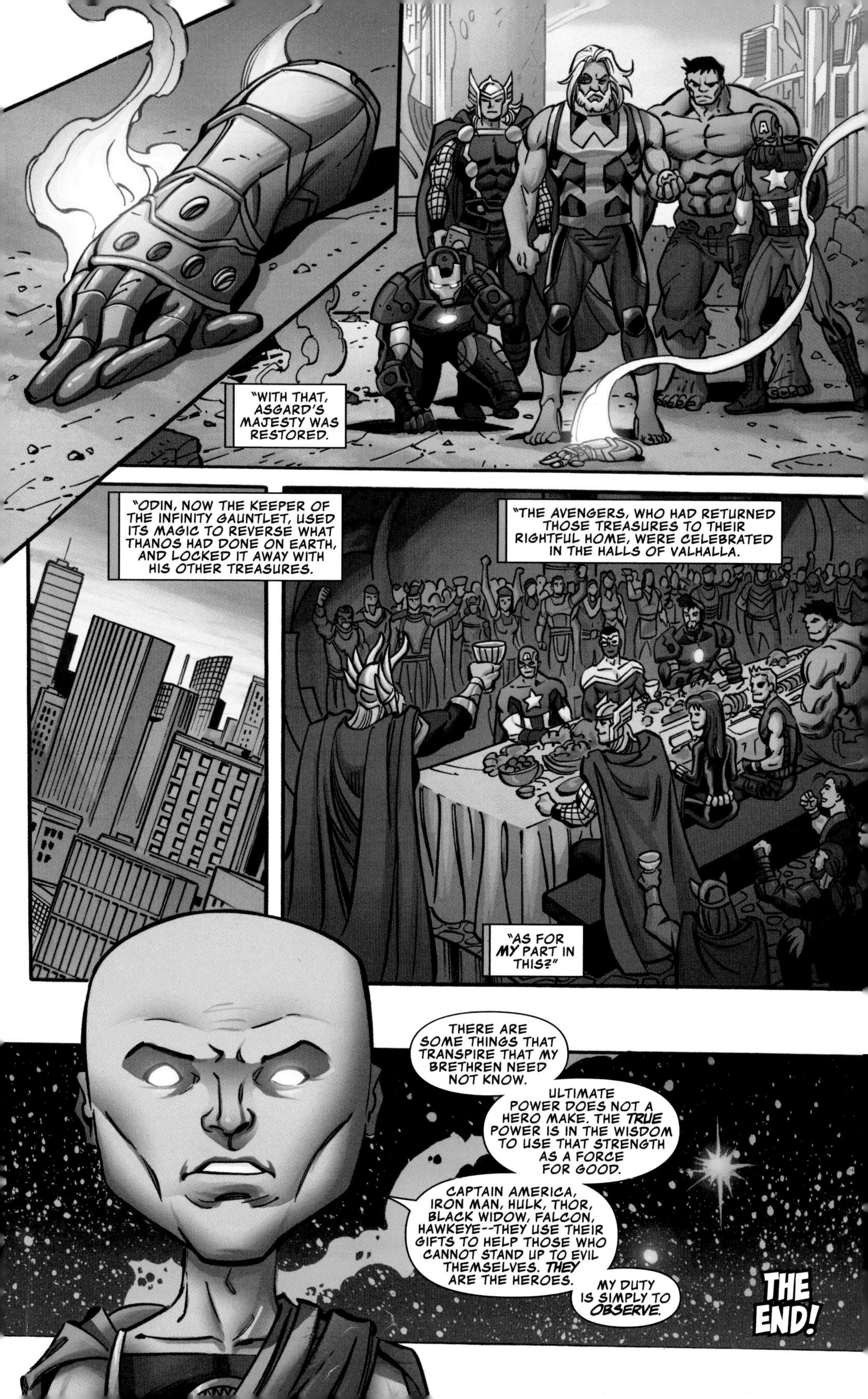
"WITH THAT, ASGARD'S MAJESTY WAS RESTORED.
"ODIN, NOW THE KEEPER OF THE INFINITY GAUNTLET, USED ITS MAGIC TO REVERSE WHAT THANOS HAD DONE ON EARTH, AND LOCKED IT AWAY WITH HIS OTHER TREASURES.
"THE AVENGERS, WHO HAD RETURNED THOSE TREASURES TO THEIR RIGHTFUL HOME, WERE CELEBRATED IN THE HALLS OF VALHALLA.
"AS FOR *MY* PART IN THIS?"
THERE ARE SOME THINGS THAT TRANSPIRE THAT MY BRETHREN NEED NOT KNOW.
ULTIMATE POWER DOES NOT A HERO MAKE. THE *TRUE* POWER IS IN THE WISDOM TO USE THAT STRENGTH AS A FORCE FOR GOOD.
CAPTAIN AMERICA, IRON MAN, HULK, THOR, BLACK WIDOW, FALCON, HAWKEYE--THEY USE THEIR GIFTS TO HELP THOSE WHO CANNOT STAND UP TO EVIL THEMSELVES. *THEY* ARE THE HEROES.
MY DUTY IS SIMPLY TO *OBSERVE*.
THE END!

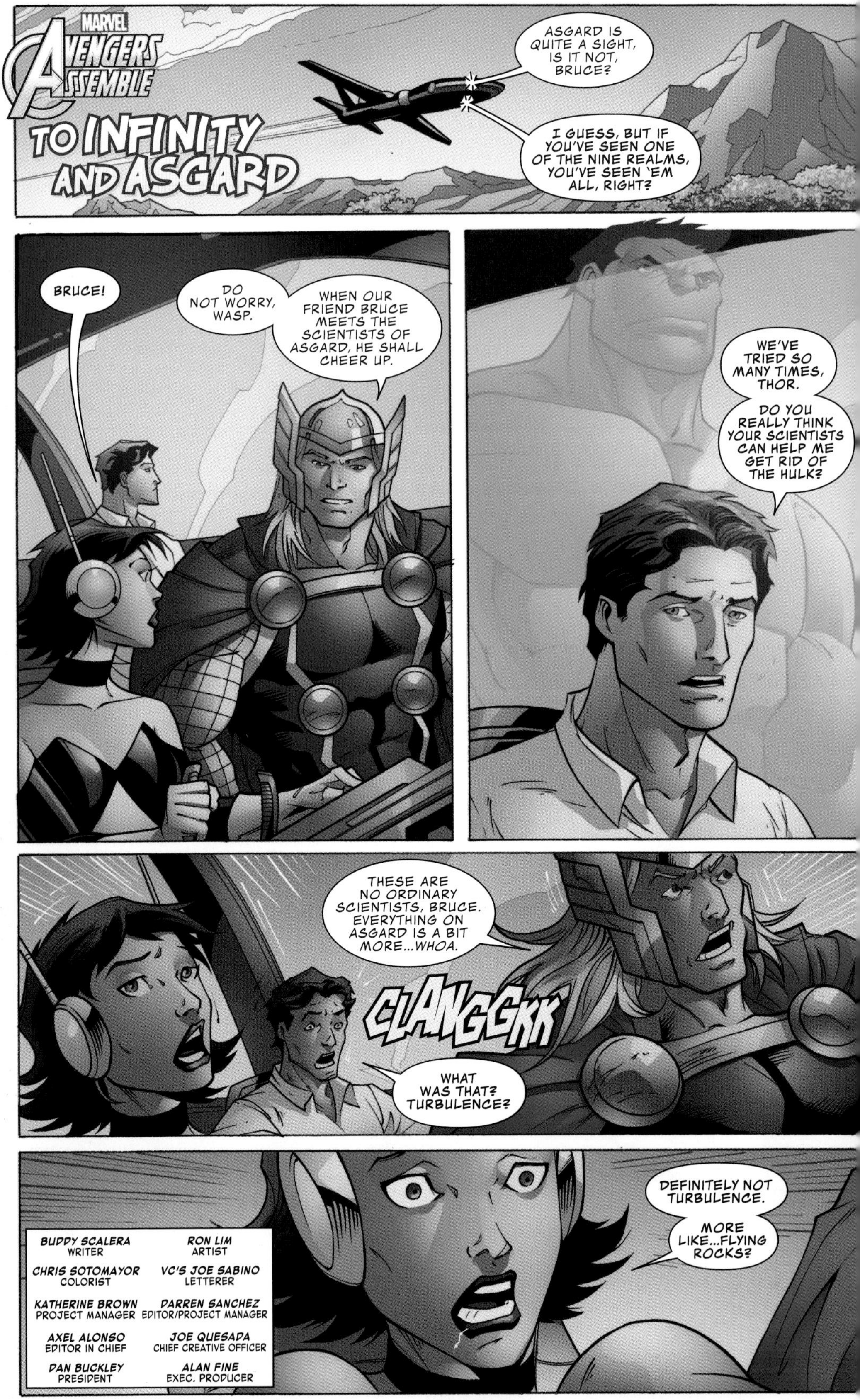
MARVEL
AVENGERS ASSEMBLE
TO INFINITY AND ASGARD
ASGARD IS QUITE A SIGHT, IS IT NOT, BRUCE?
I GUESS, BUT IF YOU'VE SEEN ONE OF THE NINE REALMS, YOU'VE SEEN 'EM ALL, RIGHT?
BRUCE!
DO NOT WORRY, WASP.
WHEN OUR FRIEND BRUCE MEETS THE SCIENTISTS OF ASGARD, HE SHALL CHEER UP.
WE'VE TRIED SO MANY TIMES, THOR.
DO YOU REALLY THINK YOUR SCIENTISTS CAN HELP ME GET RID OF THE HULK?
THESE ARE NO ORDINARY SCIENTISTS, BRUCE. EVERYTHING ON ASGARD IS A BIT MORE...WHOA.
CLANGGKK
WHAT WAS THAT? TURBULENCE?
DEFINITELY NOT TURBULENCE.
MORE LIKE...FLYING ROCKS?
BUDDY SCALERA WRITER
RON LIM ARTIST
CHRIS SOTOMAYOR COLORIST
VC'S JOE SABINO LETTERER
KATHERINE BROWN PROJECT MANAGER
DARREN SANCHEZ EDITOR/PROJECT MANAGER
AXEL ALONSO EDITOR IN CHIEF
JOE QUESADA CHIEF CREATIVE OFFICER
DAN BUCKLEY PRESIDENT
ALAN FINE EXEC. PRODUCER

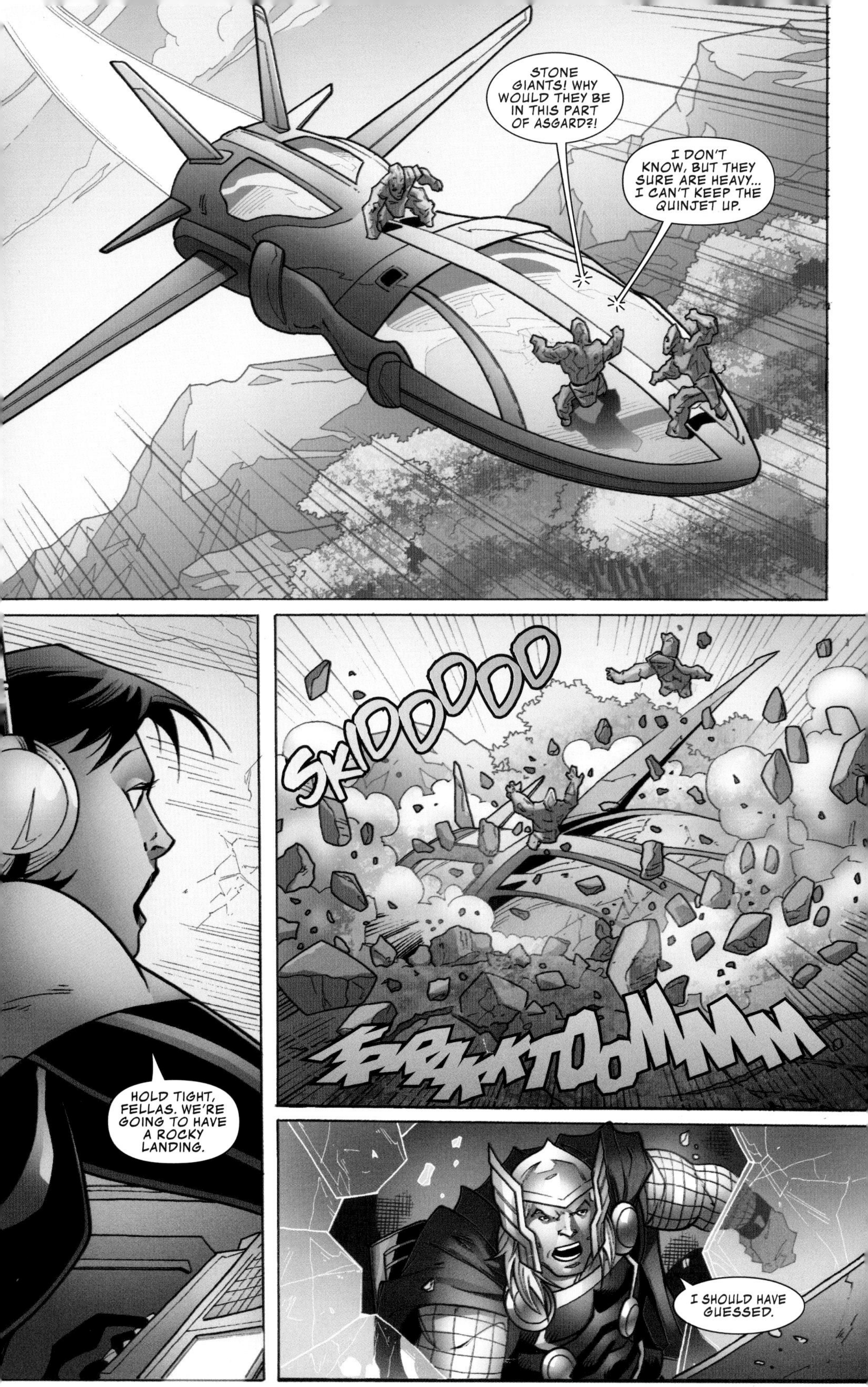
STONE GIANTS! WHY WOULD THEY BE IN THIS PART OF ASGARD?!
I DON'T KNOW, BUT THEY SURE ARE HEAVY... I CAN'T KEEP THE QUINJET UP.
HOLD TIGHT, FELLAS. WE'RE GOING TO HAVE A ROCKY LANDING.
SKIDDDDDD
I SHOULD HAVE GUESSED.

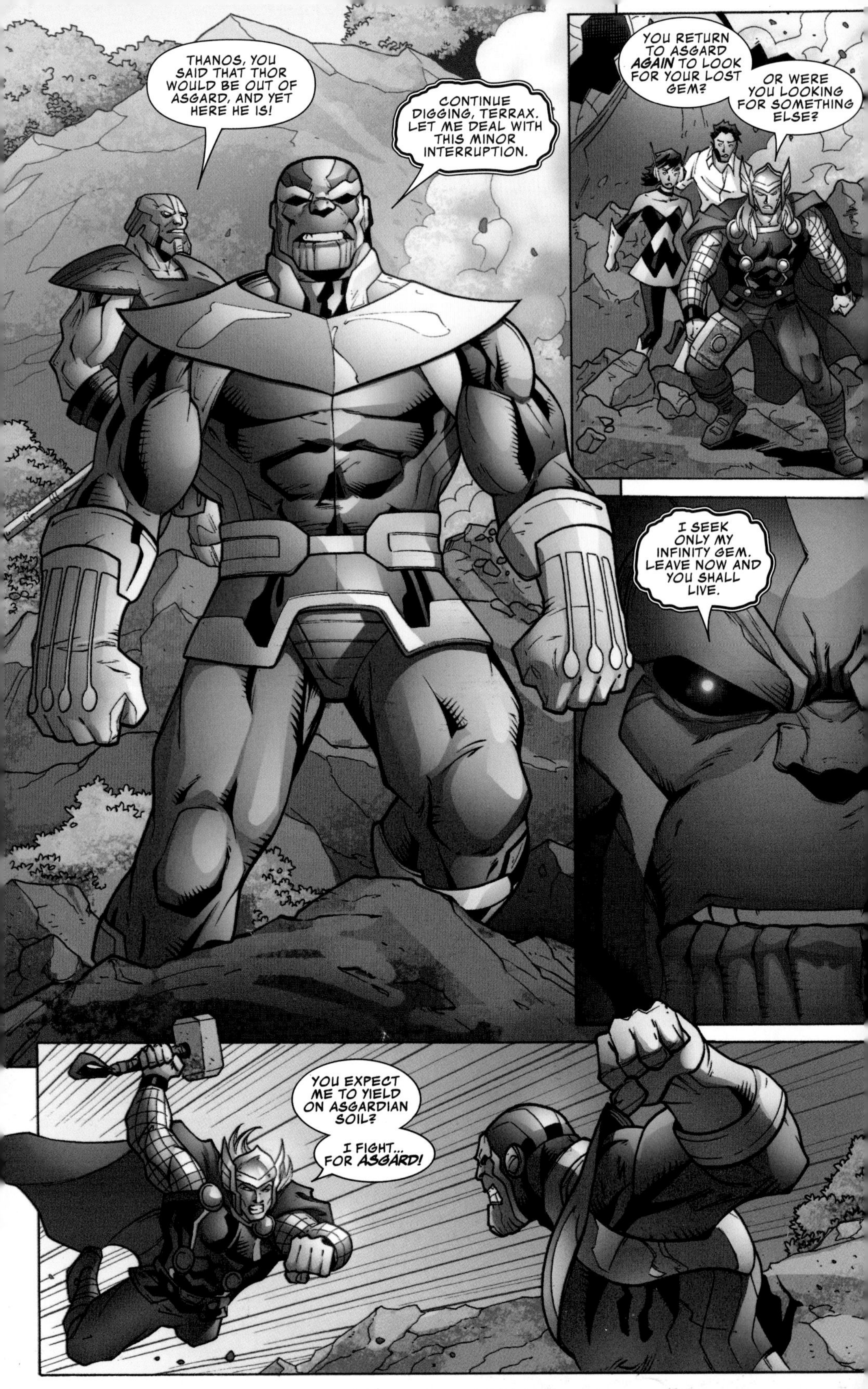
THANOS, YOU SAID THAT THOR WOULD BE OUT OF ASGARD, AND YET HERE HE IS!
CONTINUE DIGGING, TERRAX. LET ME DEAL WITH THIS MINOR INTERRUPTION.
YOU RETURN TO ASGARD AGAIN TO LOOK FOR YOUR LOST GEM?
OR WERE YOU LOOKING FOR SOMETHING ELSE?
I SEEK ONLY MY INFINITY GEM. LEAVE NOW AND YOU SHALL LIVE.
YOU EXPECT ME TO YIELD ON ASGARDIAN SOIL?
I FIGHT... FOR ASGARD!

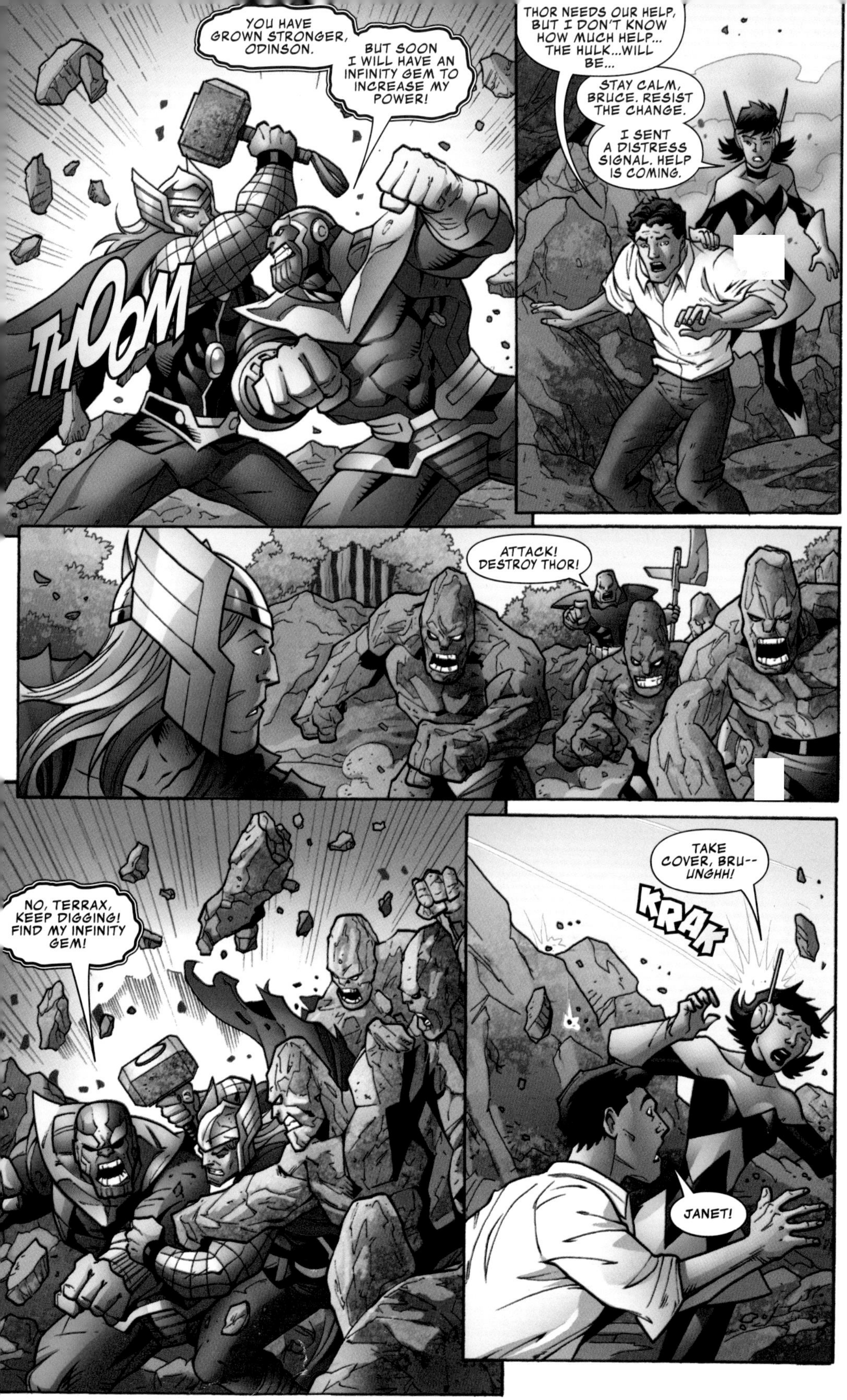
YOU HAVE GROWN STRONGER, ODINSON.
BUT SOON I WILL HAVE AN INFINITY GEM TO INCREASE MY POWER!
THOOM
THOR NEEDS OUR HELP, BUT I DON'T KNOW HOW MUCH HELP... THE HULK...WILL BE...
STAY CALM, BRUCE. RESIST THE CHANGE.
I SENT A DISTRESS SIGNAL. HELP IS COMING.
ATTACK! DESTROY THOR!
NO, TERRAX, KEEP DIGGING! FIND MY INFINITY GEM!
TAKE COVER, BRU-- UNGHH!
KRAK
JANET!

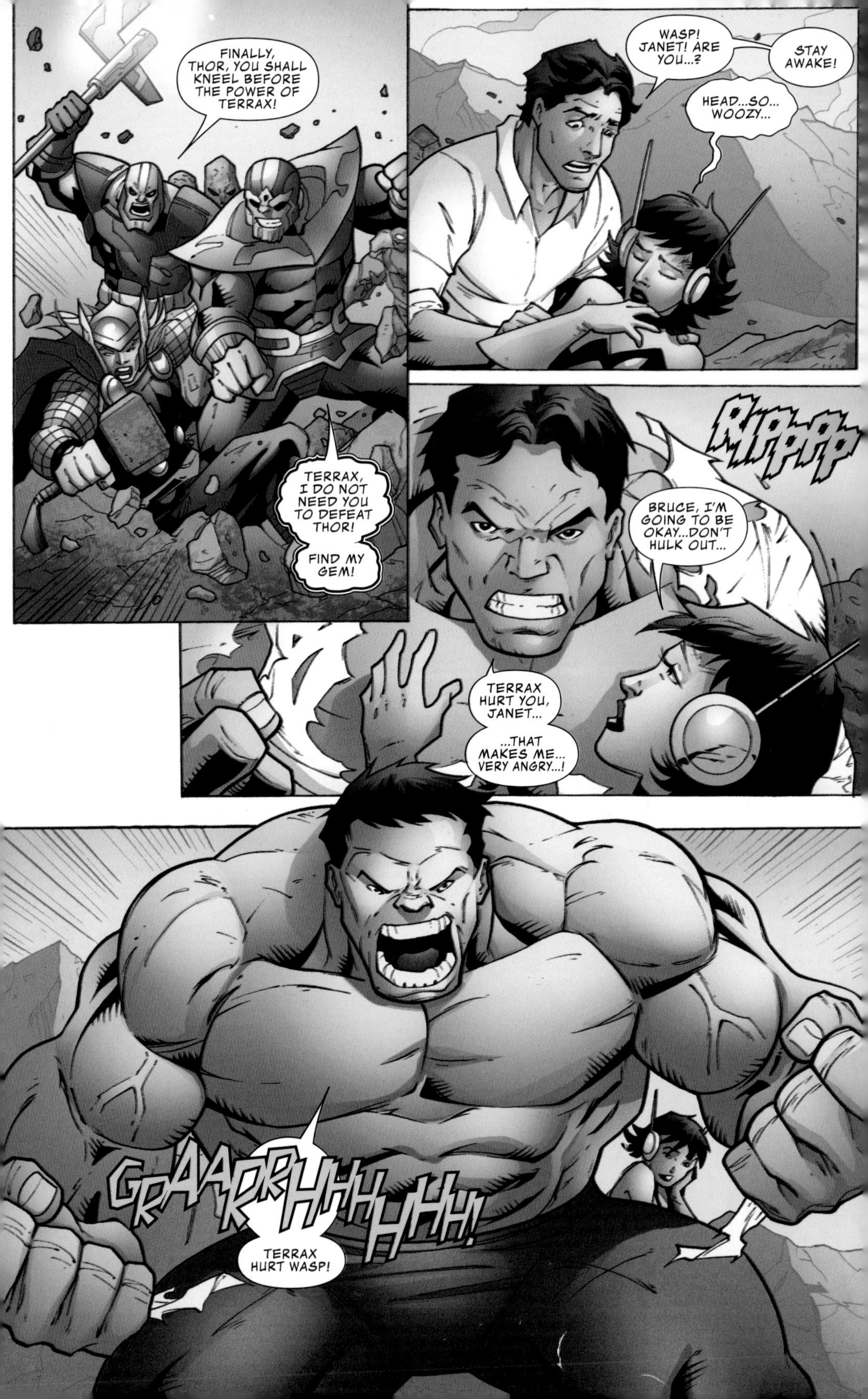
FINALLY, THOR, YOU SHALL KNEEL BEFORE THE POWER OF TERRAX!
TERRAX, I DO NOT NEED YOU TO DEFEAT THOR!
FIND MY GEM!
WASP! JANET! ARE YOU...?
STAY AWAKE!
HEAD...SO... WOOZY...
RIPPP
BRUCE, I'M GOING TO BE OKAY...DON'T HULK OUT...
TERRAX HURT YOU, JANET...
...THAT MAKES ME... VERY ANGRY...!
GRAAARRHHHHHHH!
TERRAX HURT WASP!

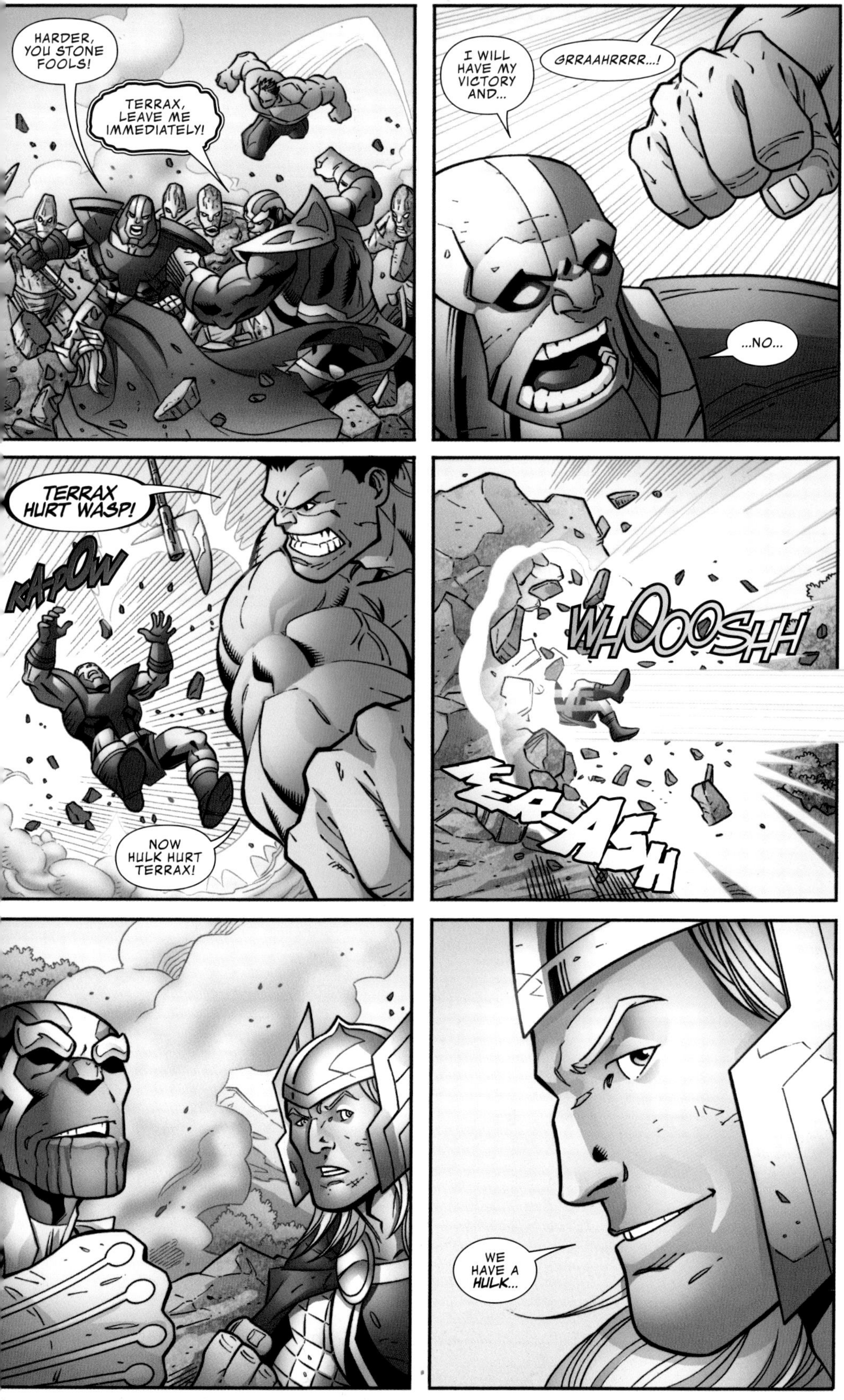

HARDER, YOU STONE FOOLS!
TERRAX, LEAVE ME IMMEDIATELY!
I WILL HAVE MY VICTORY AND...
GRRAAHRRRR...!
...NO...
TERRAX HURT WASP!
KA-POW
NOW HULK HURT TERRAX!
WHOOOOSHH
KER-RASH
WE HAVE A HULK...

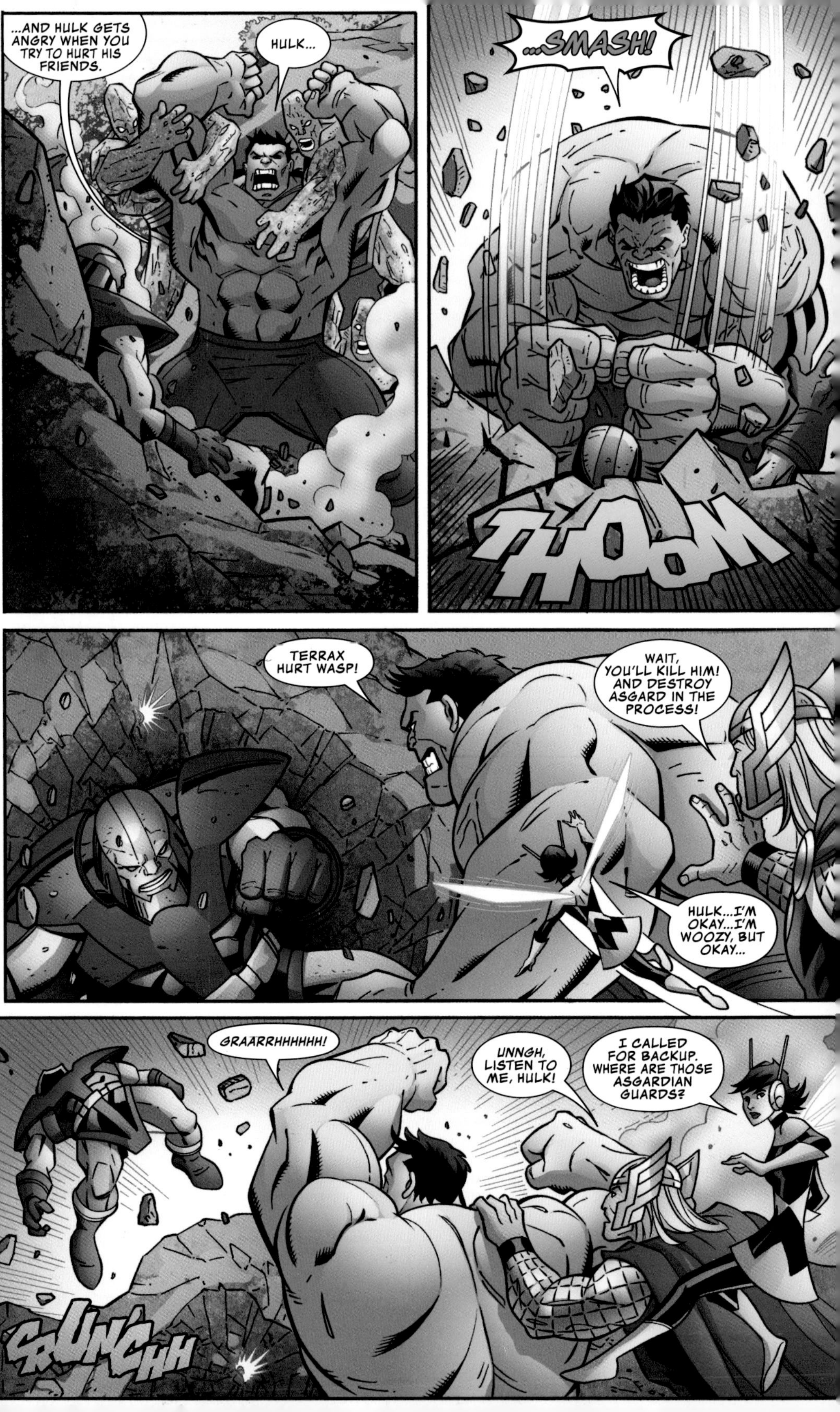
...AND HULK GETS ANGRY WHEN YOU TRY TO HURT HIS FRIENDS.
HULK...
...SMASH!
THOOM
TERRAX HURT WASP!
WAIT, YOU'LL KILL HIM! AND DESTROY ASGARD IN THE PROCESS!
HULK...I'M OKAY...I'M WOOZY, BUT OKAY...
GRAARRHHHHHH!
UNNGH, LISTEN TO ME, HULK!
I CALLED FOR BACKUP. WHERE ARE THOSE ASGARDIAN GUARDS?
CRUNCHH

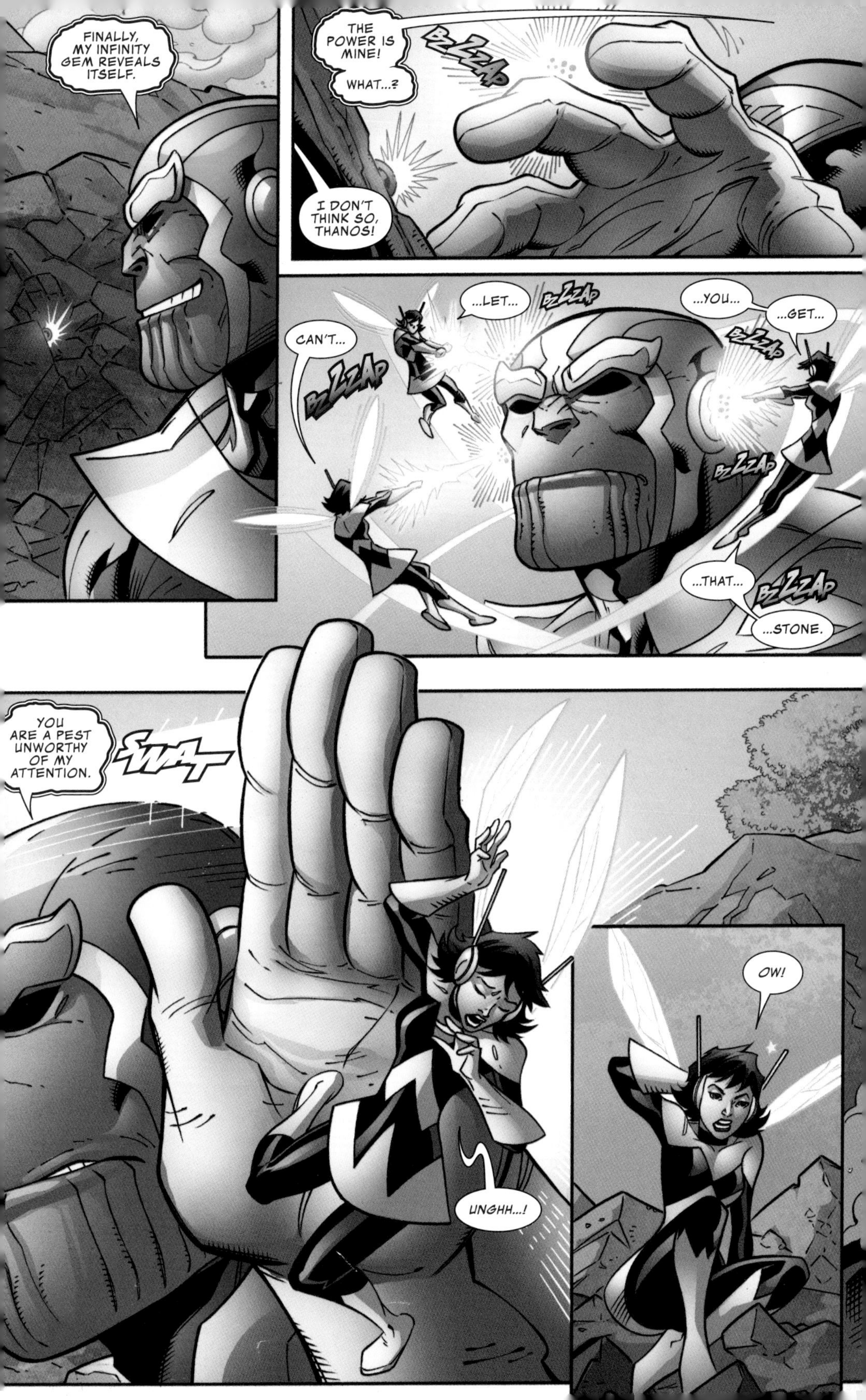
FINALLY, MY INFINITY GEM REVEALS ITSELF.
THE POWER IS MINE!
WHAT...?
BZZZAP
I DON'T THINK SO, THANOS!
CAN'T...
BZZZAP
...LET...
BZZZAP
...YOU...
...GET...
BZZZAP
BZZZAP
...THAT...
BZZZAP
...STONE.
YOU ARE A PEST UNWORTHY OF MY ATTENTION.
SWAT
UNGHH...!
OW!

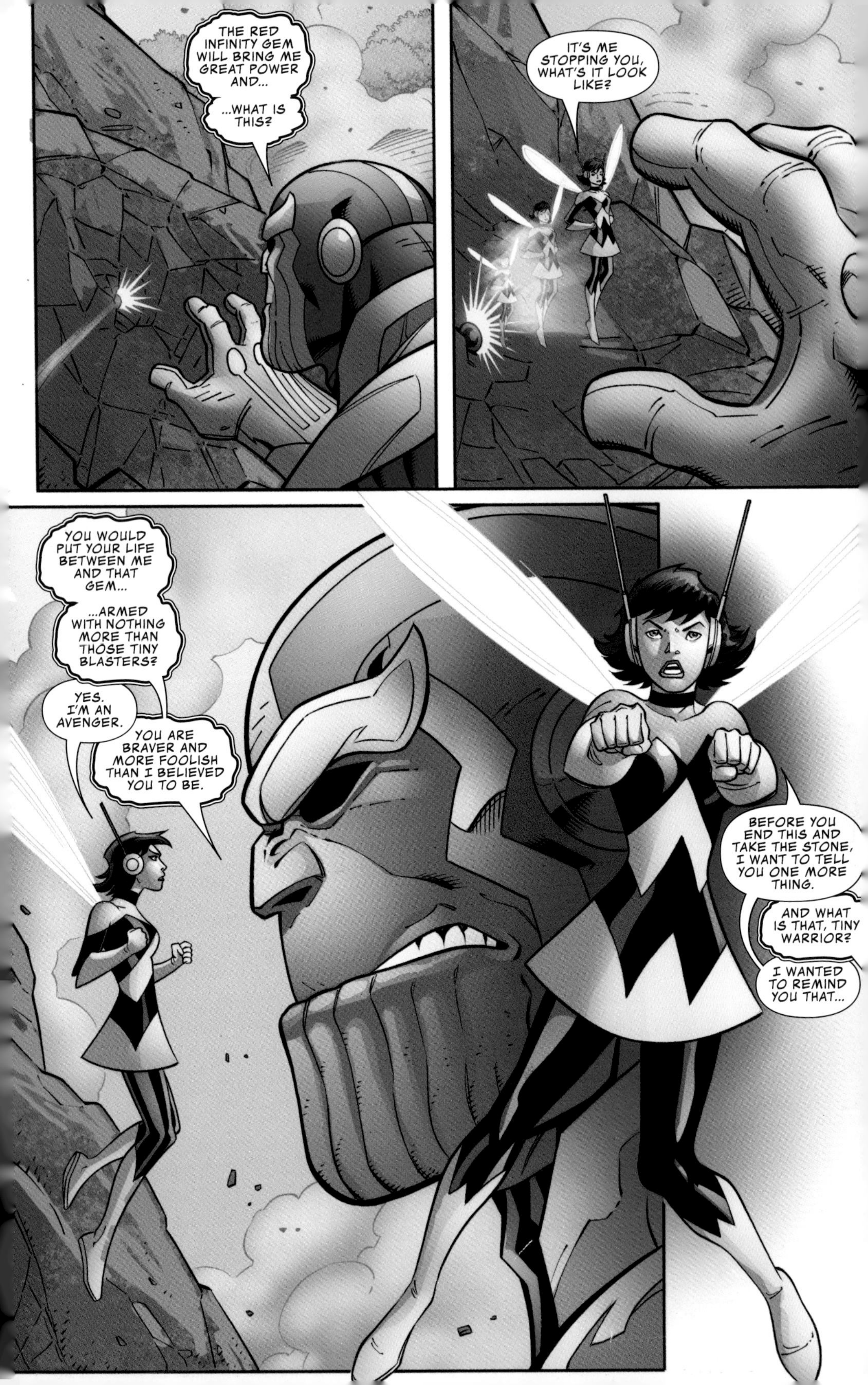
THE RED INFINITY GEM WILL BRING ME GREAT POWER AND...
...WHAT IS THIS?
IT'S ME STOPPING YOU, WHAT'S IT LOOK LIKE?
YOU WOULD PUT YOUR LIFE BETWEEN ME AND THAT GEM...
...ARMED WITH NOTHING MORE THAN THOSE TINY BLASTERS?
YES. I'M AN AVENGER.
YOU ARE BRAVER AND MORE FOOLISH THAN I BELIEVED YOU TO BE.
BEFORE YOU END THIS AND TAKE THE STONE, I WANT TO TELL YOU ONE MORE THING.
AND WHAT IS THAT, TINY WARRIOR?
I WANTED TO REMIND YOU THAT...

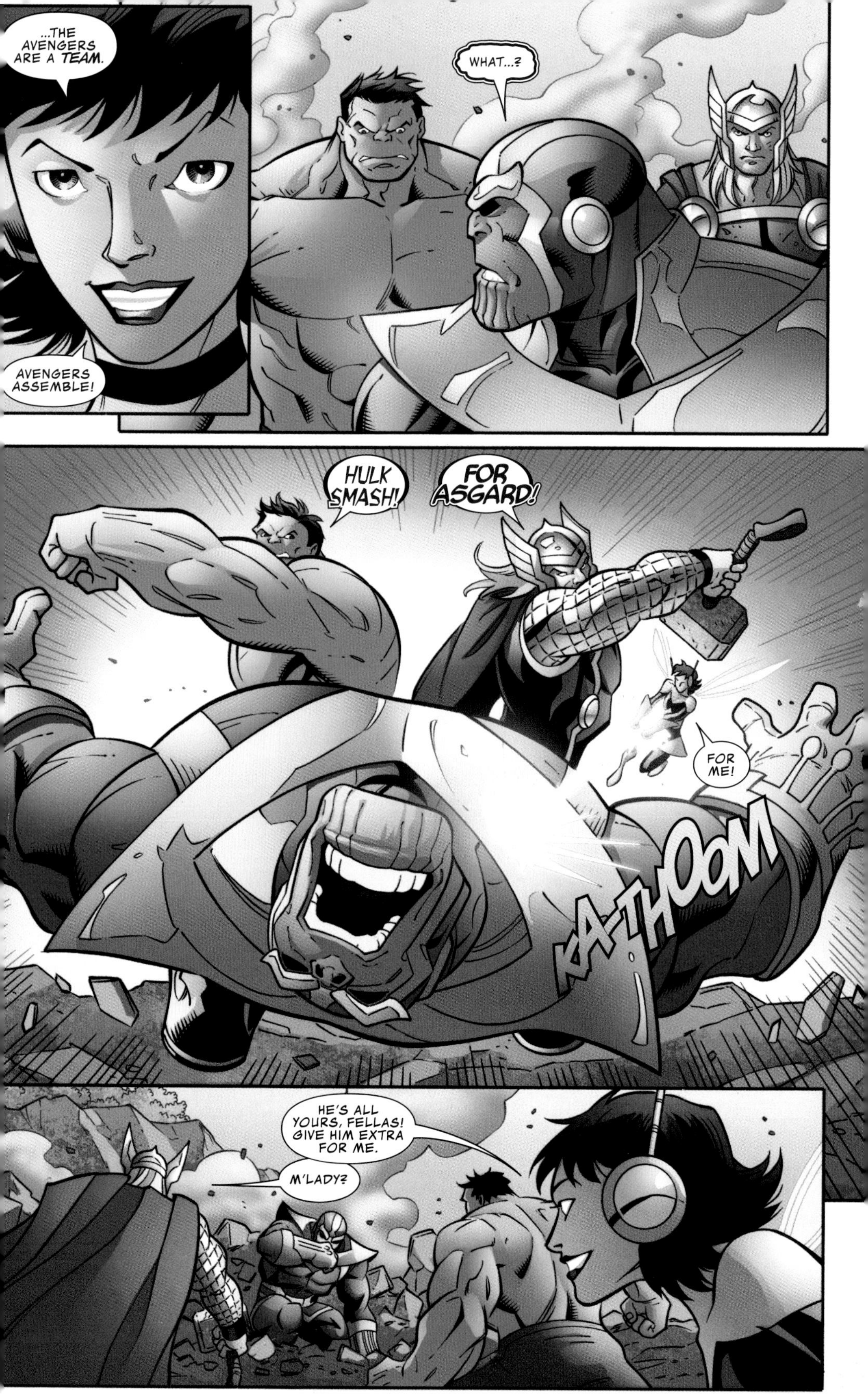
...THE AVENGERS ARE A TEAM.
AVENGERS ASSEMBLE!
WHAT...?
HULK SMASH!
FOR ASGARD!
FOR ME!
KA-THOOM
HE'S ALL YOURS, FELLAS! GIVE HIM EXTRA FOR ME.
M'LADY?

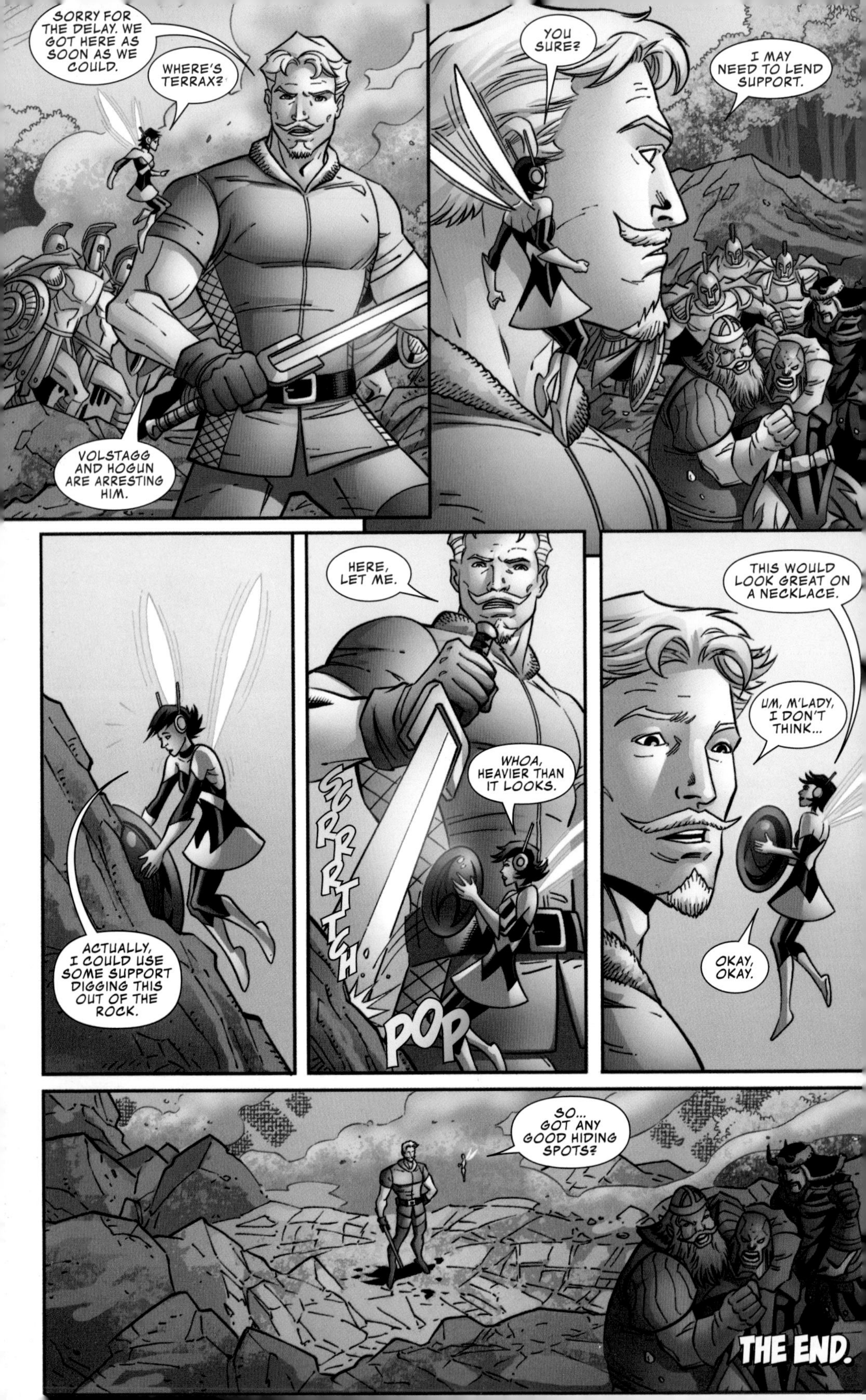
SORRY FOR THE DELAY. WE GOT HERE AS SOON AS WE COULD.
WHERE'S TERRAX?
VOLSTAGG AND HOGUN ARE ARRESTING HIM.
YOU SURE?
I MAY NEED TO LEND SUPPORT.
ACTUALLY, I COULD USE SOME SUPPORT DIGGING THIS OUT OF THE ROCK.
HERE, LET ME.
WHOA, HEAVIER THAN IT LOOKS.
SCRRRITCH
POP
THIS WOULD LOOK GREAT ON A NECKLACE.
UM, M'LADY, I DON'T THINK...
OKAY, OKAY.
SO... GOT ANY GOOD HIDING SPOTS?
THE END.

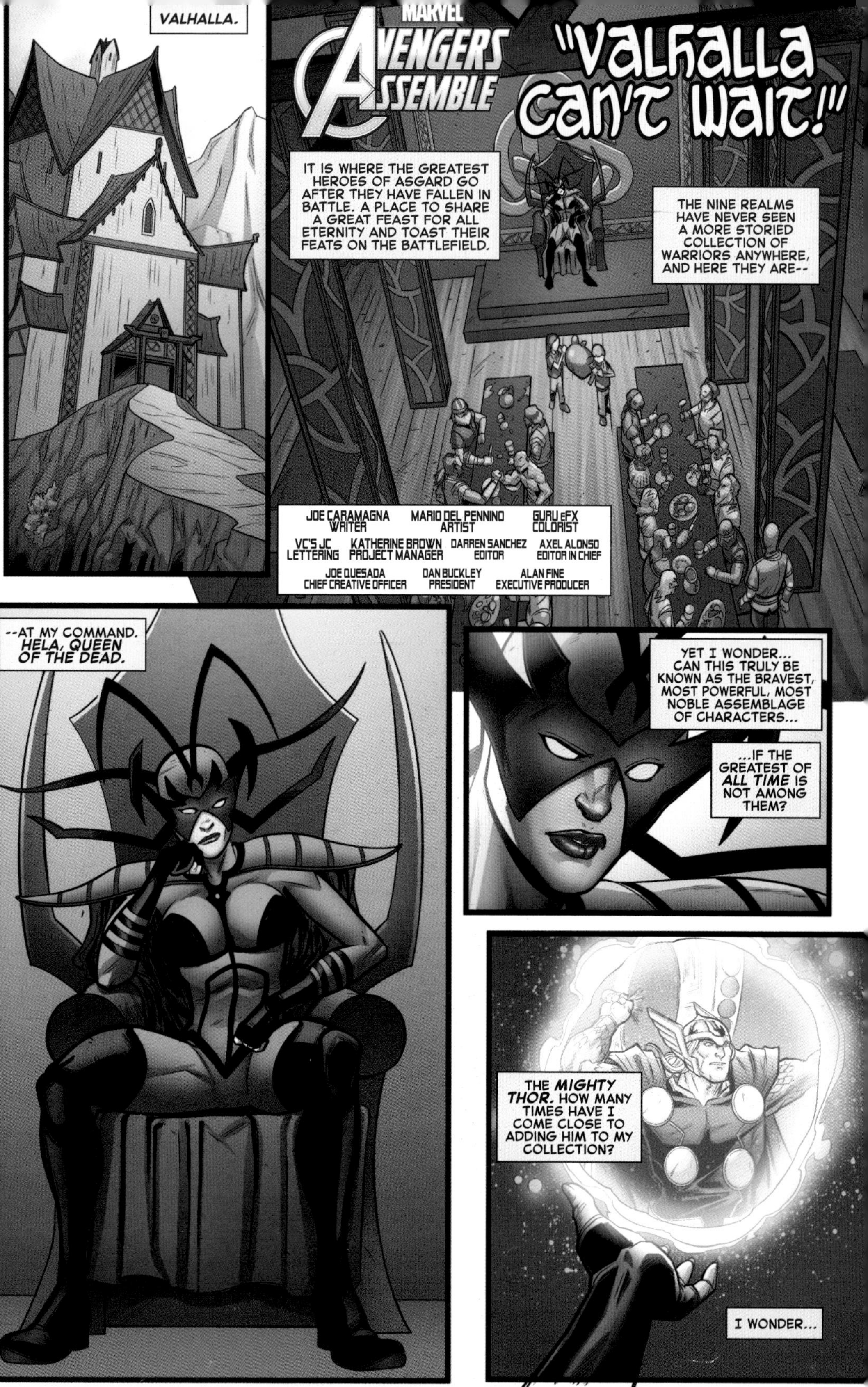
VALHALLA.
MARVEL
AVENGERS ASSEMBLE
"VALHALLA CAN'T WAIT!"
IT IS WHERE THE GREATEST HEROES OF ASGARD GO AFTER THEY HAVE FALLEN IN BATTLE. A PLACE TO SHARE A GREAT FEAST FOR ALL ETERNITY AND TOAST THEIR FEATS ON THE BATTLEFIELD.
THE NINE REALMS HAVE NEVER SEEN A MORE STORIED COLLECTION OF WARRIORS ANYWHERE, AND HERE THEY ARE--
JOE CARAMAGNA WRITER
MARIO DEL PENNINO ARTIST
GURU eFX COLORIST
VC'S JC LETTERING
KATHERINE BROWN PROJECT MANAGER
DARREN SANCHEZ EDITOR
AXEL ALONSO EDITOR IN CHIEF
JOE QUESADA CHIEF CREATIVE OFFICER
DAN BUCKLEY PRESIDENT
ALAN FINE EXECUTIVE PRODUCER
--AT MY COMMAND. HELA, QUEEN OF THE DEAD.
YET I WONDER... CAN THIS TRULY BE KNOWN AS THE BRAVEST, MOST POWERFUL, MOST NOBLE ASSEMBLAGE OF CHARACTERS...
...IF THE GREATEST OF ALL TIME IS NOT AMONG THEM?
THE MIGHTY THOR. HOW MANY TIMES HAVE I COME CLOSE TO ADDING HIM TO MY COLLECTION?
I WONDER...

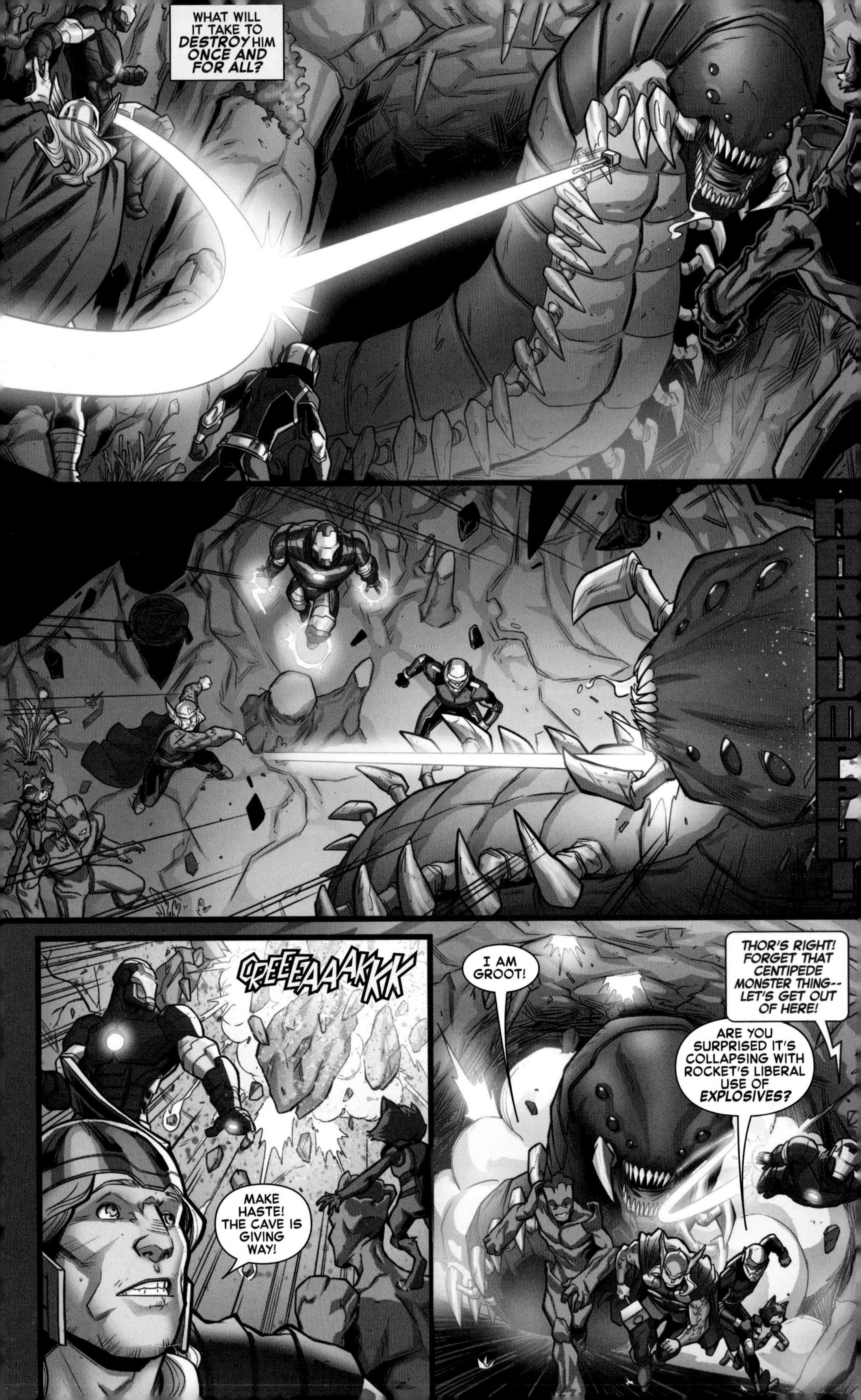
WHAT WILL IT TAKE TO DESTROY HIM ONCE AND FOR ALL?
CREEEAAAKKK
MAKE HASTE! THE CAVE IS GIVING WAY!
I AM GROOT!
THOR'S RIGHT! FORGET THAT CENTIPEDE MONSTER THING-- LET'S GET OUT OF HERE!
ARE YOU SURPRISED IT'S COLLAPSING WITH ROCKET'S LIBERAL USE OF EXPLOSIVES?

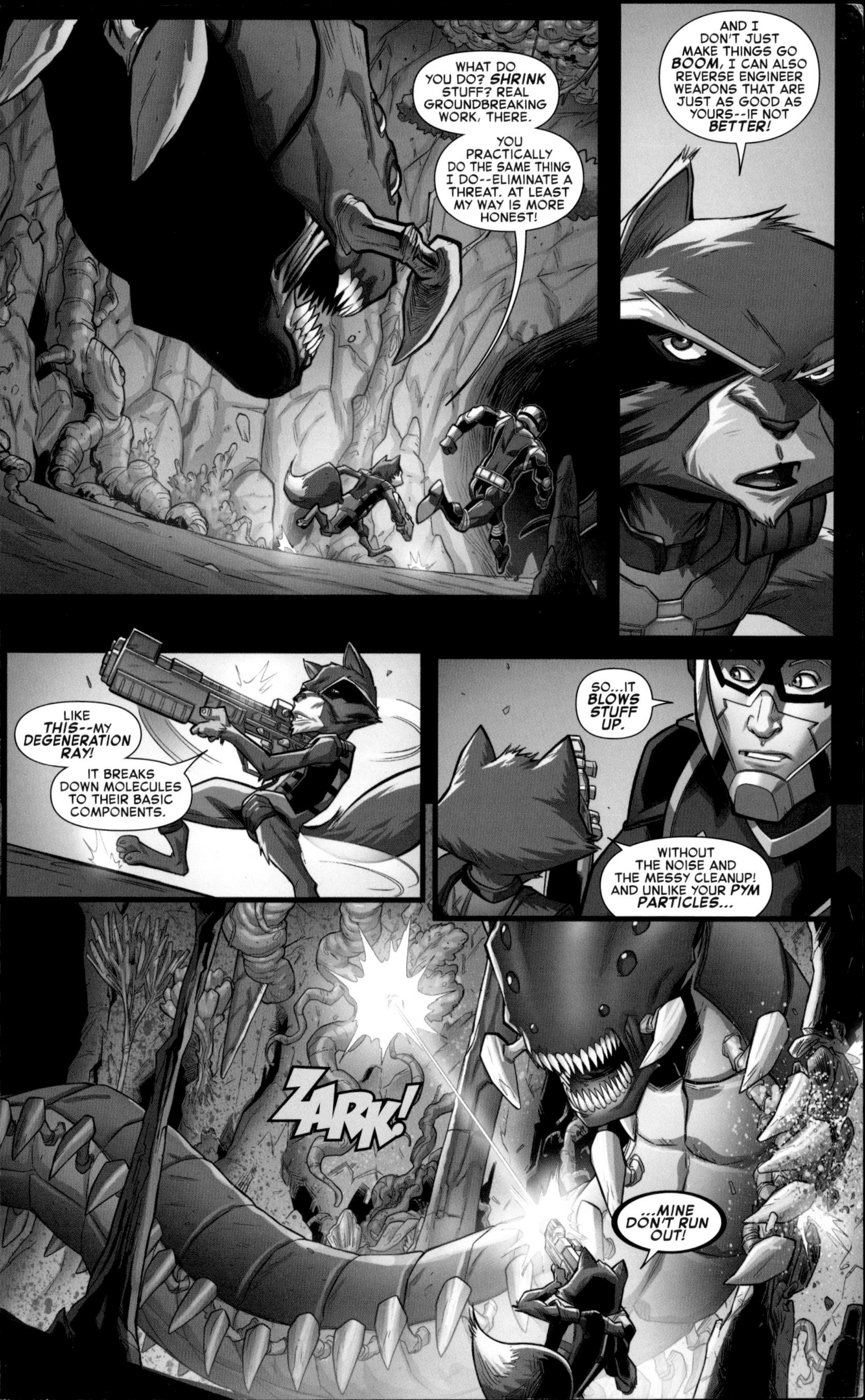
WHAT DO YOU DO? SHRINK STUFF? REAL GROUNDBREAKING WORK, THERE.
YOU PRACTICALLY DO THE SAME THING I DO--ELIMINATE A THREAT. AT LEAST MY WAY IS MORE HONEST!
AND I DON'T JUST MAKE THINGS GO BOOM, I CAN ALSO REVERSE ENGINEER WEAPONS THAT ARE JUST AS GOOD AS YOURS--IF NOT BETTER!
LIKE THIS--MY DEGENERATION RAY!
IT BREAKS DOWN MOLECULES TO THEIR BASIC COMPONENTS.
SO...IT BLOWS STUFF UP.
WITHOUT THE NOISE AND THE MESSY CLEANUP! AND UNLIKE YOUR PYM PARTICLES...
ZARK!
...MINE DON'T RUN OUT!

HUNH?

YOU ACTUALLY **STIMULATED** GROWTH! YOUR RAY IS **FERTILIZER!**

BRKKKOOOOM!

I AM GROOT!

AAAAARRRGGHH!

GREAT FORTUNE HAS SMILED UPON ME THIS DAY! THE MIGHTY THOR-- SO CLOSE TO HIS DEMISE AFTER SO MANY ATTEMPTS.

IT APPEARS HE COULD USE A PUSH.

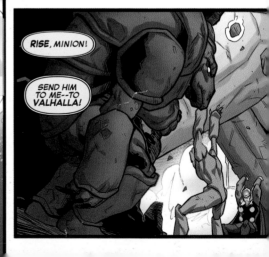

RISE, MINION!

SEND HIM TO ME--TO VALHALLA!

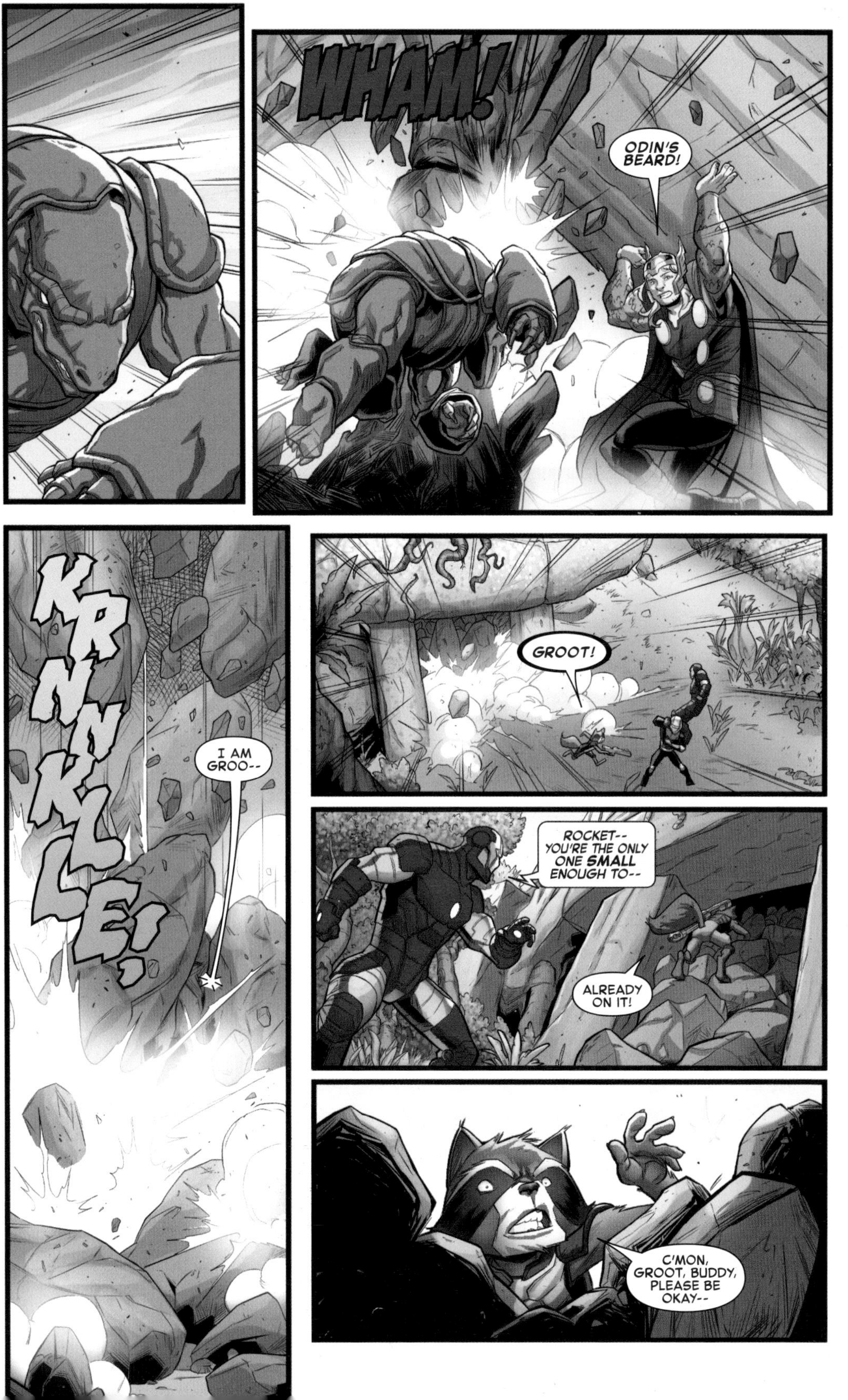
WHAM!
ODIN'S BEARD!
KRNNKLE!
I AM GROO--
GROOT!
ROCKET-- YOU'RE THE ONLY ONE SMALL ENOUGH TO--
ALREADY ON IT!
C'MON, GROOT, BUDDY, PLEASE BE OKAY--

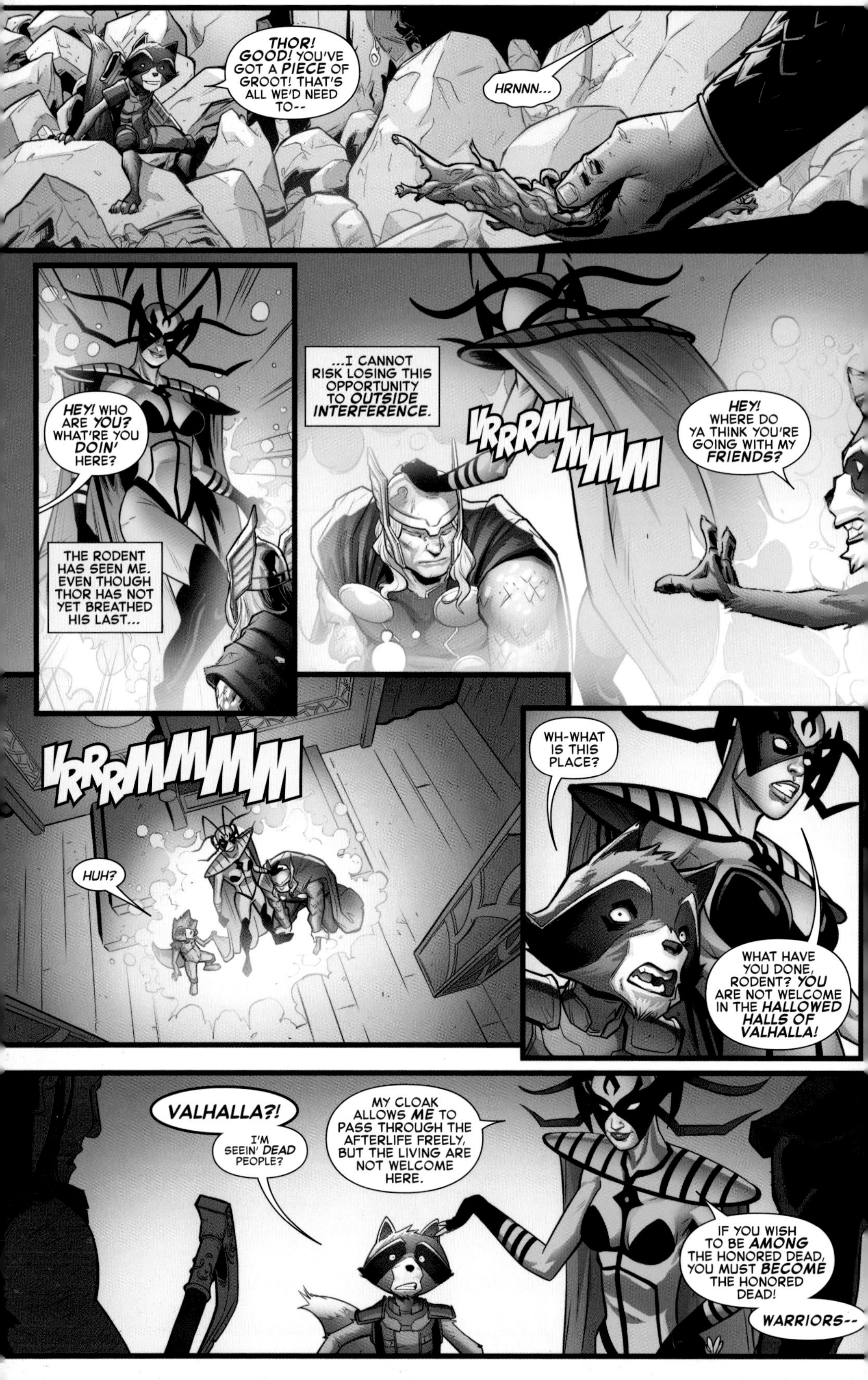
THOR! GOOD! YOU'VE GOT A PIECE OF GROOT! THAT'S ALL WE'D NEED TO--
HRNNN...
HEY! WHO ARE YOU? WHAT'RE YOU DOIN' HERE?
THE RODENT HAS SEEN ME. EVEN THOUGH THOR HAS NOT YET BREATHED HIS LAST...
...I CANNOT RISK LOSING THIS OPPORTUNITY TO OUTSIDE INTERFERENCE.
VRRRMMMMM
HEY! WHERE DO YA THINK YOU'RE GOING WITH MY FRIENDS?
VRRRMMMMMM
HUH?
WH-WHAT IS THIS PLACE?
WHAT HAVE YOU DONE, RODENT? YOU ARE NOT WELCOME IN THE HALLOWED HALLS OF VALHALLA!
VALHALLA?!
I'M SEEIN' DEAD PEOPLE?
MY CLOAK ALLOWS ME TO PASS THROUGH THE AFTERLIFE FREELY, BUT THE LIVING ARE NOT WELCOME HERE.
IF YOU WISH TO BE AMONG THE HONORED DEAD, YOU MUST BECOME THE HONORED DEAD!
WARRIORS--

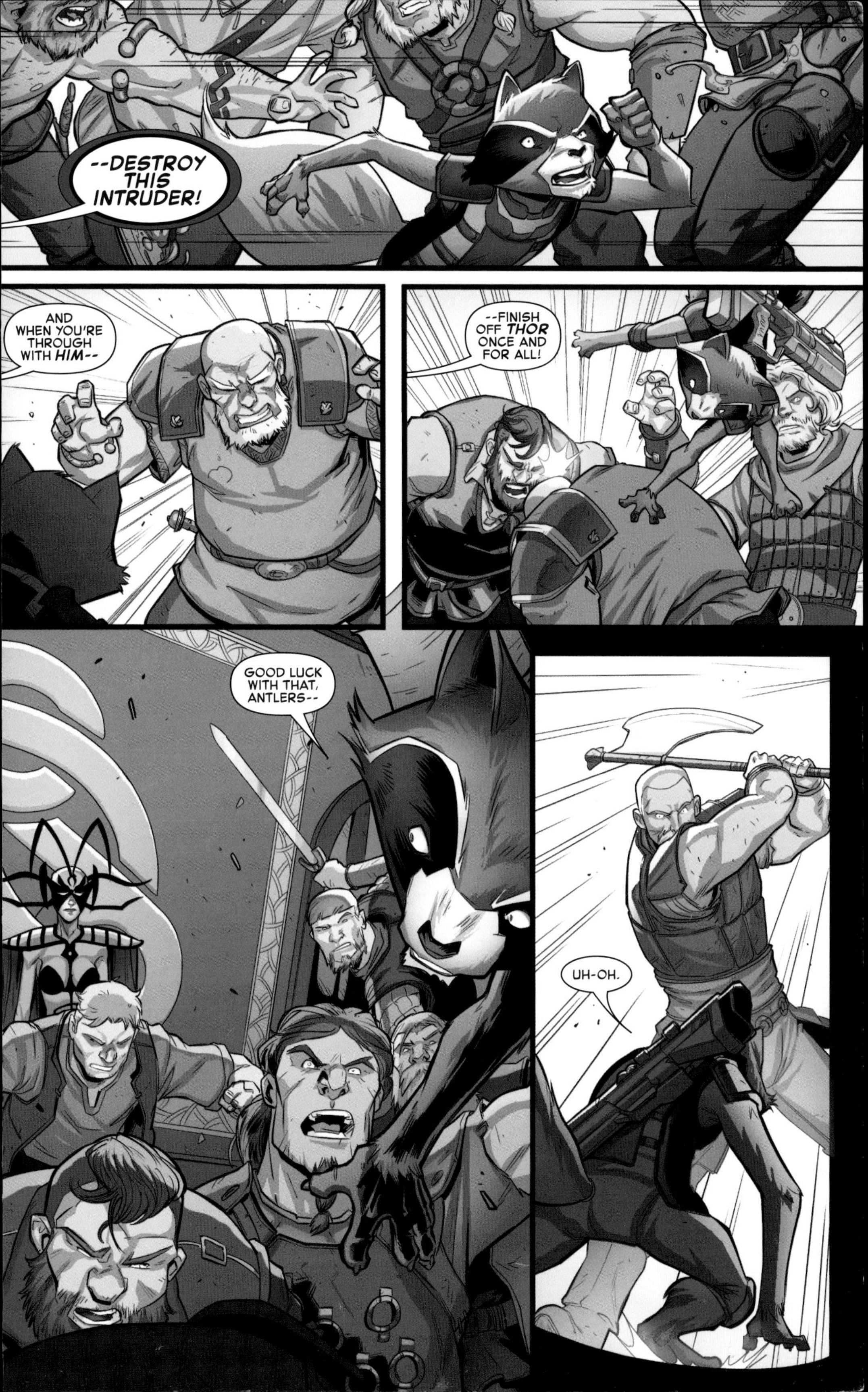
--DESTROY THIS INTRUDER!
AND WHEN YOU'RE THROUGH WITH *HIM*--
--FINISH OFF *THOR* ONCE AND FOR ALL!
GOOD LUCK WITH THAT, ANTLERS--
UH-OH.

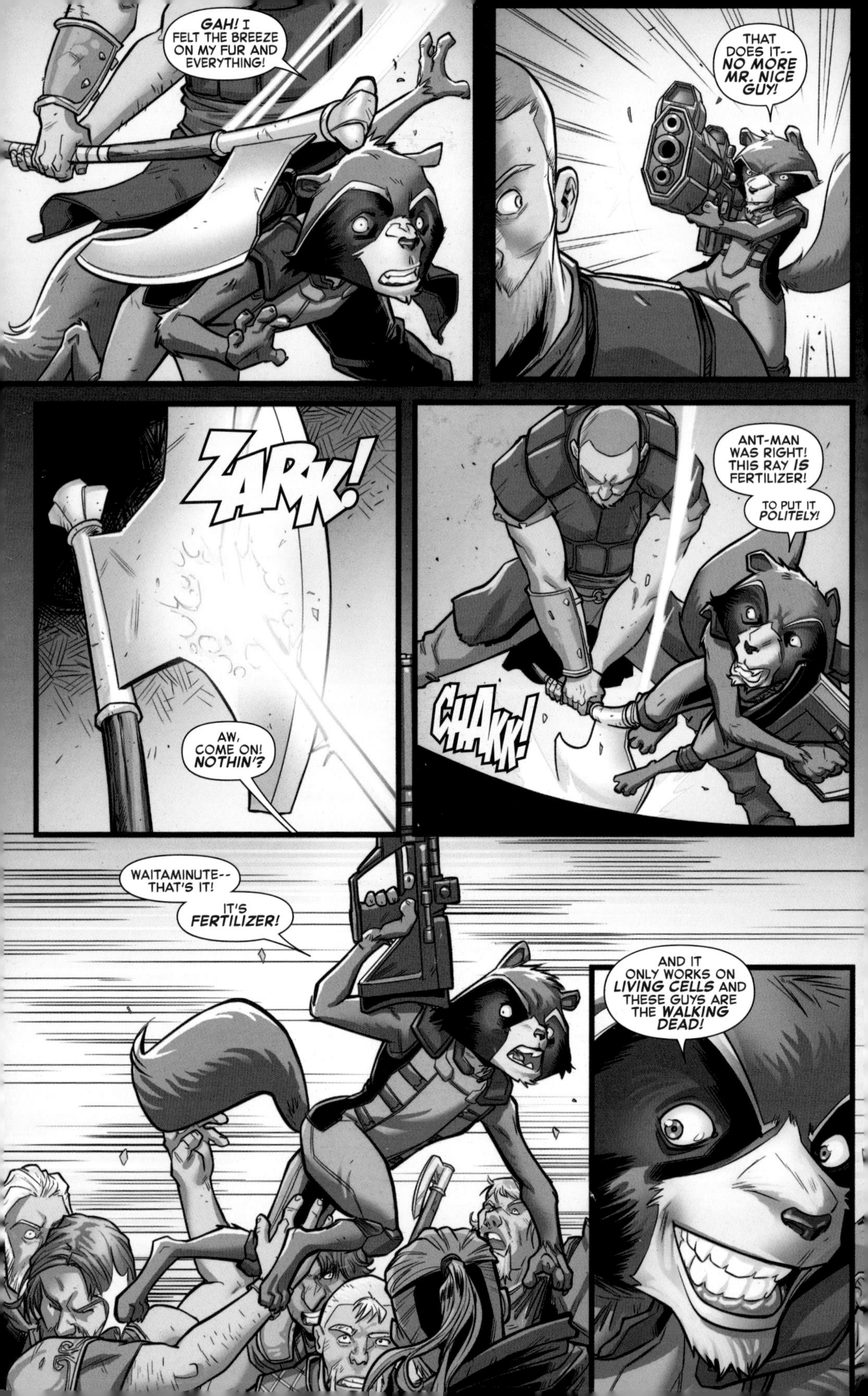
GAH! I FELT THE BREEZE ON MY FUR AND EVERYTHING!
THAT DOES IT-- NO MORE MR. NICE GUY!
ZARK!
AW, COME ON! NOTHIN'?
ANT-MAN WAS RIGHT! THIS RAY IS FERTILIZER!
TO PUT IT POLITELY!
CHAKK!
WAITAMINUTE-- THAT'S IT!
IT'S FERTILIZER!
AND IT ONLY WORKS ON LIVING CELLS AND THESE GUYS ARE THE WALKING DEAD!

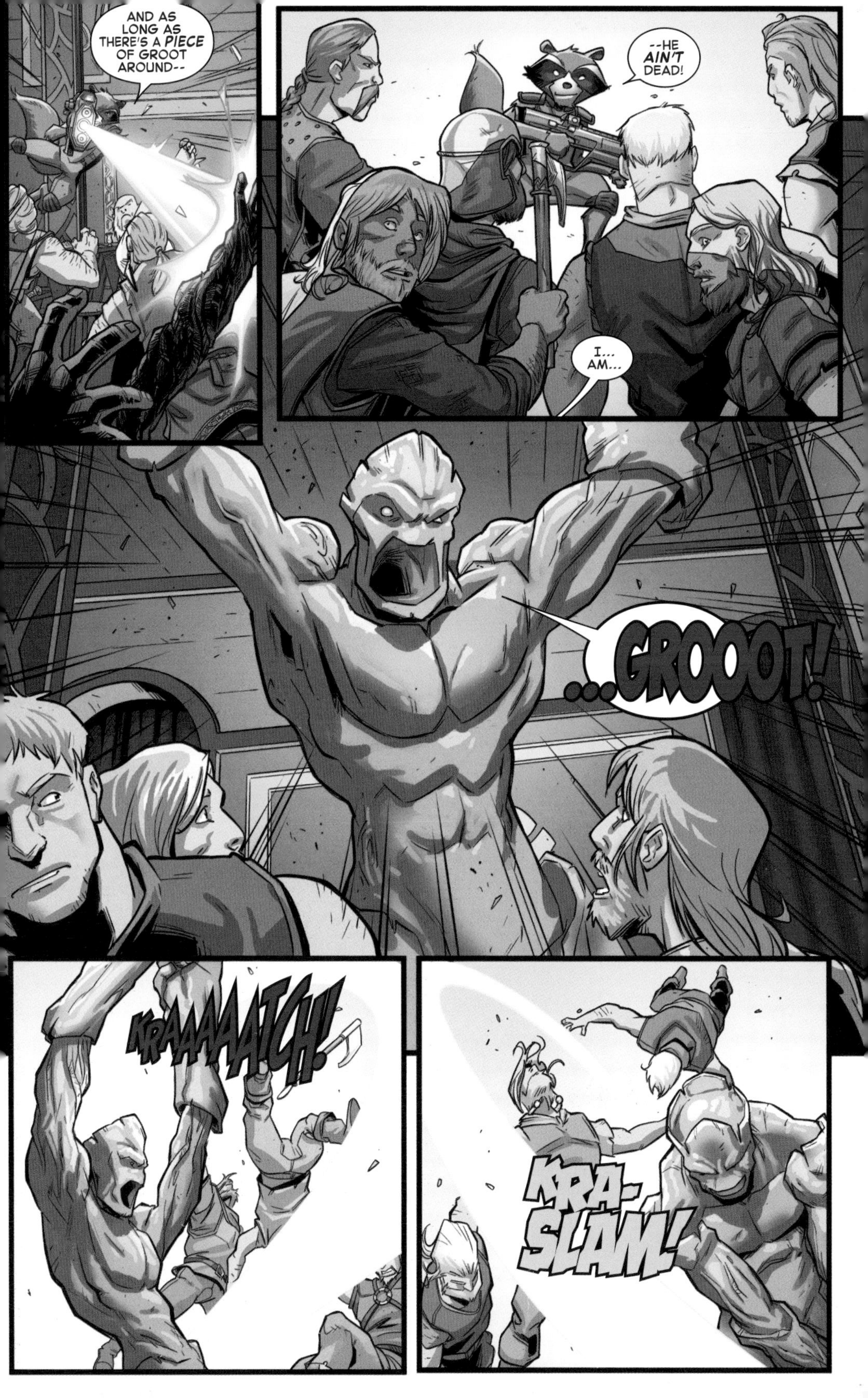
AND AS LONG AS THERE'S A *PIECE* OF GROOT AROUND--
--HE *AIN'T* DEAD!
I... AM...
....GROOOT!
KRAAAAATCH!
KRA-SLAM!

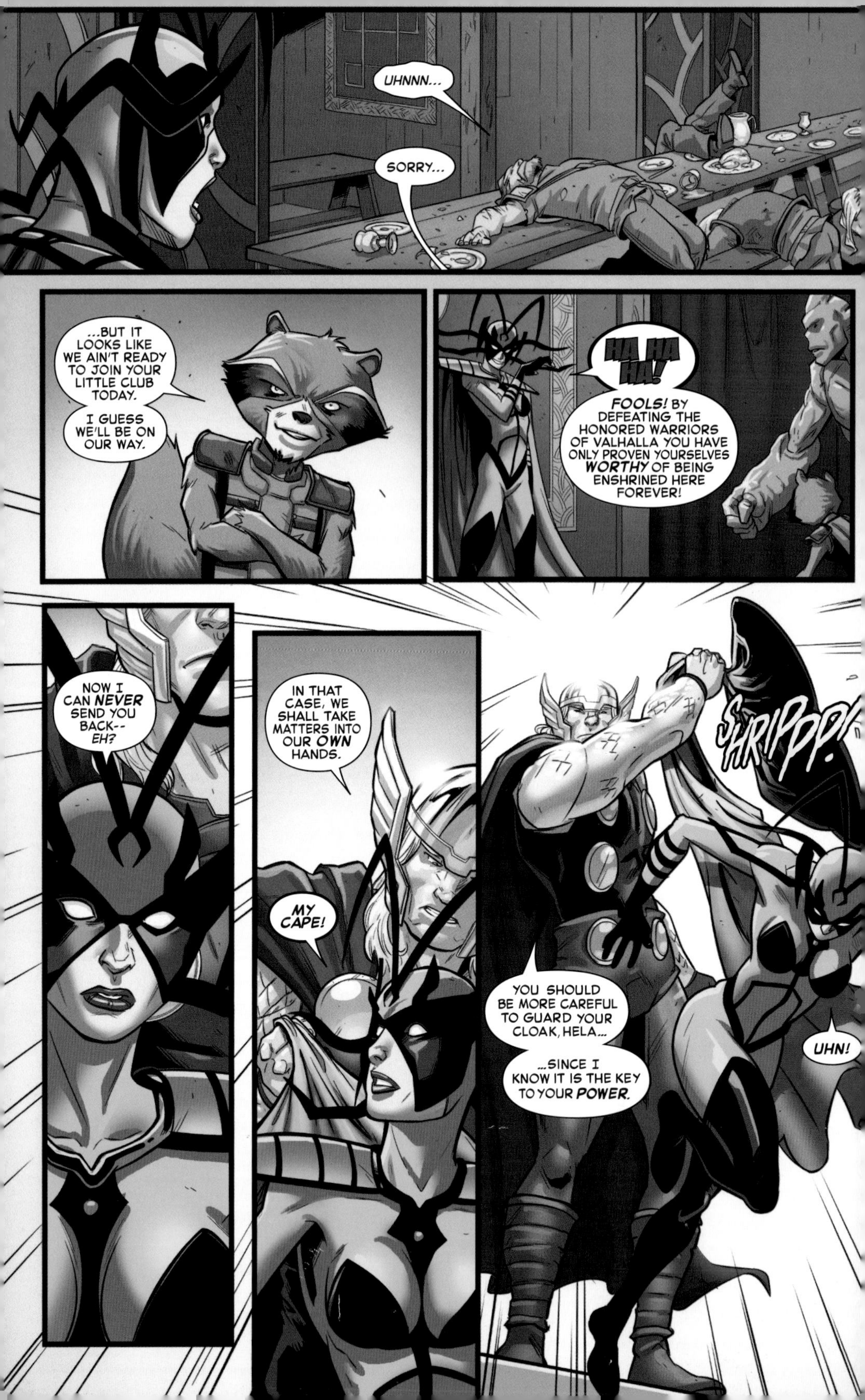

UHNNN...
SORRY...
...BUT IT LOOKS LIKE WE AIN'T READY TO JOIN YOUR LITTLE CLUB TODAY.
I GUESS WE'LL BE ON OUR WAY.
HA HA HA!
FOOLS! BY DEFEATING THE HONORED WARRIORS OF VALHALLA YOU HAVE ONLY PROVEN YOURSELVES WORTHY OF BEING ENSHRINED HERE FOREVER!
NOW I CAN NEVER SEND YOU BACK--EH?
IN THAT CASE, WE SHALL TAKE MATTERS INTO OUR OWN HANDS.
MY CAPE!
SHRIPPP!
YOU SHOULD BE MORE CAREFUL TO GUARD YOUR CLOAK, HELA...
...SINCE I KNOW IT IS THE KEY TO YOUR POWER.
UHN!

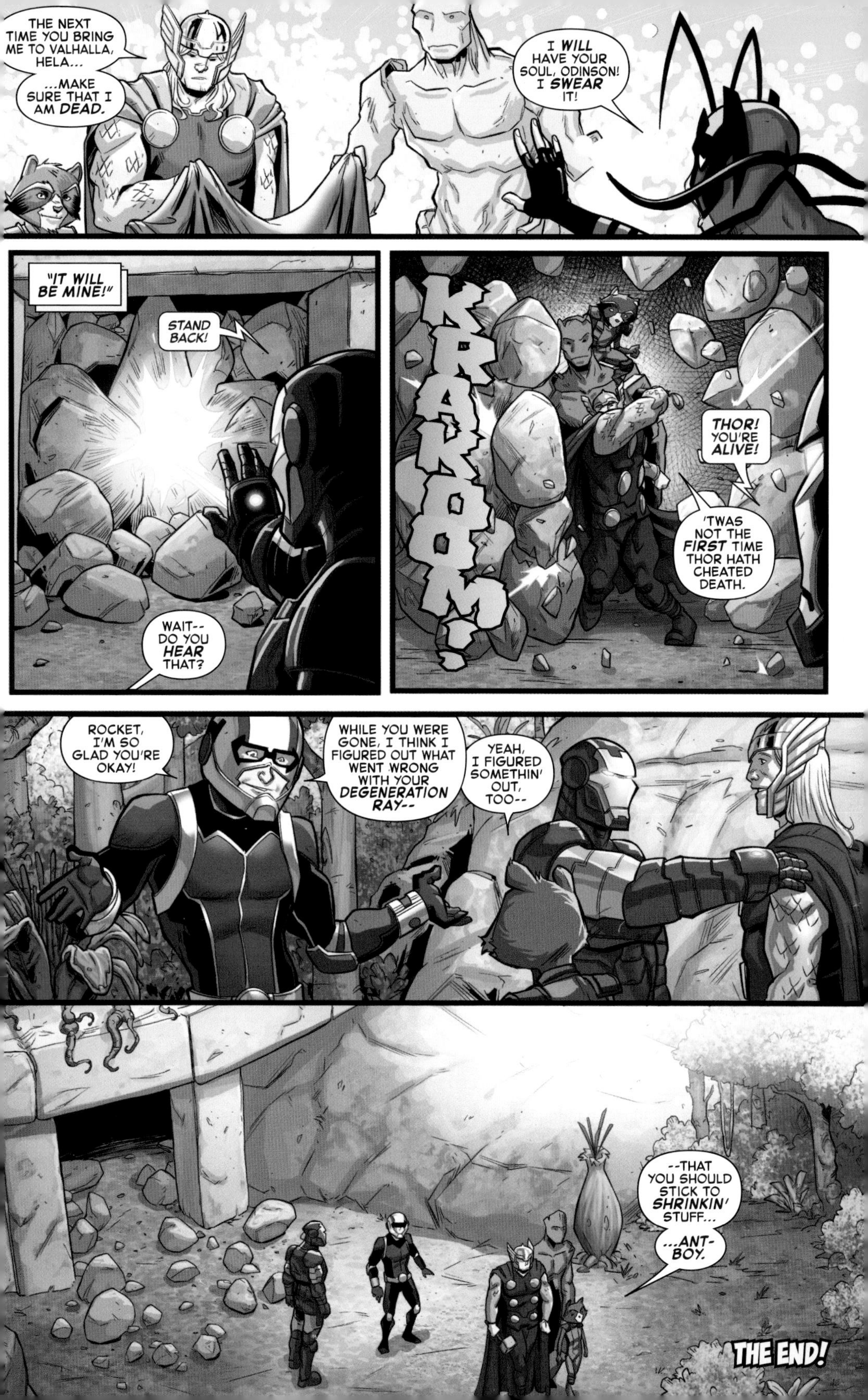
THE NEXT TIME YOU BRING ME TO VALHALLA, HELA...
...MAKE SURE THAT I AM DEAD.
I WILL HAVE YOUR SOUL, ODINSON! I SWEAR IT!
"IT WILL BE MINE!"
STAND BACK!
WAIT-- DO YOU HEAR THAT?
KRAKOOM!
THOR! YOU'RE ALIVE!
'TWAS NOT THE FIRST TIME THOR HATH CHEATED DEATH.
ROCKET, I'M SO GLAD YOU'RE OKAY!
WHILE YOU WERE GONE, I THINK I FIGURED OUT WHAT WENT WRONG WITH YOUR DEGENERATION RAY--
YEAH, I FIGURED SOMETHIN' OUT, TOO--
--THAT YOU SHOULD STICK TO SHRINKIN' STUFF...
...ANT-BOY.
THE END!

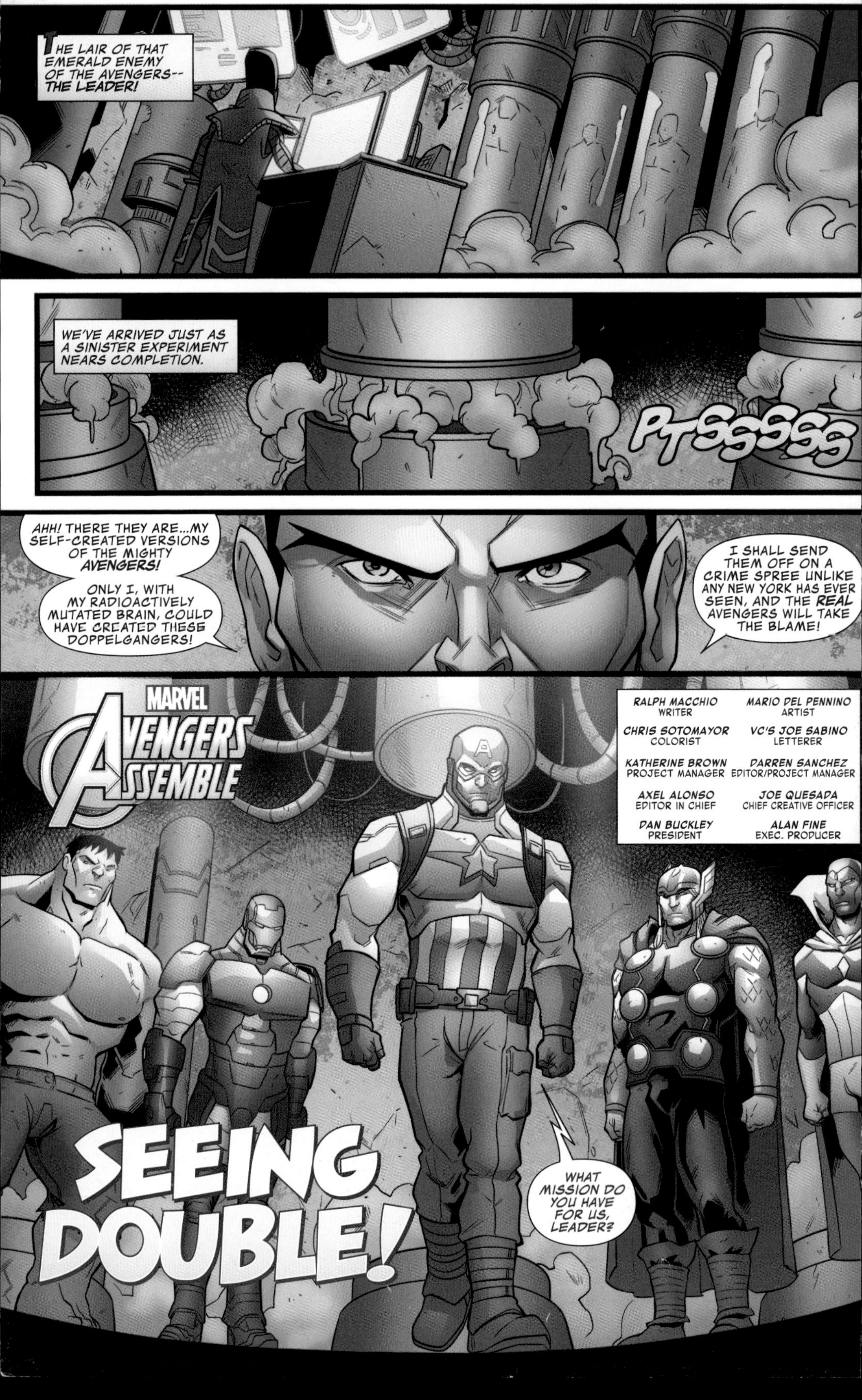
THE LAIR OF THAT EMERALD ENEMY OF THE AVENGERS-- THE LEADER!
WE'VE ARRIVED JUST AS A SINISTER EXPERIMENT NEARS COMPLETION.
PTSSSSS
AHH! THERE THEY ARE...MY SELF-CREATED VERSIONS OF THE MIGHTY AVENGERS!
ONLY I, WITH MY RADIOACTIVELY MUTATED BRAIN, COULD HAVE CREATED THESE DOPPELGANGERS!
I SHALL SEND THEM OFF ON A CRIME SPREE UNLIKE ANY NEW YORK HAS EVER SEEN, AND THE REAL AVENGERS WILL TAKE THE BLAME!
MARVEL AVENGERS ASSEMBLE
RALPH MACCHIO WRITER
MARIO DEL PENNINO ARTIST
CHRIS SOTOMAYOR COLORIST
VC'S JOE SABINO LETTERER
KATHERINE BROWN PROJECT MANAGER
DARREN SANCHEZ EDITOR/PROJECT MANAGER
AXEL ALONSO EDITOR IN CHIEF
JOE QUESADA CHIEF CREATIVE OFFICER
DAN BUCKLEY PRESIDENT
ALAN FINE EXEC. PRODUCER
SEEING DOUBLE!
WHAT MISSION DO YOU HAVE FOR US, LEADER?

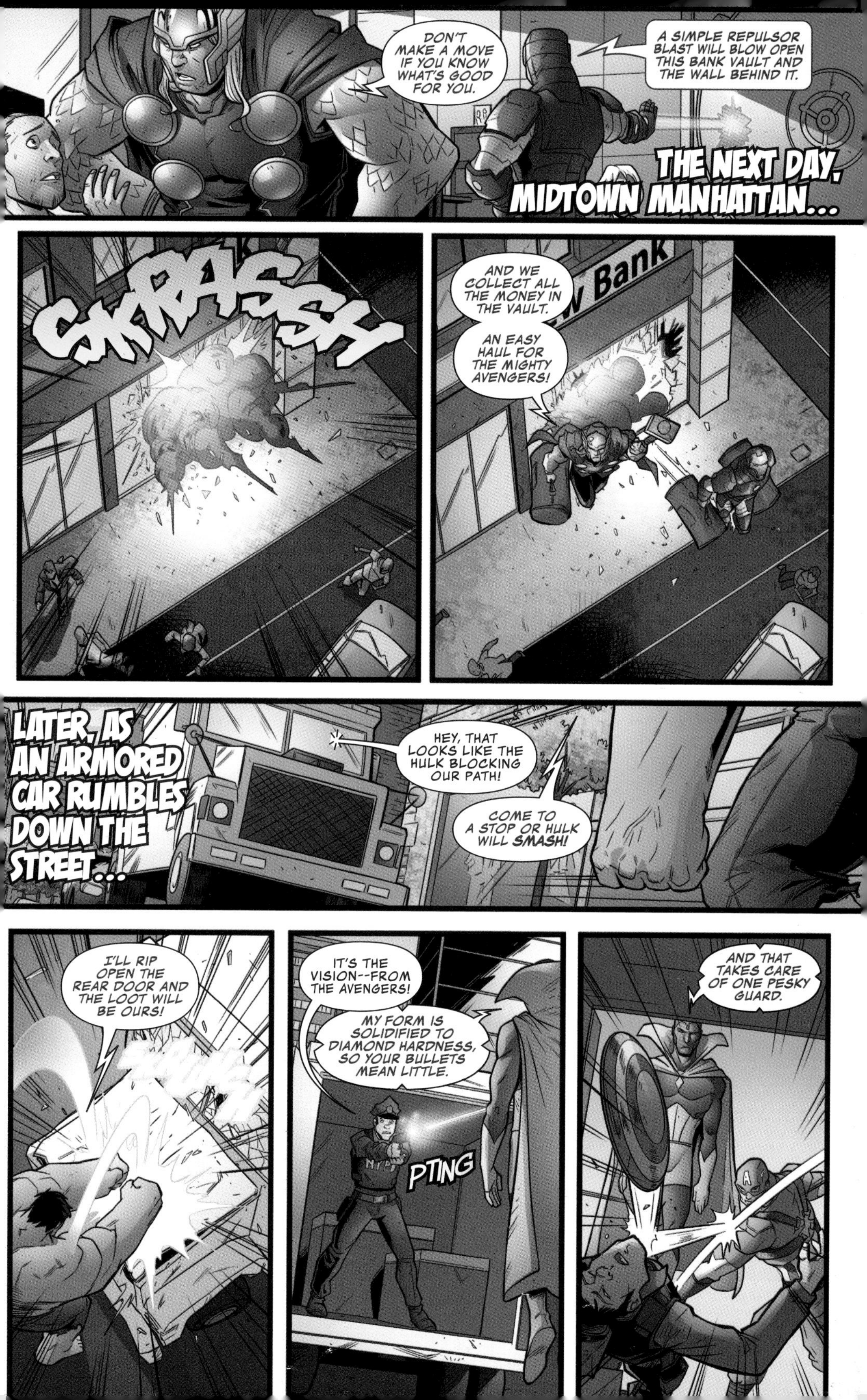
DON'T MAKE A MOVE IF YOU KNOW WHAT'S GOOD FOR YOU.
A SIMPLE REPULSOR BLAST WILL BLOW OPEN THIS BANK VAULT AND THE WALL BEHIND IT.
THE NEXT DAY, MIDTOWN MANHATTAN...
CKRASSH
AND WE COLLECT ALL THE MONEY IN THE VAULT.
AN EASY HAUL FOR THE MIGHTY AVENGERS!
LATER, AS AN ARMORED CAR RUMBLES DOWN THE STREET...
HEY, THAT LOOKS LIKE THE HULK BLOCKING OUR PATH!
COME TO A STOP OR HULK WILL SMASH!
I'LL RIP OPEN THE REAR DOOR AND THE LOOT WILL BE OURS!
IT'S THE VISION--FROM THE AVENGERS!
MY FORM IS SOLIDIFIED TO DIAMOND HARDNESS, SO YOUR BULLETS MEAN LITTLE.
PTING
AND THAT TAKES CARE OF ONE PESKY GUARD.

AVENGERS TOWER, HEADQUARTERS OF EARTH'S MIGHTIEST HEROES.

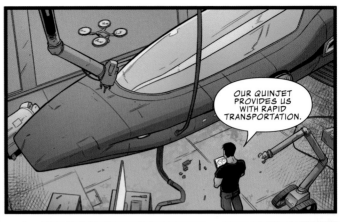

OUR QUINJET PROVIDES US WITH RAPID TRANSPORTATION.

BUT I'VE FIGURED OUT HOW TO MODIFY THIS ONE SO IT'LL MOVE AT HYPERSONIC SPEEDS.

THIS IS A TASK TONY STARK IS FAR BETTER EQUIPPED TO HANDLE THAN MY IRON MAN ALTER EGO.

EXERCISE ROOM

THE REST OF THE AVENGERS ARE BEING PUT THROUGH THEIR PACES BY CAPTAIN AMERICA.

I'VE PRESET THE THREAT LEVEL TO FIVE, SO GET READY TO HONE YOUR SKILLS TO PREPARE US FOR ANY FOE.

AYE, CAPTAIN. WE COULD USE SUCH TRAINING SESSIONS FOR THE WARRIORS IN FAR-OFF ASGARD.

LET THE TRAINING EXERCISE BEGIN.

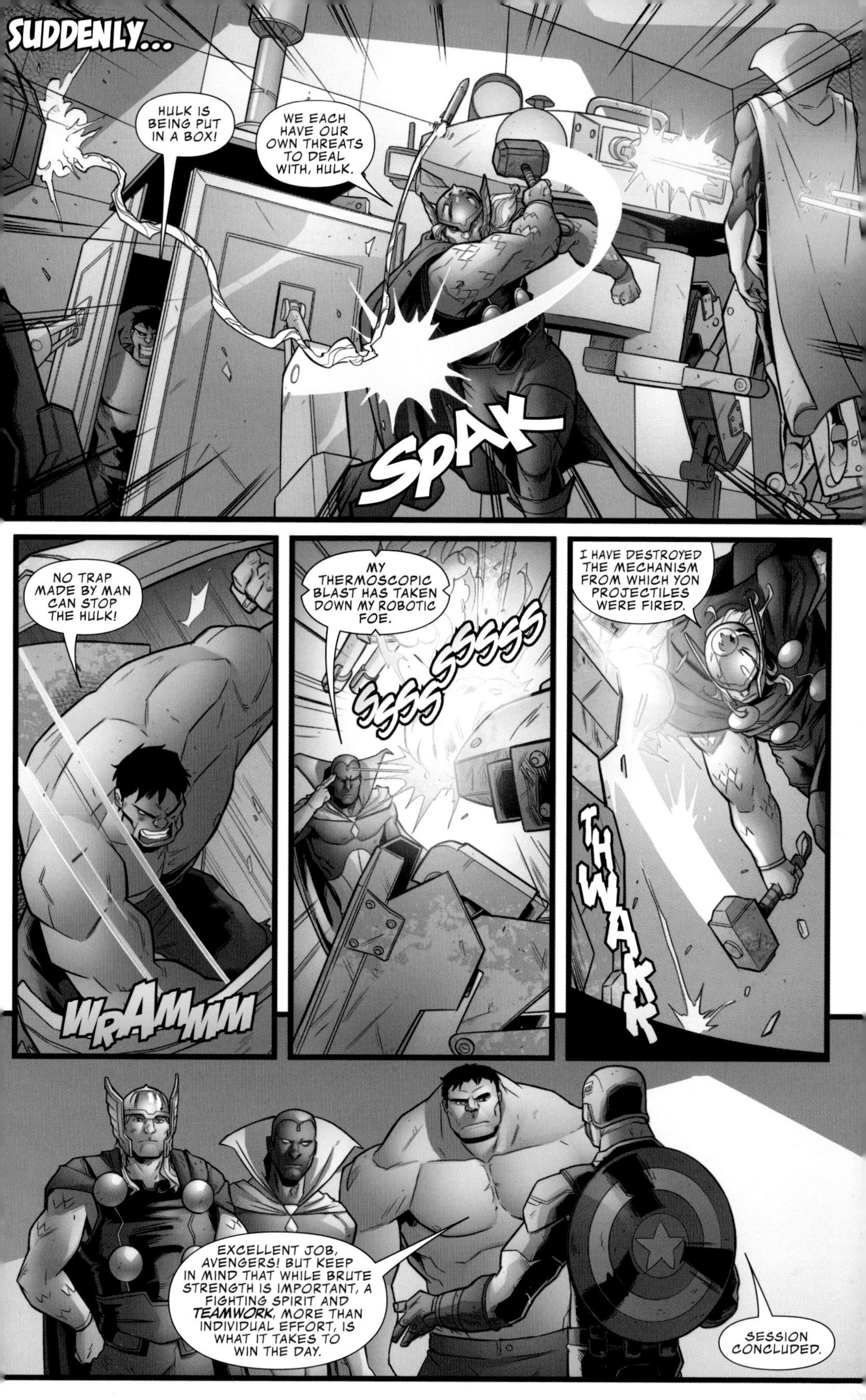
SUDDENLY...
HULK IS BEING PUT IN A BOX!
WE EACH HAVE OUR OWN THREATS TO DEAL WITH, HULK.
SPAK
NO TRAP MADE BY MAN CAN STOP THE HULK!
WRAMMMM
MY THERMOSCOPIC BLAST HAS TAKEN DOWN MY ROBOTIC FOE.
SSSSSSSSSS
I HAVE DESTROYED THE MECHANISM FROM WHICH YON PROJECTILES WERE FIRED.
THWAKK
EXCELLENT JOB, AVENGERS! BUT KEEP IN MIND THAT WHILE BRUTE STRENGTH IS IMPORTANT, A FIGHTING SPIRIT AND TEAMWORK, MORE THAN INDIVIDUAL EFFORT, IS WHAT IT TAKES TO WIN THE DAY.
SESSION CONCLUDED.

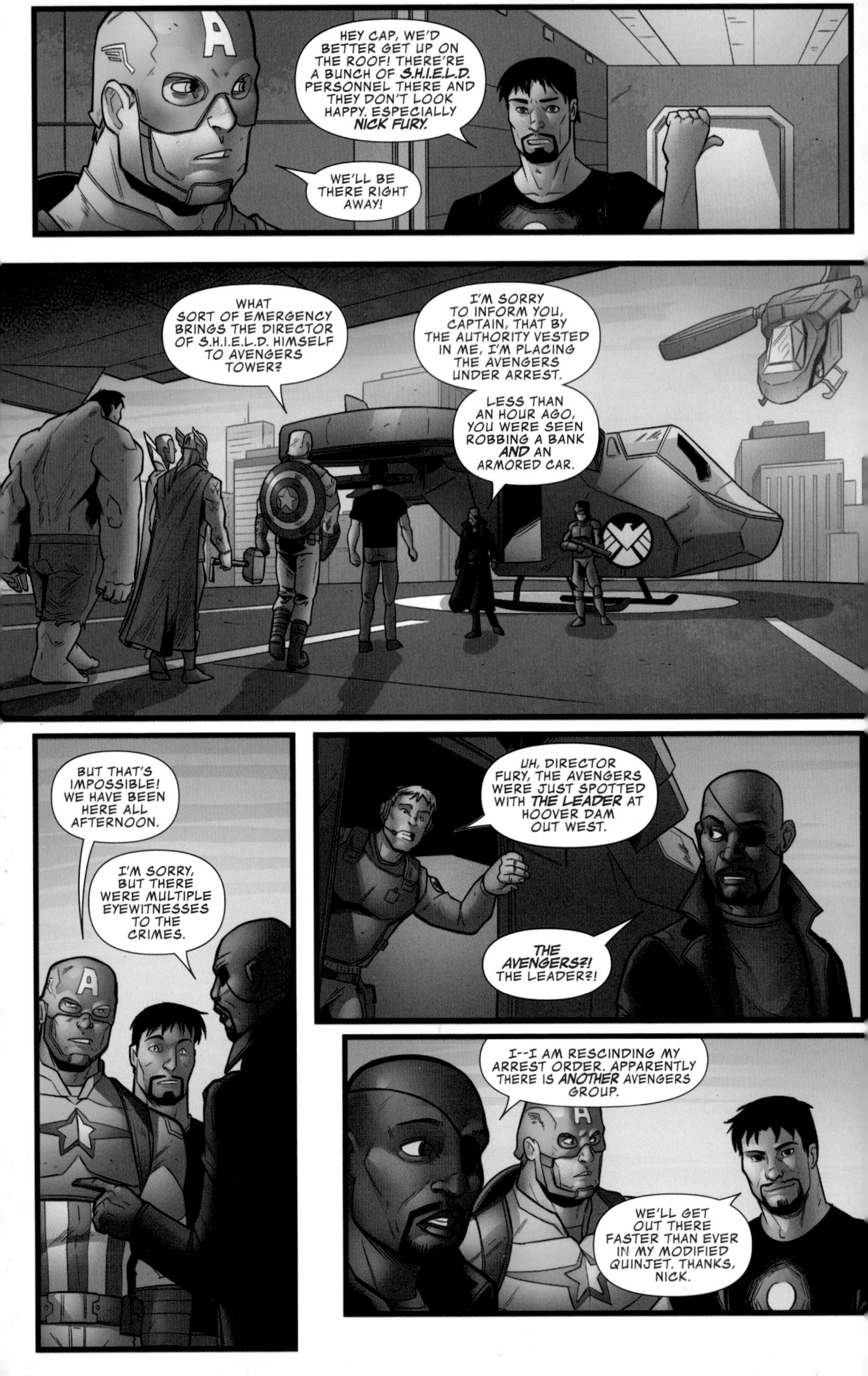
HEY CAP, WE'D BETTER GET UP ON THE ROOF! THERE'RE A BUNCH OF S.H.I.E.L.D. PERSONNEL THERE AND THEY DON'T LOOK HAPPY. ESPECIALLY NICK FURY.
WE'LL BE THERE RIGHT AWAY!
WHAT SORT OF EMERGENCY BRINGS THE DIRECTOR OF S.H.I.E.L.D. HIMSELF TO AVENGERS TOWER?
I'M SORRY TO INFORM YOU, CAPTAIN, THAT BY THE AUTHORITY VESTED IN ME, I'M PLACING THE AVENGERS UNDER ARREST.
LESS THAN AN HOUR AGO, YOU WERE SEEN ROBBING A BANK AND AN ARMORED CAR.
BUT THAT'S IMPOSSIBLE! WE HAVE BEEN HERE ALL AFTERNOON.
I'M SORRY, BUT THERE WERE MULTIPLE EYEWITNESSES TO THE CRIMES.
UH, DIRECTOR FURY, THE AVENGERS WERE JUST SPOTTED WITH THE LEADER AT HOOVER DAM OUT WEST.
THE AVENGERS?! THE LEADER?!
I--I AM RESCINDING MY ARREST ORDER. APPARENTLY THERE IS ANOTHER AVENGERS GROUP.
WE'LL GET OUT THERE FASTER THAN EVER IN MY MODIFIED QUINJET. THANKS, NICK.

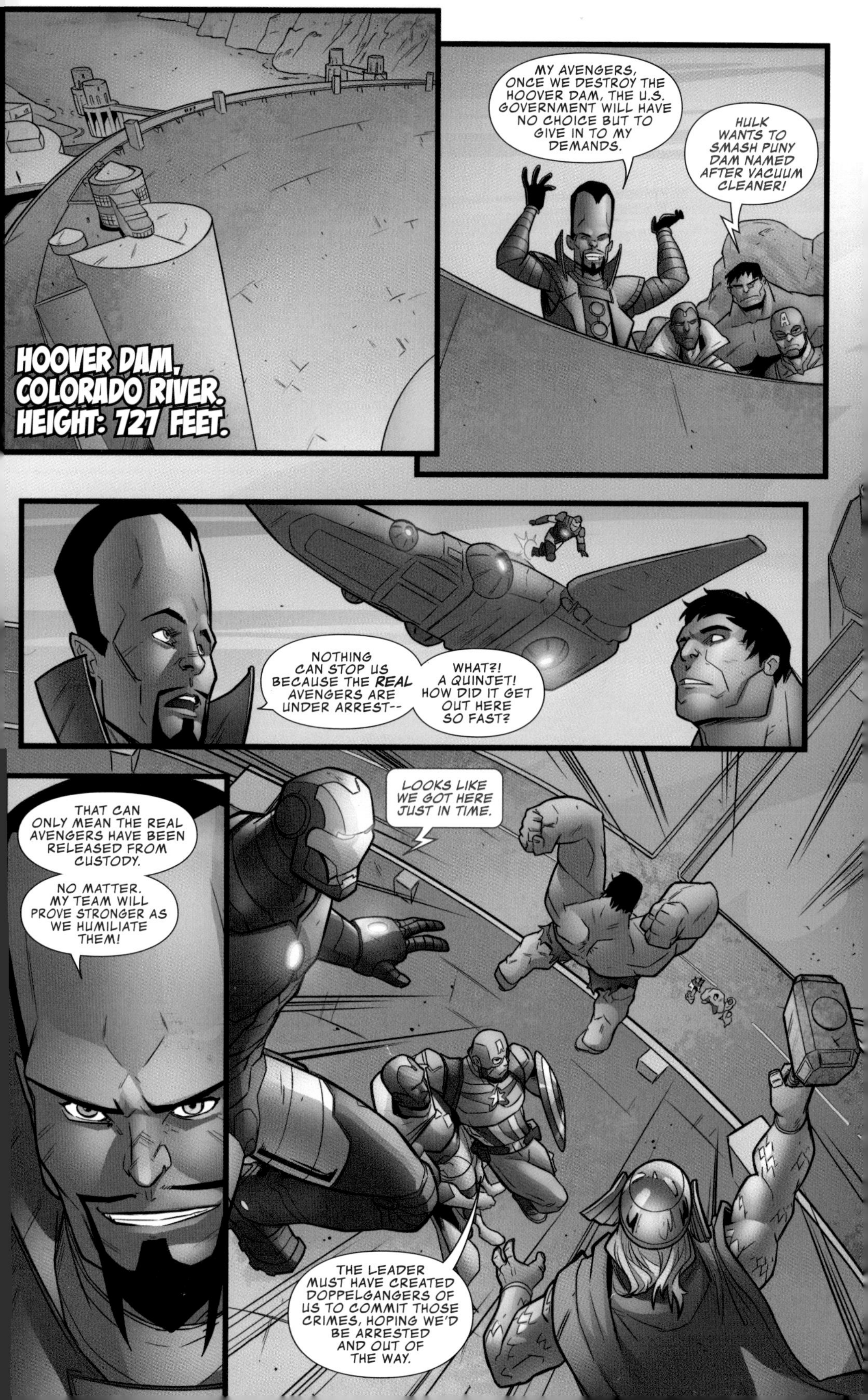
HOOVER DAM, COLORADO RIVER. HEIGHT: 727 FEET.
MY AVENGERS, ONCE WE DESTROY THE HOOVER DAM, THE U.S. GOVERNMENT WILL HAVE NO CHOICE BUT TO GIVE IN TO MY DEMANDS.
HULK WANTS TO SMASH PUNY DAM NAMED AFTER VACUUM CLEANER!
NOTHING CAN STOP US BECAUSE THE REAL AVENGERS ARE UNDER ARREST--
WHAT?! A QUINJET! HOW DID IT GET OUT HERE SO FAST?
THAT CAN ONLY MEAN THE REAL AVENGERS HAVE BEEN RELEASED FROM CUSTODY.
NO MATTER. MY TEAM WILL PROVE STRONGER AS WE HUMILIATE THEM!
LOOKS LIKE WE GOT HERE JUST IN TIME.
THE LEADER MUST HAVE CREATED DOPPELGANGERS OF US TO COMMIT THOSE CRIMES, HOPING WE'D BE ARRESTED AND OUT OF THE WAY.

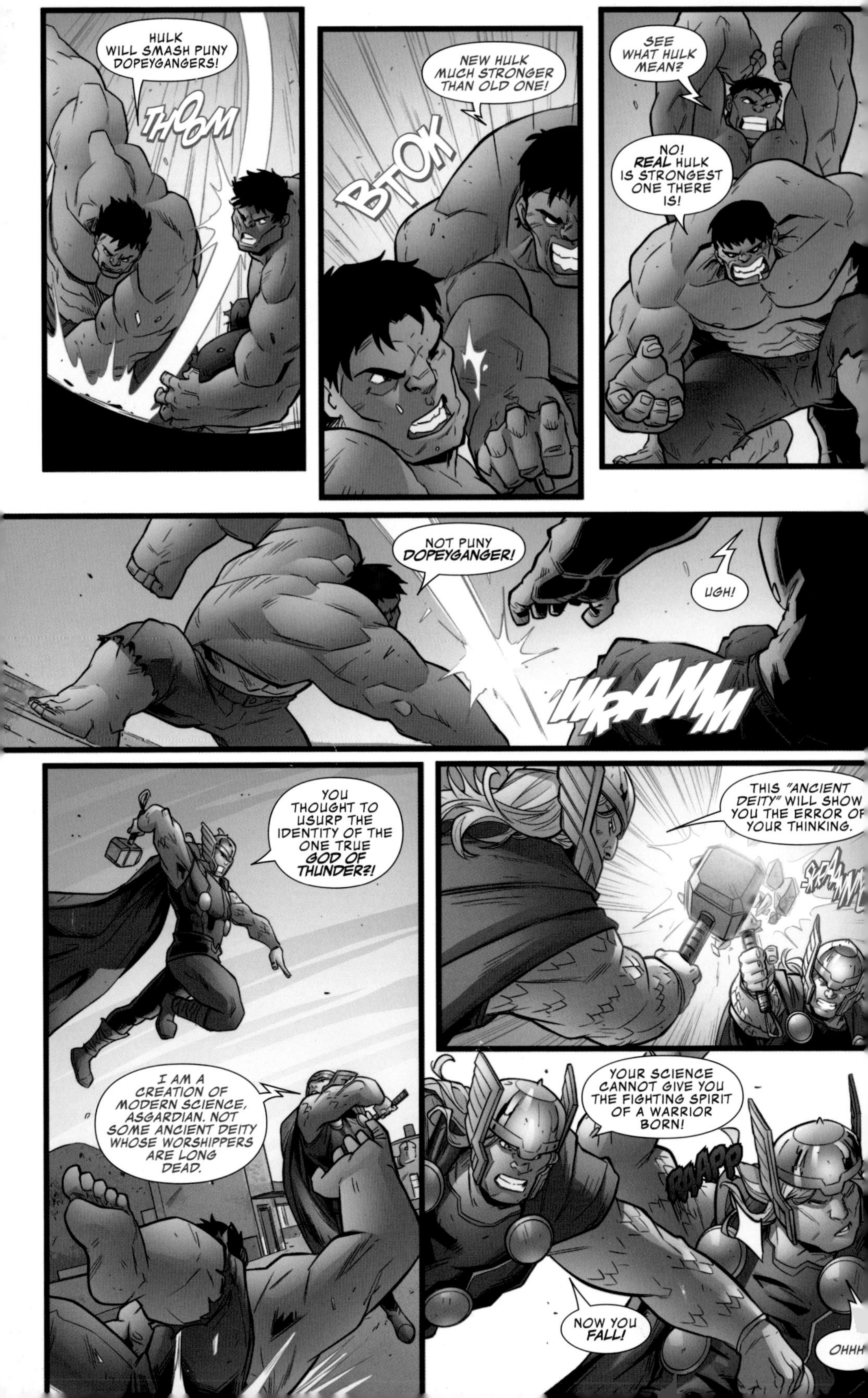
HULK WILL SMASH PUNY DOPEYGANGERS!
THOOOM
NEW HULK MUCH STRONGER THAN OLD ONE!
BTOK
SEE WHAT HULK MEAN?
NO! REAL HULK IS STRONGEST ONE THERE IS!
NOT PUNY DOPEYGANGER!
UGH!
WRAMMM
YOU THOUGHT TO USURP THE IDENTITY OF THE ONE TRUE GOD OF THUNDER?!
THIS "ANCIENT DEITY" WILL SHOW YOU THE ERROR OF YOUR THINKING.
I AM A CREATION OF MODERN SCIENCE, ASGARDIAN. NOT SOME ANCIENT DEITY WHOSE WORSHIPPERS ARE LONG DEAD.
YOUR SCIENCE CANNOT GIVE YOU THE FIGHTING SPIRIT OF A WARRIOR BORN!
RAAPP
NOW YOU FALL!
OHHH

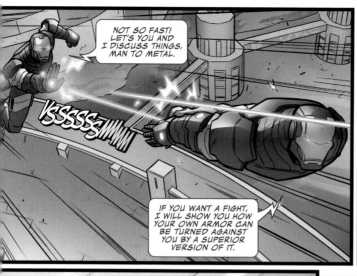

NOT SO FAST! LET'S YOU AND I DISCUSS THINGS, MAN TO METAL.

IF YOU WANT A FIGHT, I WILL SHOW YOU HOW YOUR OWN ARMOR CAN BE TURNED AGAINST YOU BY A SUPERIOR VERSION OF IT.

VSSSSSSWWWWW

I HAVE LEARNED EVERY STRENGTH THIS GLEAMING SUIT POSSESSES!

MAYBE SO, BUT I'LL BET YOU DON'T KNOW ALL ITS WEAKNESSES!

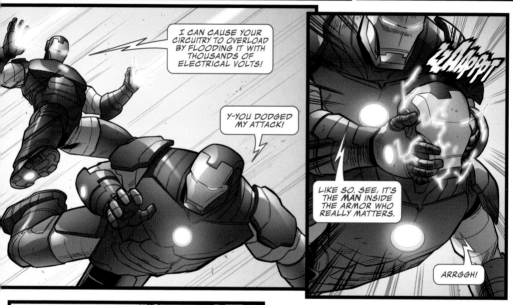

I CAN CAUSE YOUR CIRCUITRY TO OVERLOAD BY FLOODING IT WITH THOUSANDS OF ELECTRICAL VOLTS!

Y-YOU DODGED MY ATTACK!

KZAAPFT

LIKE SO. SEE, IT'S THE MAN INSIDE THE ARMOR WHO REALLY MATTERS.

ARRGGH!

HAPPY LANDINGS!

HOW YOU DOING, VISION?

WE SEEM EVENLY MATCHED, IRON MAN. AFTER ALL, WE ARE BOTH ANDROIDS.

THWAK

THOUGH I HAVE THE GREAT ADVANTAGE OF BEING TAUGHT THE FULLEST USE OF MY POWERS BY CAPTAIN AMERICA!

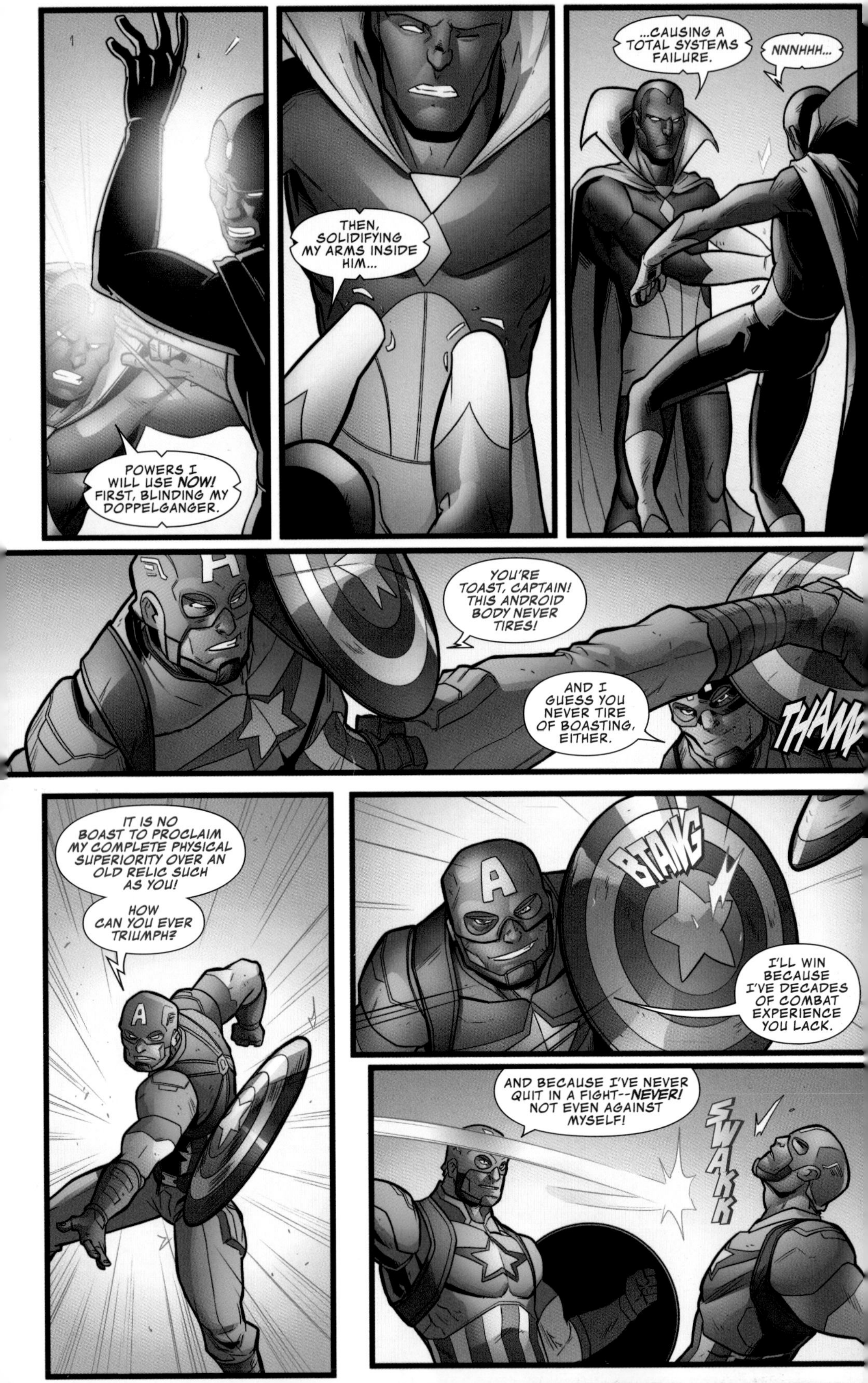
POWERS I WILL USE *NOW!* FIRST, BLINDING MY DOPPELGANGER.
THEN, SOLIDIFYING MY ARMS INSIDE HIM...
...CAUSING A TOTAL SYSTEMS FAILURE.
NNNHHH...
YOU'RE TOAST, CAPTAIN! THIS ANDROID BODY NEVER TIRES!
AND I GUESS YOU NEVER TIRE OF BOASTING, EITHER.
THAM
IT IS NO BOAST TO PROCLAIM MY COMPLETE PHYSICAL SUPERIORITY OVER AN OLD RELIC SUCH AS YOU!
HOW CAN YOU EVER TRIUMPH?
BTANG
I'LL WIN BECAUSE I'VE DECADES OF COMBAT EXPERIENCE YOU LACK.
AND BECAUSE I'VE NEVER QUIT IN A FIGHT--*NEVER!* NOT EVEN AGAINST MYSELF!
SWAKK

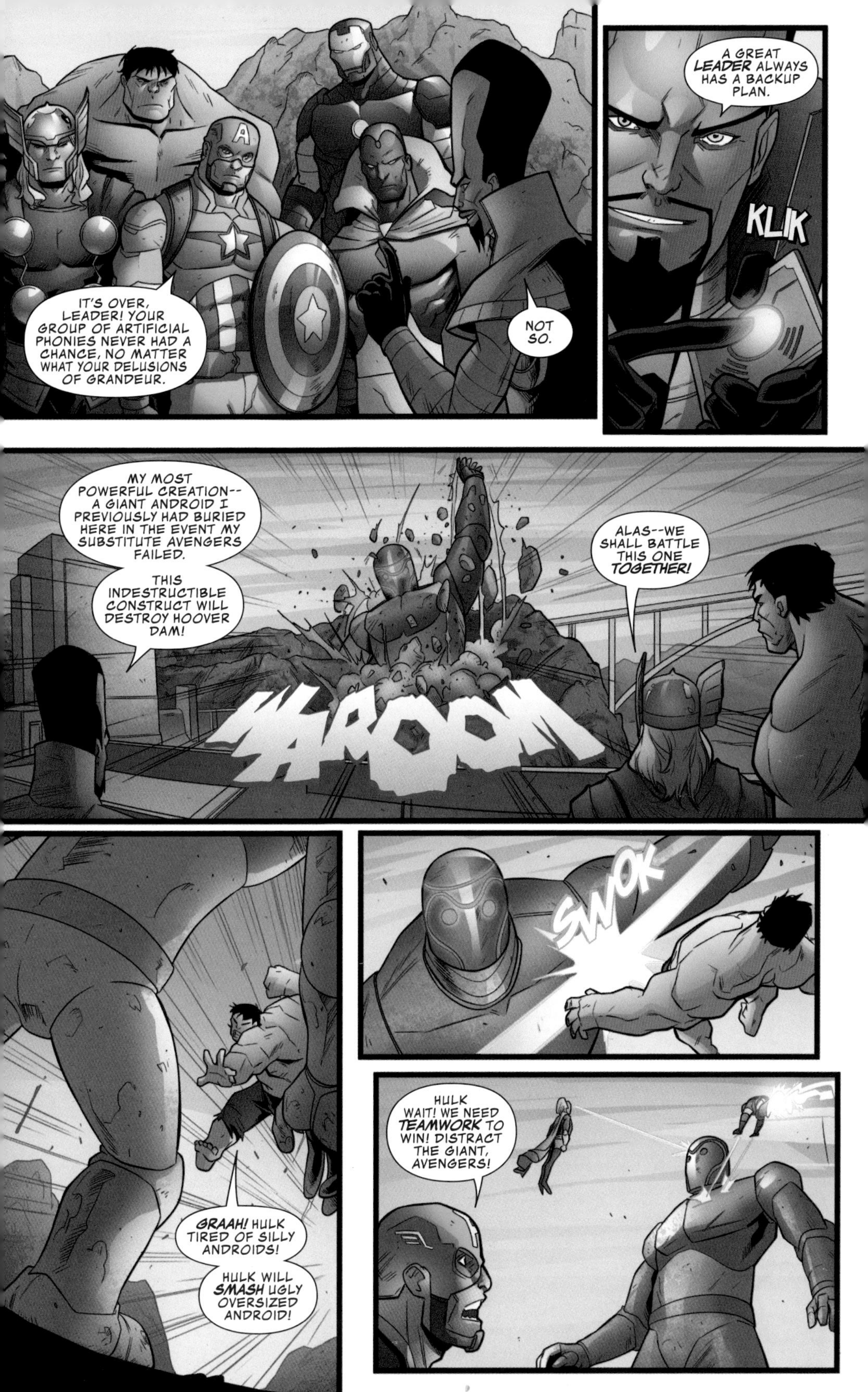
IT'S OVER, LEADER! YOUR GROUP OF ARTIFICIAL PHONIES NEVER HAD A CHANCE, NO MATTER WHAT YOUR DELUSIONS OF GRANDEUR.
NOT SO.
A GREAT LEADER ALWAYS HAS A BACKUP PLAN.
KLIK
MY MOST POWERFUL CREATION-- A GIANT ANDROID I PREVIOUSLY HAD BURIED HERE IN THE EVENT MY SUBSTITUTE AVENGERS FAILED.
THIS INDESTRUCTIBLE CONSTRUCT WILL DESTROY HOOVER DAM!
ALAS--WE SHALL BATTLE THIS ONE TOGETHER!
GRAAH! HULK TIRED OF SILLY ANDROIDS!
HULK WILL SMASH UGLY OVERSIZED ANDROID!
SWOK
HULK WAIT! WE NEED TEAMWORK TO WIN! DISTRACT THE GIANT, AVENGERS!

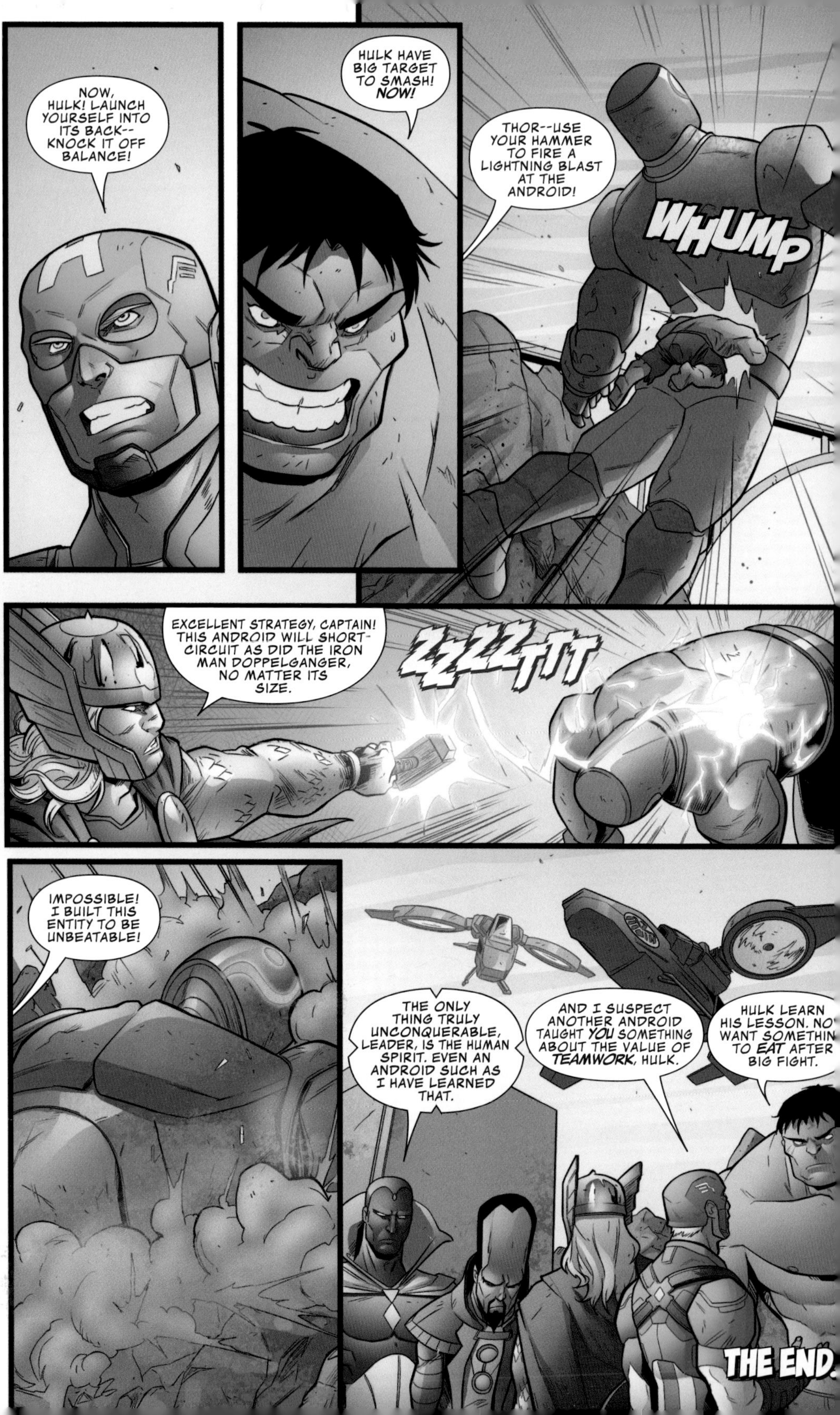
NOW, HULK! LAUNCH YOURSELF INTO ITS BACK-- KNOCK IT OFF BALANCE!
HULK HAVE BIG TARGET TO SMASH! NOW!
THOR--USE YOUR HAMMER TO FIRE A LIGHTNING BLAST AT THE ANDROID!
WHUMP
EXCELLENT STRATEGY, CAPTAIN! THIS ANDROID WILL SHORT-CIRCUIT AS DID THE IRON MAN DOPPELGANGER, NO MATTER ITS SIZE.
ZZZZTTT
IMPOSSIBLE! I BUILT THIS ENTITY TO BE UNBEATABLE!
THE ONLY THING TRULY UNCONQUERABLE, LEADER, IS THE HUMAN SPIRIT. EVEN AN ANDROID SUCH AS I HAVE LEARNED THAT.
AND I SUSPECT ANOTHER ANDROID TAUGHT YOU SOMETHING ABOUT THE VALUE OF TEAMWORK, HULK.
THE END.

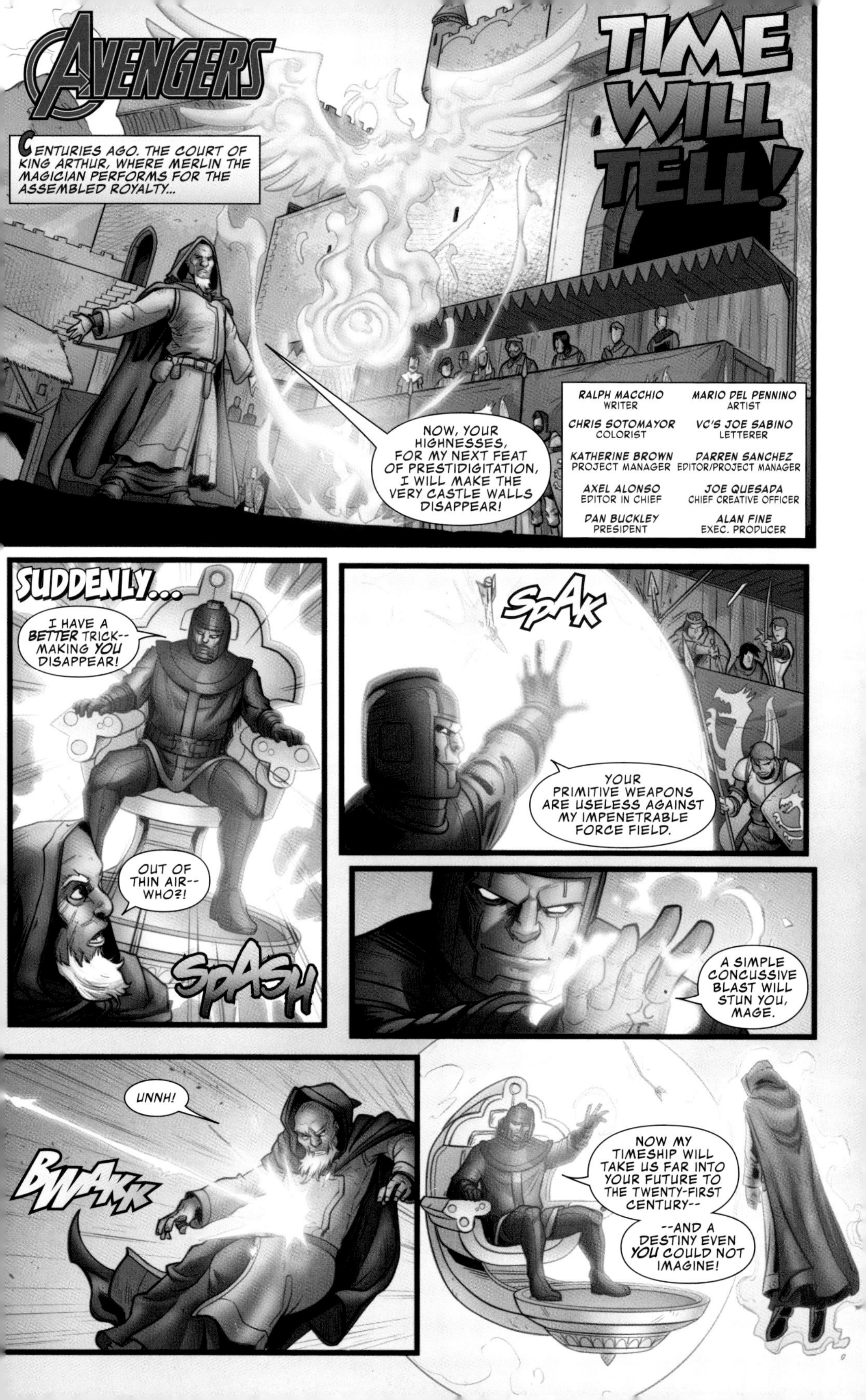
AVENGERS
TIME WILL TELL!
CENTURIES AGO. THE COURT OF KING ARTHUR, WHERE MERLIN THE MAGICIAN PERFORMS FOR THE ASSEMBLED ROYALTY...
NOW, YOUR HIGHNESSES, FOR MY NEXT FEAT OF PRESTIDIGITATION, I WILL MAKE THE VERY CASTLE WALLS DISAPPEAR!
RALPH MACCHIO WRITER
MARIO DEL PENNINO ARTIST
CHRIS SOTOMAYOR COLORIST
VC'S JOE SABINO LETTERER
KATHERINE BROWN PROJECT MANAGER
DARREN SANCHEZ EDITOR/PROJECT MANAGER
AXEL ALONSO EDITOR IN CHIEF
JOE QUESADA CHIEF CREATIVE OFFICER
DAN BUCKLEY PRESIDENT
ALAN FINE EXEC. PRODUCER
SUDDENLY...
I HAVE A BETTER TRICK-- MAKING YOU DISAPPEAR!
OUT OF THIN AIR-- WHO?!
SPASH
SPAK
YOUR PRIMITIVE WEAPONS ARE USELESS AGAINST MY IMPENETRABLE FORCE FIELD.
A SIMPLE CONCUSSIVE BLAST WILL STUN YOU, MAGE.
UNNH!
BWAKK
NOW MY TIMESHIP WILL TAKE US FAR INTO YOUR FUTURE TO THE TWENTY-FIRST CENTURY--
--AND A DESTINY EVEN YOU COULD NOT IMAGINE!

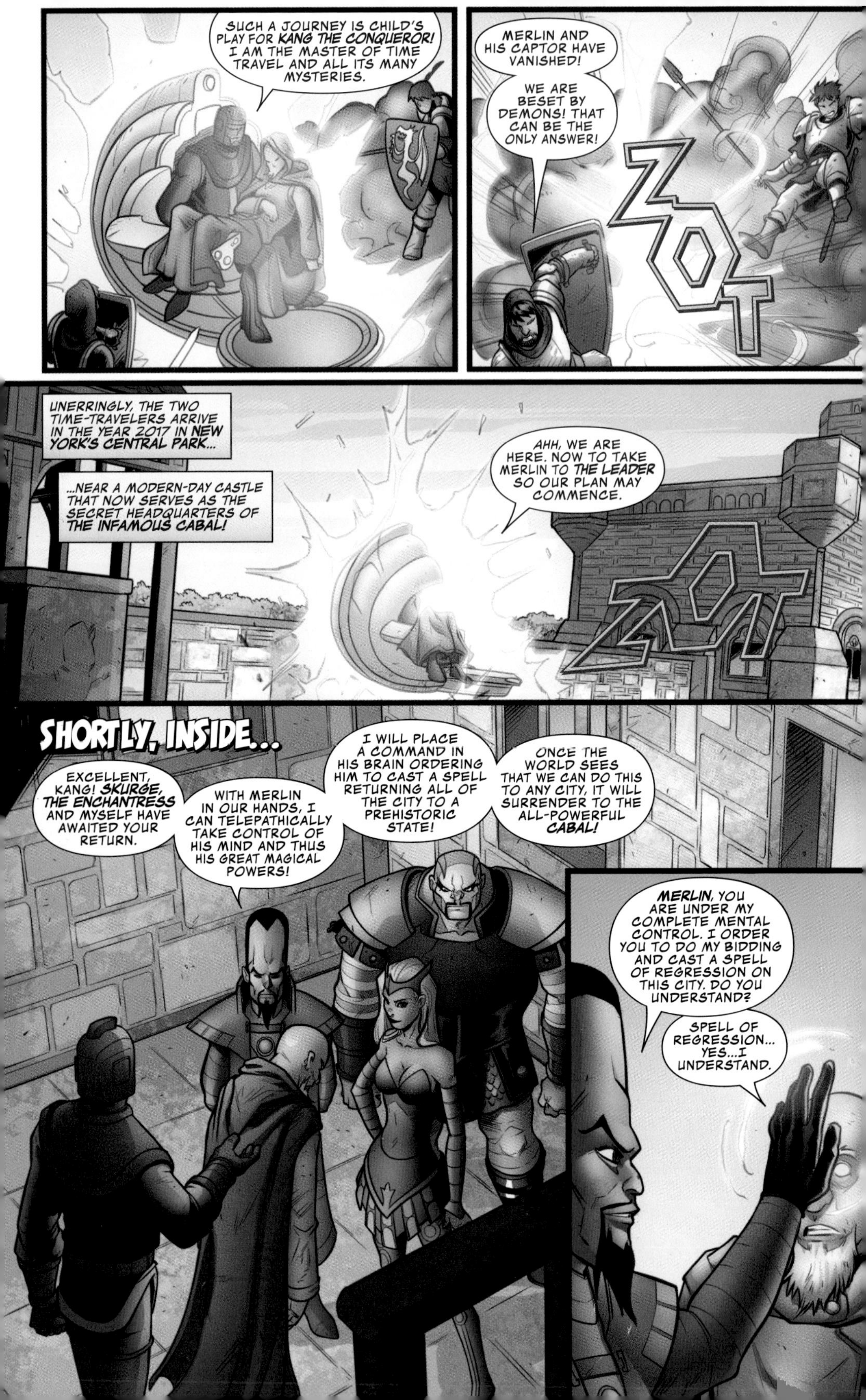
SUCH A JOURNEY IS CHILD'S PLAY FOR KANG THE CONQUEROR! I AM THE MASTER OF TIME TRAVEL AND ALL ITS MANY MYSTERIES.
MERLIN AND HIS CAPTOR HAVE VANISHED!
WE ARE BESET BY DEMONS! THAT CAN BE THE ONLY ANSWER!
ZOT
UNERRINGLY, THE TWO TIME-TRAVELERS ARRIVE IN THE YEAR 2017 IN NEW YORK'S CENTRAL PARK...
...NEAR A MODERN-DAY CASTLE THAT NOW SERVES AS THE SECRET HEADQUARTERS OF THE INFAMOUS CABAL!
AHH, WE ARE HERE. NOW TO TAKE MERLIN TO THE LEADER SO OUR PLAN MAY COMMENCE.
ZOT
SHORTLY, INSIDE...
EXCELLENT, KANG! SKURGE, THE ENCHANTRESS AND MYSELF HAVE AWAITED YOUR RETURN.
WITH MERLIN IN OUR HANDS, I CAN TELEPATHICALLY TAKE CONTROL OF HIS MIND AND THUS HIS GREAT MAGICAL POWERS!
I WILL PLACE A COMMAND IN HIS BRAIN ORDERING HIM TO CAST A SPELL RETURNING ALL OF THE CITY TO A PREHISTORIC STATE!
ONCE THE WORLD SEES THAT WE CAN DO THIS TO ANY CITY, IT WILL SURRENDER TO THE ALL-POWERFUL CABAL!
MERLIN, YOU ARE UNDER MY COMPLETE MENTAL CONTROL. I ORDER YOU TO DO MY BIDDING AND CAST A SPELL OF REGRESSION ON THIS CITY. DO YOU UNDERSTAND?
SPELL OF REGRESSION... YES...I UNDERSTAND.

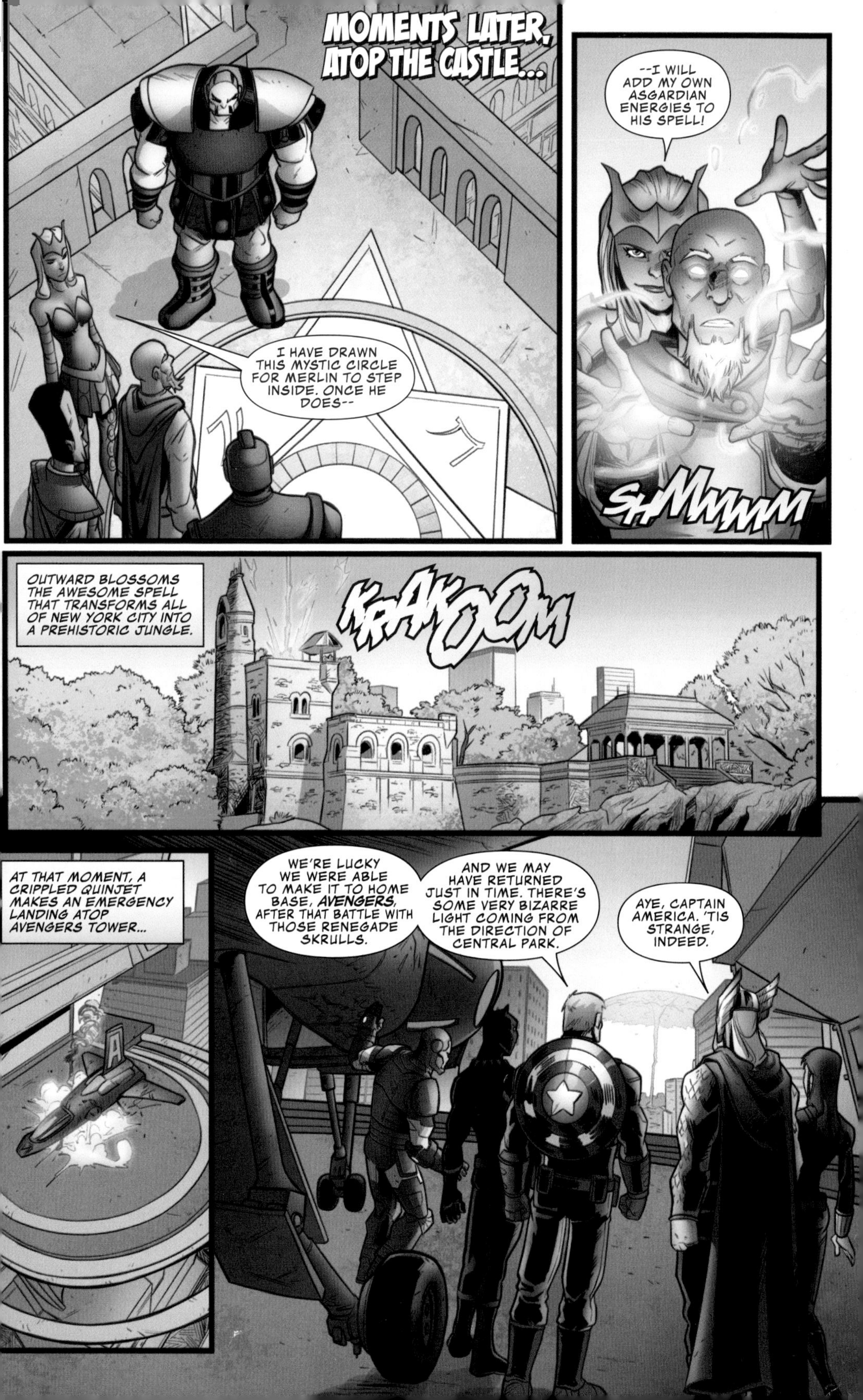
MOMENTS LATER, ATOP THE CASTLE...
I HAVE DRAWN THIS MYSTIC CIRCLE FOR MERLIN TO STEP INSIDE. ONCE HE DOES--
--I WILL ADD MY OWN ASGARDIAN ENERGIES TO HIS SPELL!
SHMMMMM
OUTWARD BLOSSOMS THE AWESOME SPELL THAT TRANSFORMS ALL OF NEW YORK CITY INTO A PREHISTORIC JUNGLE.
KRAKOOM
AT THAT MOMENT, A CRIPPLED QUINJET MAKES AN EMERGENCY LANDING ATOP AVENGERS TOWER...
WE'RE LUCKY WE WERE ABLE TO MAKE IT TO HOME BASE, AVENGERS, AFTER THAT BATTLE WITH THOSE RENEGADE SKRULLS.
AND WE MAY HAVE RETURNED JUST IN TIME. THERE'S SOME VERY BIZARRE LIGHT COMING FROM THE DIRECTION OF CENTRAL PARK.
AYE, CAPTAIN AMERICA. 'TIS STRANGE, INDEED.

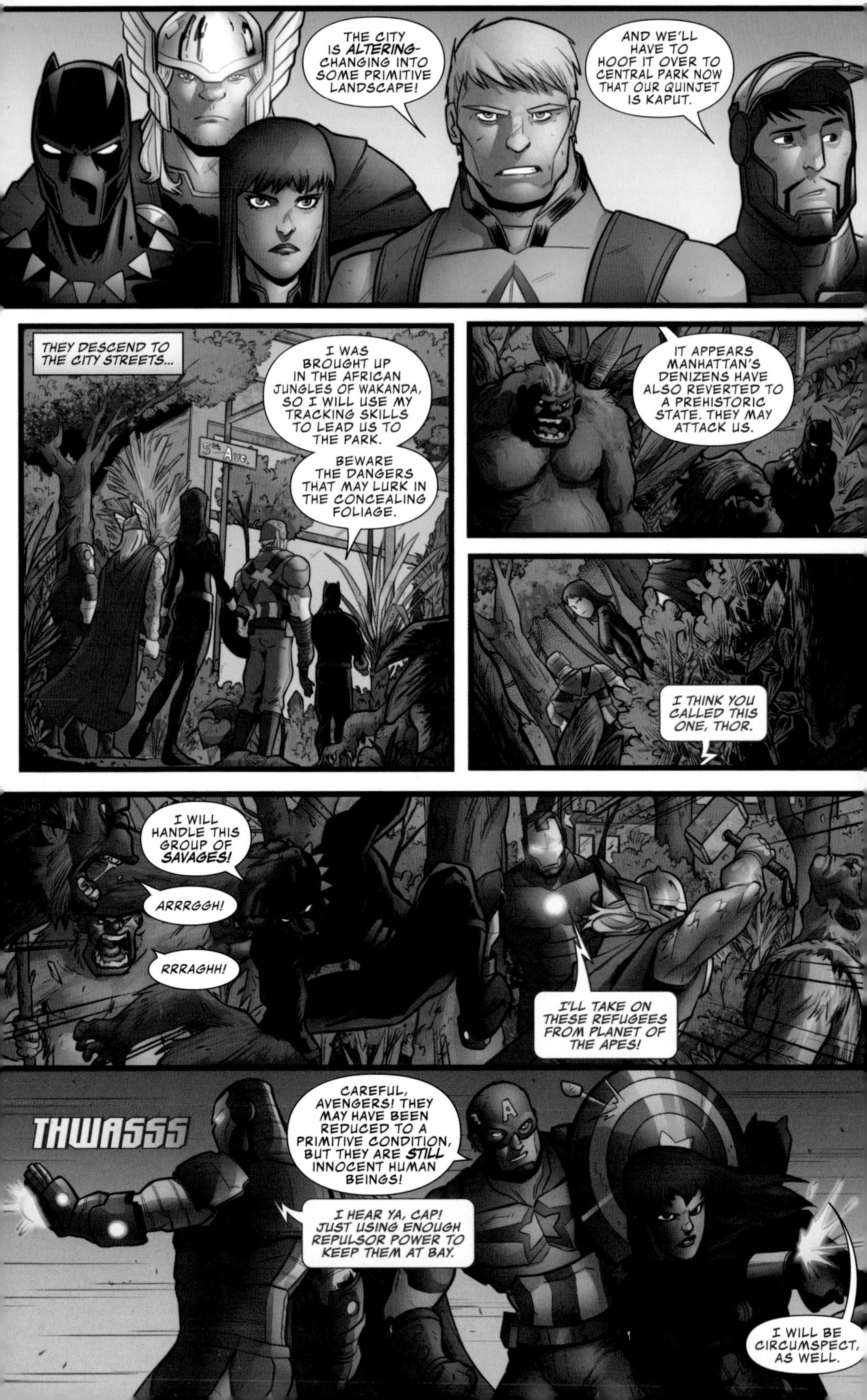
THE CITY IS ALTERING-CHANGING INTO SOME PRIMITIVE LANDSCAPE!
AND WE'LL HAVE TO HOOF IT OVER TO CENTRAL PARK NOW THAT OUR QUINJET IS KAPUT.
THEY DESCEND TO THE CITY STREETS...
I WAS BROUGHT UP IN THE AFRICAN JUNGLES OF WAKANDA, SO I WILL USE MY TRACKING SKILLS TO LEAD US TO THE PARK.
BEWARE THE DANGERS THAT MAY LURK IN THE CONCEALING FOLIAGE.
5th Ave.
IT APPEARS MANHATTAN'S DENIZENS HAVE ALSO REVERTED TO A PREHISTORIC STATE. THEY MAY ATTACK US.
I THINK YOU CALLED THIS ONE, THOR.
I WILL HANDLE THIS GROUP OF SAVAGES!
ARRRGGH!
RRRAGHH!
I'LL TAKE ON THESE REFUGEES FROM PLANET OF THE APES!
THWASSS
CAREFUL, AVENGERS! THEY MAY HAVE BEEN REDUCED TO A PRIMITIVE CONDITION, BUT THEY ARE STILL INNOCENT HUMAN BEINGS!
I HEAR YA, CAP! JUST USING ENOUGH REPULSOR POWER TO KEEP THEM AT BAY.
I WILL BE CIRCUMSPECT, AS WELL.

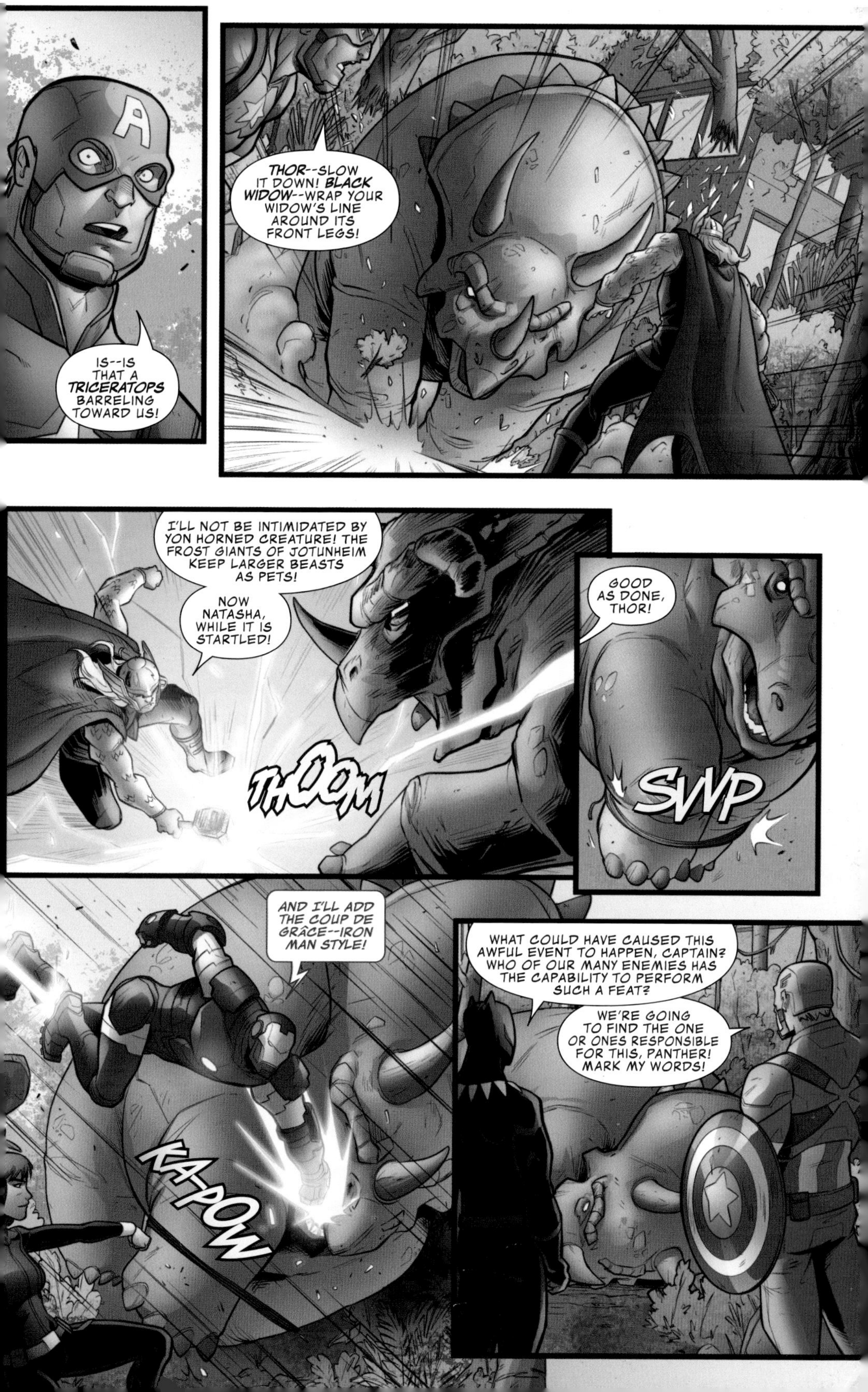
IS--IS THAT A TRICERATOPS BARRELING TOWARD US!
THOR--SLOW IT DOWN! BLACK WIDOW--WRAP YOUR WIDOW'S LINE AROUND ITS FRONT LEGS!
I'LL NOT BE INTIMIDATED BY YON HORNED CREATURE! THE FROST GIANTS OF JOTUNHEIM KEEP LARGER BEASTS AS PETS!
NOW NATASHA, WHILE IT IS STARTLED!
THOOM
GOOD AS DONE, THOR!
SVVP
AND I'LL ADD THE COUP DE GRÂCE--IRON MAN STYLE!
KA-POW
WHAT COULD HAVE CAUSED THIS AWFUL EVENT TO HAPPEN, CAPTAIN? WHO OF OUR MANY ENEMIES HAS THE CAPABILITY TO PERFORM SUCH A FEAT?
WE'RE GOING TO FIND THE ONE OR ONES RESPONSIBLE FOR THIS, PANTHER! MARK MY WORDS!

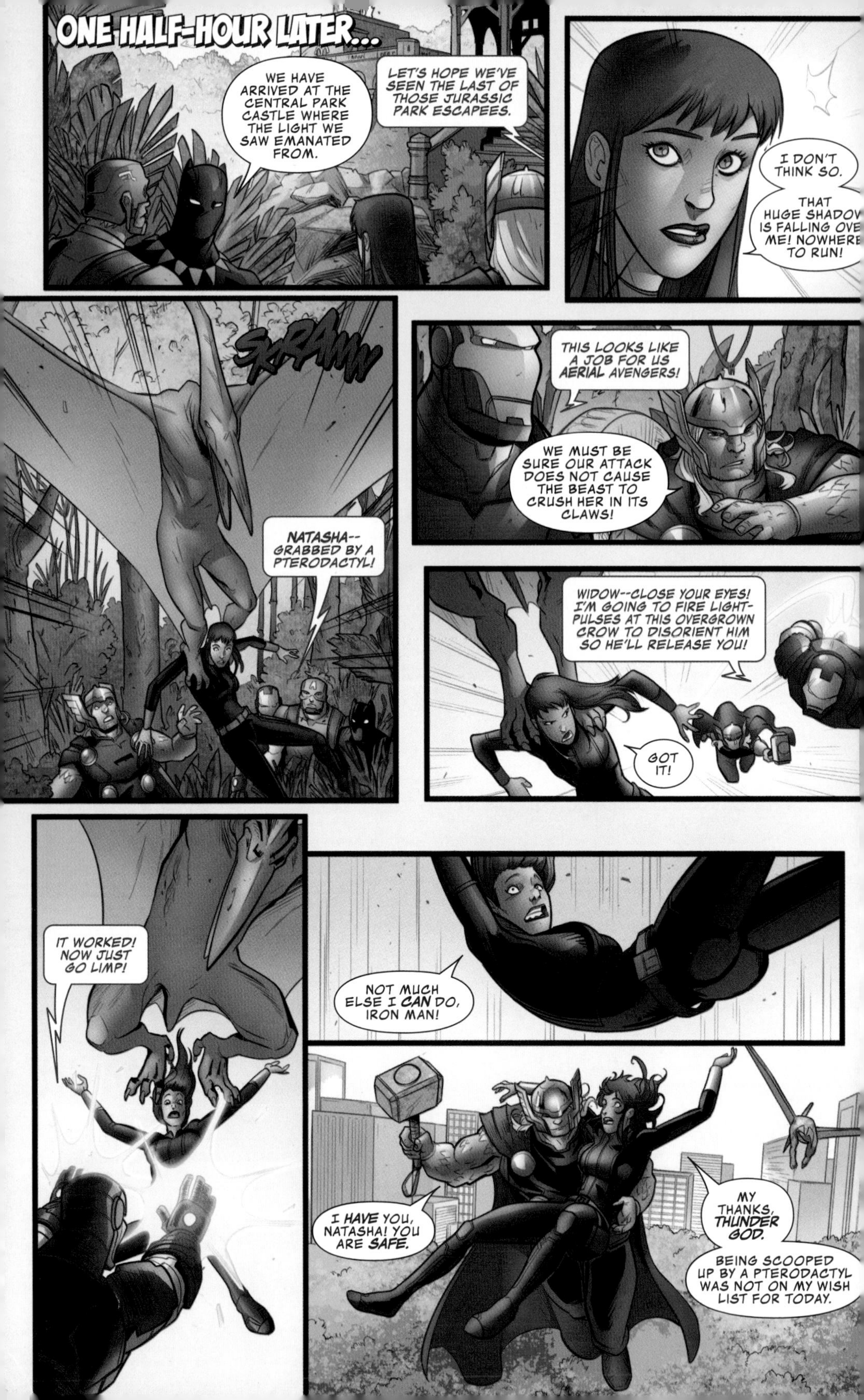
ONE HALF-HOUR LATER...
WE HAVE ARRIVED AT THE CENTRAL PARK CASTLE WHERE THE LIGHT WE SAW EMANATED FROM.
LET'S HOPE WE'VE SEEN THE LAST OF THOSE JURASSIC PARK ESCAPEES.
I DON'T THINK SO.
THAT HUGE SHADOW IS FALLING OVER ME! NOWHERE TO RUN!
SKRAWW
NATASHA-- GRABBED BY A PTERODACTYL!
THIS LOOKS LIKE A JOB FOR US AERIAL AVENGERS!
WE MUST BE SURE OUR ATTACK DOES NOT CAUSE THE BEAST TO CRUSH HER IN ITS CLAWS!
WIDOW--CLOSE YOUR EYES! I'M GOING TO FIRE LIGHT-PULSES AT THIS OVERGROWN CROW TO DISORIENT HIM SO HE'LL RELEASE YOU!
GOT IT!
IT WORKED! NOW JUST GO LIMP!
NOT MUCH ELSE I CAN DO, IRON MAN!
I HAVE YOU, NATASHA! YOU ARE SAFE.
MY THANKS, THUNDER GOD.
BEING SCOOPED UP BY A PTERODACTYL WAS NOT ON MY WISH LIST FOR TODAY.

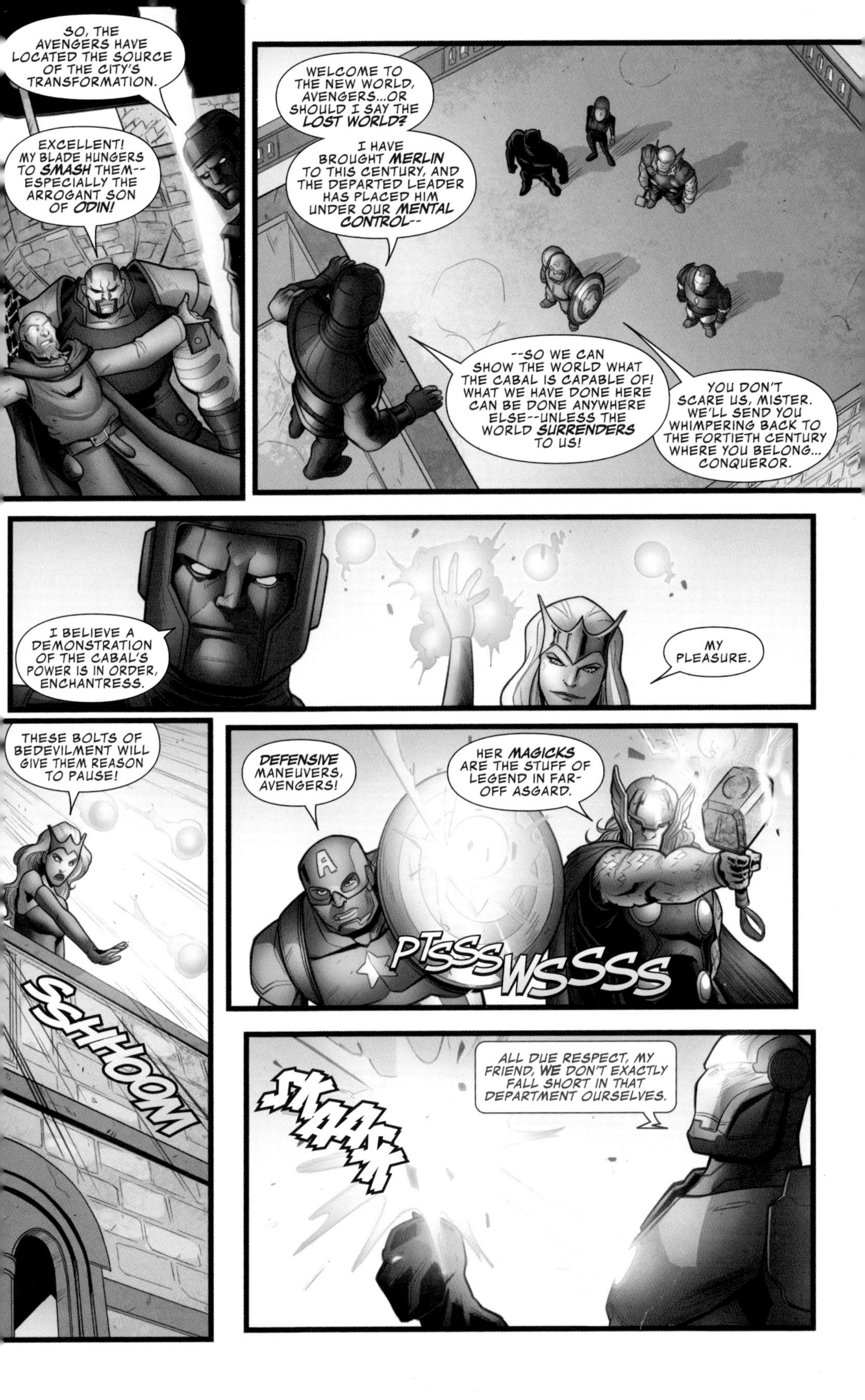
SO, THE AVENGERS HAVE LOCATED THE SOURCE OF THE CITY'S TRANSFORMATION.
EXCELLENT! MY BLADE HUNGERS TO SMASH THEM--ESPECIALLY THE ARROGANT SON OF ODIN!
WELCOME TO THE NEW WORLD, AVENGERS...OR SHOULD I SAY THE LOST WORLD?
I HAVE BROUGHT MERLIN TO THIS CENTURY, AND THE DEPARTED LEADER HAS PLACED HIM UNDER OUR MENTAL CONTROL--
--SO WE CAN SHOW THE WORLD WHAT THE CABAL IS CAPABLE OF! WHAT WE HAVE DONE HERE CAN BE DONE ANYWHERE ELSE--UNLESS THE WORLD SURRENDERS TO US!
YOU DON'T SCARE US, MISTER. WE'LL SEND YOU WHIMPERING BACK TO THE FORTIETH CENTURY WHERE YOU BELONG... CONQUEROR.
I BELIEVE A DEMONSTRATION OF THE CABAL'S POWER IS IN ORDER, ENCHANTRESS.
MY PLEASURE.
THESE BOLTS OF BEDEVILMENT WILL GIVE THEM REASON TO PAUSE!
SSHOOM
DEFENSIVE MANEUVERS, AVENGERS!
HER MAGICKS ARE THE STUFF OF LEGEND IN FAR-OFF ASGARD.
PTSSSWSSSSS
SKAAK
ALL DUE RESPECT, MY FRIEND, WE DON'T EXACTLY FALL SHORT IN THAT DEPARTMENT OURSELVES.

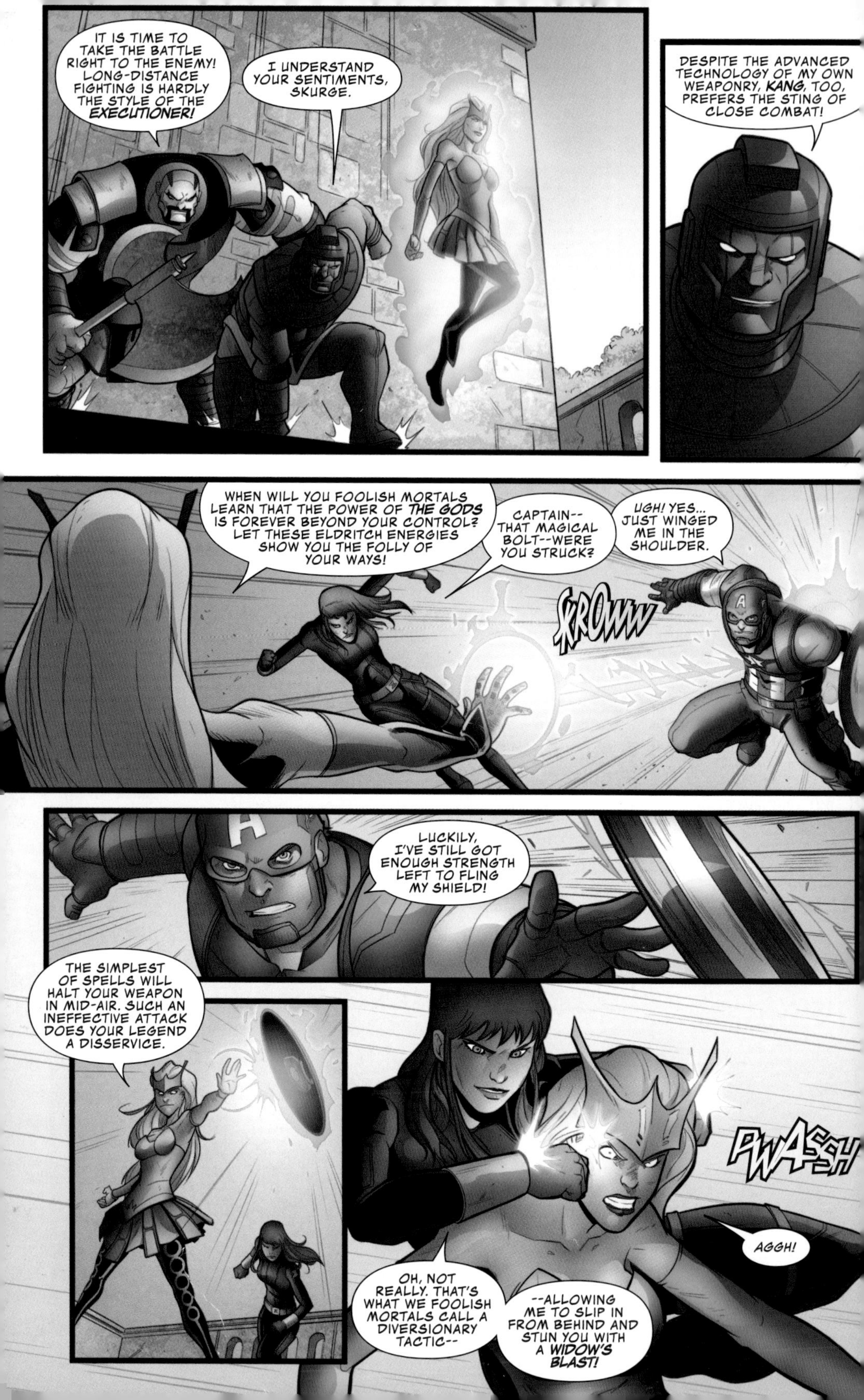

IT IS TIME TO TAKE THE BATTLE RIGHT TO THE ENEMY! LONG-DISTANCE FIGHTING IS HARDLY THE STYLE OF THE EXECUTIONER!
I UNDERSTAND YOUR SENTIMENTS, SKURGE.
DESPITE THE ADVANCED TECHNOLOGY OF MY OWN WEAPONRY, KANG, TOO, PREFERS THE STING OF CLOSE COMBAT!
WHEN WILL YOU FOOLISH MORTALS LEARN THAT THE POWER OF THE GODS IS FOREVER BEYOND YOUR CONTROL? LET THESE ELDRITCH ENERGIES SHOW YOU THE FOLLY OF YOUR WAYS!
CAPTAIN-- THAT MAGICAL BOLT--WERE YOU STRUCK?
UGH! YES... JUST WINGED ME IN THE SHOULDER.
KROWW
LUCKILY, I'VE STILL GOT ENOUGH STRENGTH LEFT TO FLING MY SHIELD!
THE SIMPLEST OF SPELLS WILL HALT YOUR WEAPON IN MID-AIR. SUCH AN INEFFECTIVE ATTACK DOES YOUR LEGEND A DISSERVICE.
PWASSH
AGGH!
OH, NOT REALLY. THAT'S WHAT WE FOOLISH MORTALS CALL A DIVERSIONARY TACTIC--
--ALLOWING ME TO SLIP IN FROM BEHIND AND STUN YOU WITH A WIDOW'S BLAST!

OUT OF THE WAY, YOU ARMORED CLOWN! SKURGE HAS BUSINESS WITH THAT LITTLE BLOND GODLING BEHIND YOU!

SAVE THAT AX FOR SLICING BALONEY, PAL! I'M NOT MOVING FROM THIS SPOT!

THIS BLADE CAN CLEAVE THE HARDEST ARMOR IN ASGARD!

SHAK!

UNNGH!

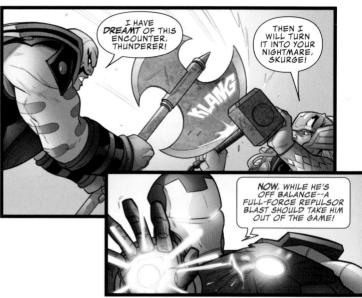

I HAVE DREAMT OF THIS ENCOUNTER, THUNDERER!

THEN I WILL TURN IT INTO YOUR NIGHTMARE, SKURGE!

KLANG

NOW, WHILE HE'S OFF BALANCE--A FULL-FORCE REPULSOR BLAST SHOULD TAKE HIM OUT OF THE GAME!

YOUR WEAPONS ARE FORMIDABLE, KANG, BUT THEY MUST STRIKE THEIR TARGET TO WORK!

ZZAPP

NOW YOU ARE MINE!

OFF WITH YOU, FELINE!

WHERE ARE YOUR BOASTS NOW AS YOU LIE ON YOUR BACK AT MY MERCY?

OOF!

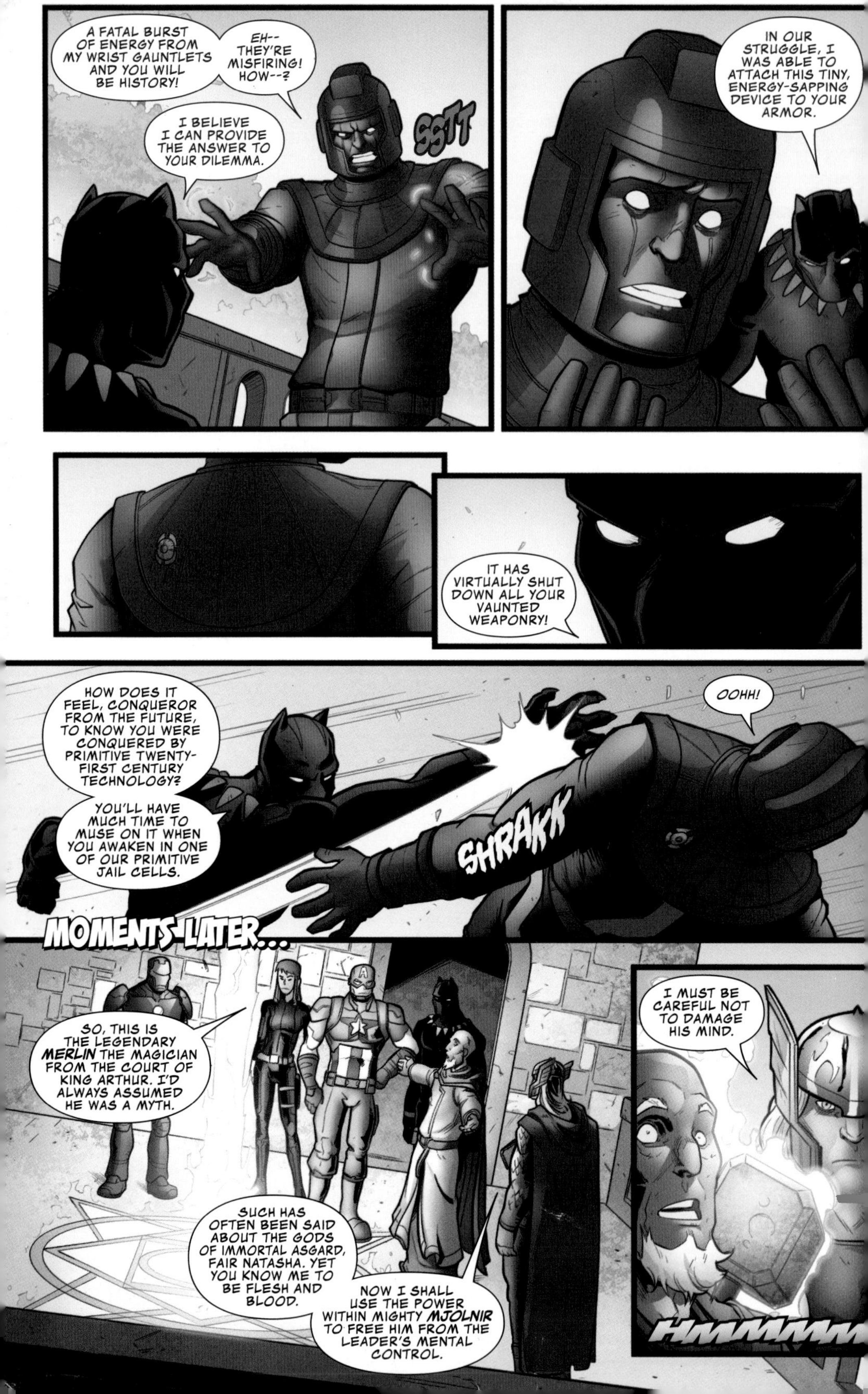
A FATAL BURST OF ENERGY FROM MY WRIST GAUNTLETS AND YOU WILL BE HISTORY!
EH-- THEY'RE MISFIRING! HOW--?
SSTT
I BELIEVE I CAN PROVIDE THE ANSWER TO YOUR DILEMMA.
IN OUR STRUGGLE, I WAS ABLE TO ATTACH THIS TINY, ENERGY-SAPPING DEVICE TO YOUR ARMOR.
IT HAS VIRTUALLY SHUT DOWN ALL YOUR VAUNTED WEAPONRY!
HOW DOES IT FEEL, CONQUEROR FROM THE FUTURE, TO KNOW YOU WERE CONQUERED BY PRIMITIVE TWENTY-FIRST CENTURY TECHNOLOGY?
YOU'LL HAVE MUCH TIME TO MUSE ON IT WHEN YOU AWAKEN IN ONE OF OUR PRIMITIVE JAIL CELLS.
OOHH!
SHRAKK
MOMENTS LATER...
SO, THIS IS THE LEGENDARY MERLIN THE MAGICIAN FROM THE COURT OF KING ARTHUR. I'D ALWAYS ASSUMED HE WAS A MYTH.
SUCH HAS OFTEN BEEN SAID ABOUT THE GODS OF IMMORTAL ASGARD, FAIR NATASHA. YET YOU KNOW ME TO BE FLESH AND BLOOD.
NOW I SHALL USE THE POWER WITHIN MIGHTY MJOLNIR TO FREE HIM FROM THE LEADER'S MENTAL CONTROL.
I MUST BE CAREFUL NOT TO DAMAGE HIS MIND.
HMMMMM

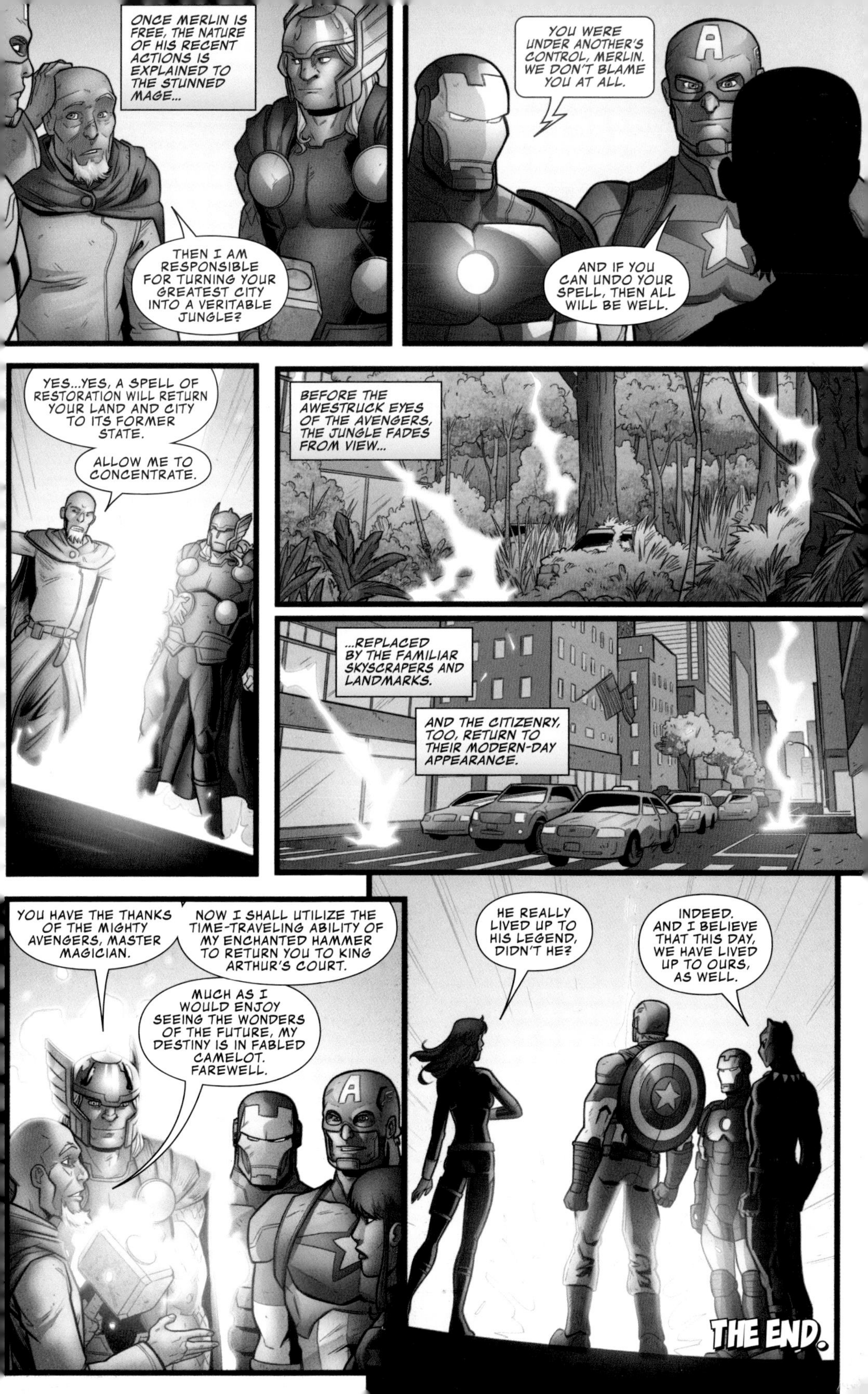
ONCE MERLIN IS FREE, THE NATURE OF HIS RECENT ACTIONS IS EXPLAINED TO THE STUNNED MAGE...
THEN I AM RESPONSIBLE FOR TURNING YOUR GREATEST CITY INTO A VERITABLE JUNGLE?
YOU WERE UNDER ANOTHER'S CONTROL, MERLIN. WE DON'T BLAME YOU AT ALL.
AND IF YOU CAN UNDO YOUR SPELL, THEN ALL WILL BE WELL.
YES...YES, A SPELL OF RESTORATION WILL RETURN YOUR LAND AND CITY TO ITS FORMER STATE.
ALLOW ME TO CONCENTRATE.
BEFORE THE AWESTRUCK EYES OF THE AVENGERS, THE JUNGLE FADES FROM VIEW...
...REPLACED BY THE FAMILIAR SKYSCRAPERS AND LANDMARKS.
AND THE CITIZENRY, TOO, RETURN TO THEIR MODERN-DAY APPEARANCE.
YOU HAVE THE THANKS OF THE MIGHTY AVENGERS, MASTER MAGICIAN.
NOW I SHALL UTILIZE THE TIME-TRAVELING ABILITY OF MY ENCHANTED HAMMER TO RETURN YOU TO KING ARTHUR'S COURT.
MUCH AS I WOULD ENJOY SEEING THE WONDERS OF THE FUTURE, MY DESTINY IS IN FABLED CAMELOT. FAREWELL.
HE REALLY LIVED UP TO HIS LEGEND, DIDN'T HE?
INDEED. AND I BELIEVE THAT THIS DAY, WE HAVE LIVED UP TO OURS, AS WELL.
THE END.

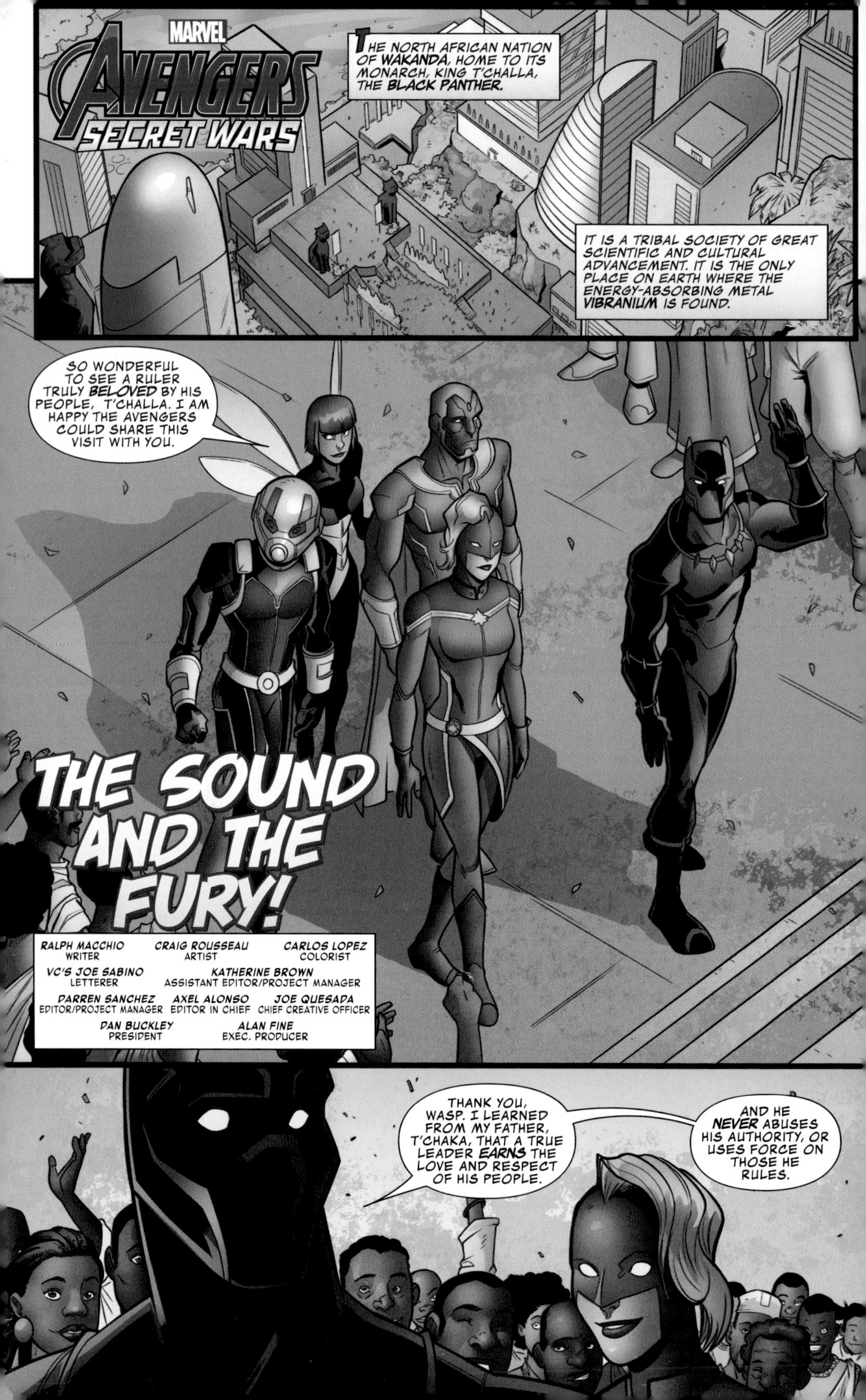
MARVEL
AVENGERS
SECRET WARS
THE NORTH AFRICAN NATION OF WAKANDA, HOME TO ITS MONARCH, KING T'CHALLA, THE BLACK PANTHER.
IT IS A TRIBAL SOCIETY OF GREAT SCIENTIFIC AND CULTURAL ADVANCEMENT. IT IS THE ONLY PLACE ON EARTH WHERE THE ENERGY-ABSORBING METAL VIBRANIUM IS FOUND.
SO WONDERFUL TO SEE A RULER TRULY BELOVED BY HIS PEOPLE, T'CHALLA. I AM HAPPY THE AVENGERS COULD SHARE THIS VISIT WITH YOU.
THE SOUND AND THE FURY!
RALPH MACCHIO WRITER
CRAIG ROUSSEAU ARTIST
CARLOS LOPEZ COLORIST
VC'S JOE SABINO LETTERER
KATHERINE BROWN ASSISTANT EDITOR/PROJECT MANAGER
DARREN SANCHEZ EDITOR/PROJECT MANAGER
AXEL ALONSO EDITOR IN CHIEF
JOE QUESADA CHIEF CREATIVE OFFICER
DAN BUCKLEY PRESIDENT
ALAN FINE EXEC. PRODUCER
THANK YOU, WASP. I LEARNED FROM MY FATHER, T'CHAKA, THAT A TRUE LEADER EARNS THE LOVE AND RESPECT OF HIS PEOPLE.
AND HE NEVER ABUSES HIS AUTHORITY, OR USES FORCE ON THOSE HE RULES.

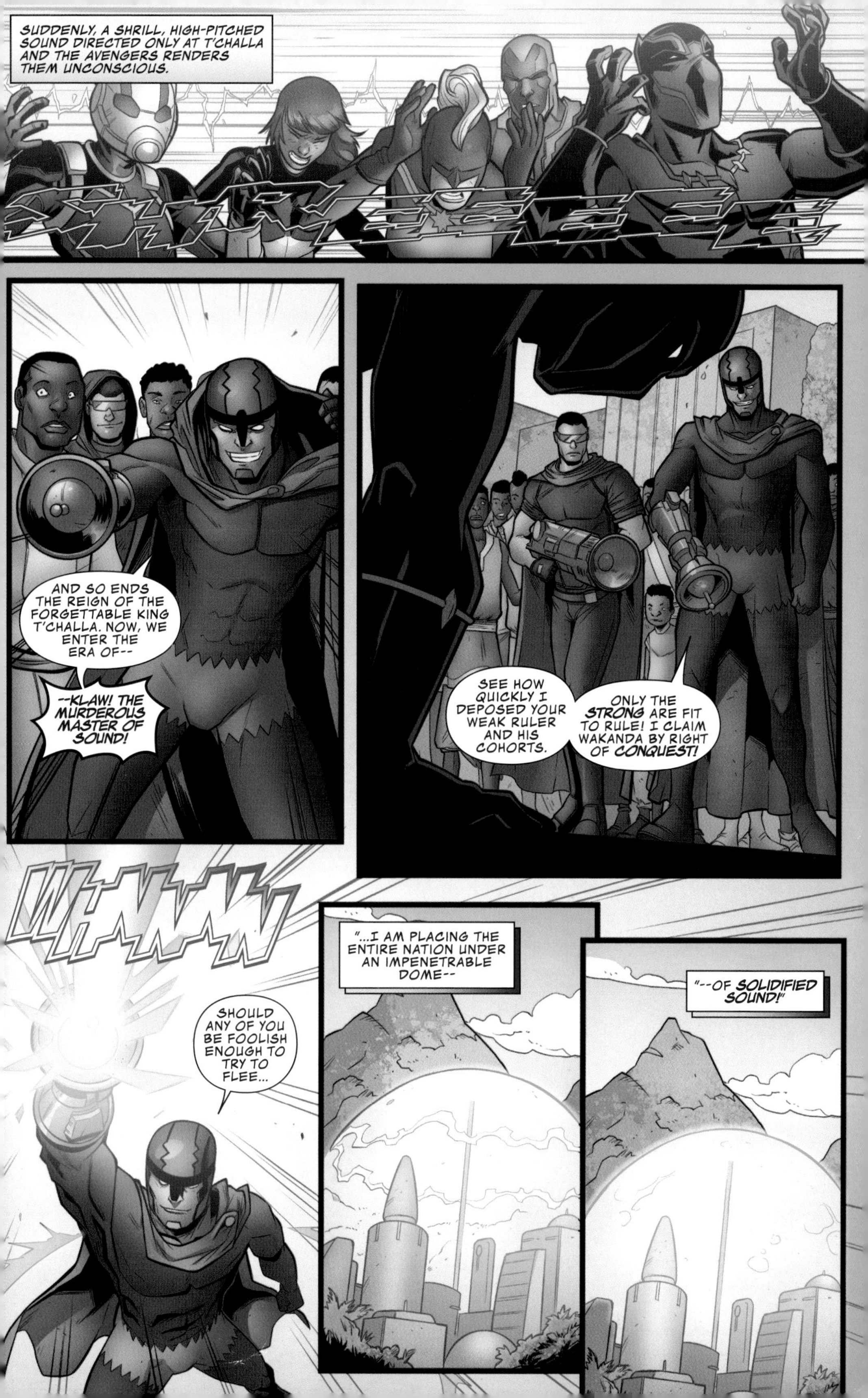
SUDDENLY, A SHRILL, HIGH-PITCHED SOUND DIRECTED ONLY AT T'CHALLA AND THE AVENGERS RENDERS THEM UNCONSCIOUS.
AND SO ENDS THE REIGN OF THE FORGETTABLE KING T'CHALLA. NOW, WE ENTER THE ERA OF--
--KLAW! THE MURDEROUS MASTER OF SOUND!
SEE HOW QUICKLY I DEPOSED YOUR WEAK RULER AND HIS COHORTS.
ONLY THE STRONG ARE FIT TO RULE! I CLAIM WAKANDA BY RIGHT OF CONQUEST!
WHNNN
SHOULD ANY OF YOU BE FOOLISH ENOUGH TO TRY TO FLEE...
"...I AM PLACING THE ENTIRE NATION UNDER AN IMPENETRABLE DOME--
"--OF SOLIDIFIED SOUND!"

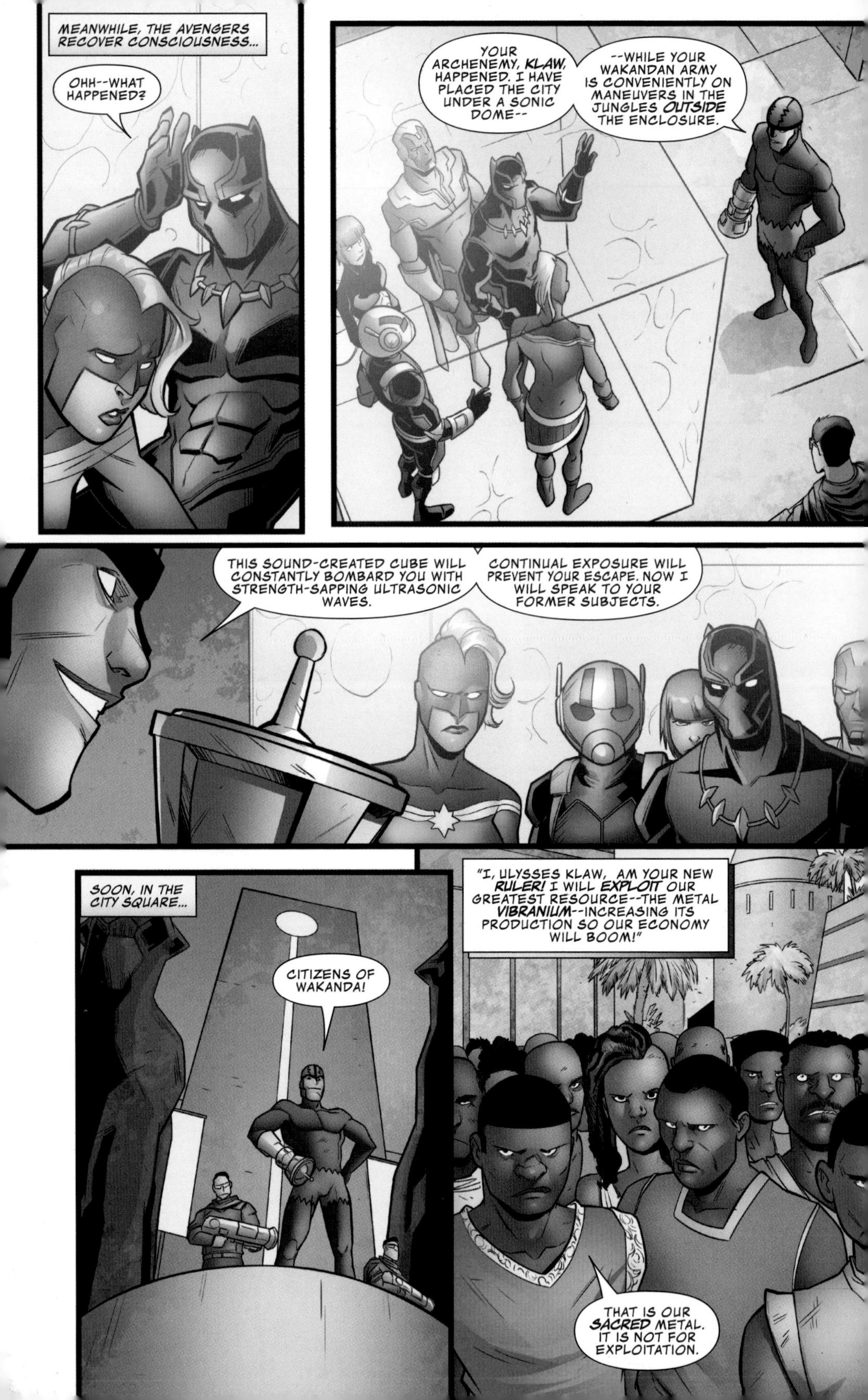
MEANWHILE, THE AVENGERS RECOVER CONSCIOUSNESS...
OHH--WHAT HAPPENED?
YOUR ARCHENEMY, KLAW, HAPPENED. I HAVE PLACED THE CITY UNDER A SONIC DOME--
--WHILE YOUR WAKANDAN ARMY IS CONVENIENTLY ON MANEUVERS IN THE JUNGLES OUTSIDE THE ENCLOSURE.
THIS SOUND-CREATED CUBE WILL CONSTANTLY BOMBARD YOU WITH STRENGTH-SAPPING ULTRASONIC WAVES.
CONTINUAL EXPOSURE WILL PREVENT YOUR ESCAPE. NOW I WILL SPEAK TO YOUR FORMER SUBJECTS.
SOON, IN THE CITY SQUARE...
CITIZENS OF WAKANDA!
"I, ULYSSES KLAW, AM YOUR NEW RULER! I WILL EXPLOIT OUR GREATEST RESOURCE--THE METAL VIBRANIUM--INCREASING ITS PRODUCTION SO OUR ECONOMY WILL BOOM!"
THAT IS OUR SACRED METAL. IT IS NOT FOR EXPLOITATION.

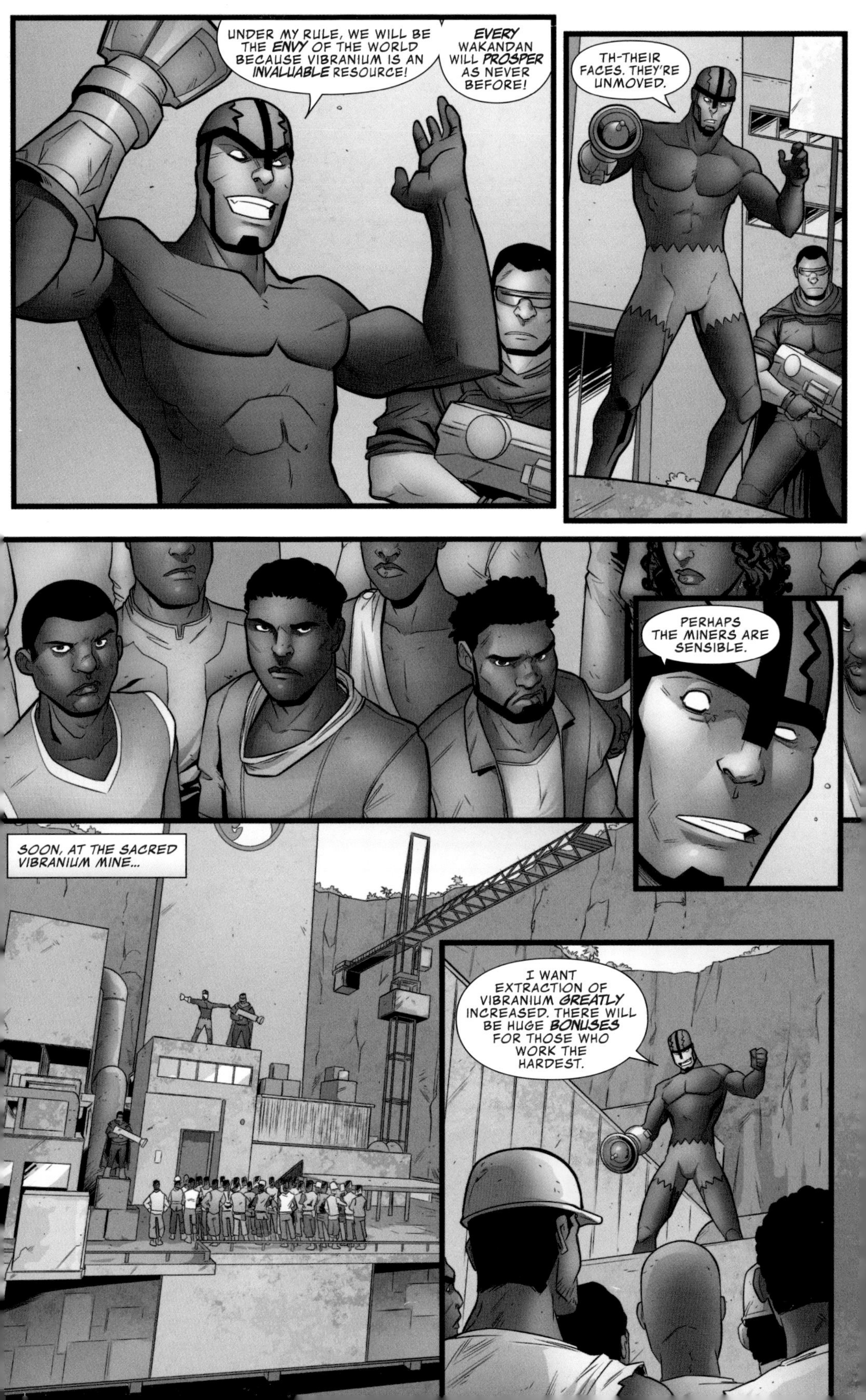
UNDER MY RULE, WE WILL BE THE ENVY OF THE WORLD BECAUSE VIBRANIUM IS AN INVALUABLE RESOURCE!
EVERY WAKANDAN WILL PROSPER AS NEVER BEFORE!
TH-THEIR FACES. THEY'RE UNMOVED.
PERHAPS THE MINERS ARE SENSIBLE.
SOON, AT THE SACRED VIBRANIUM MINE...
I WANT EXTRACTION OF VIBRANIUM GREATLY INCREASED. THERE WILL BE HUGE BONUSES FOR THOSE WHO WORK THE HARDEST.

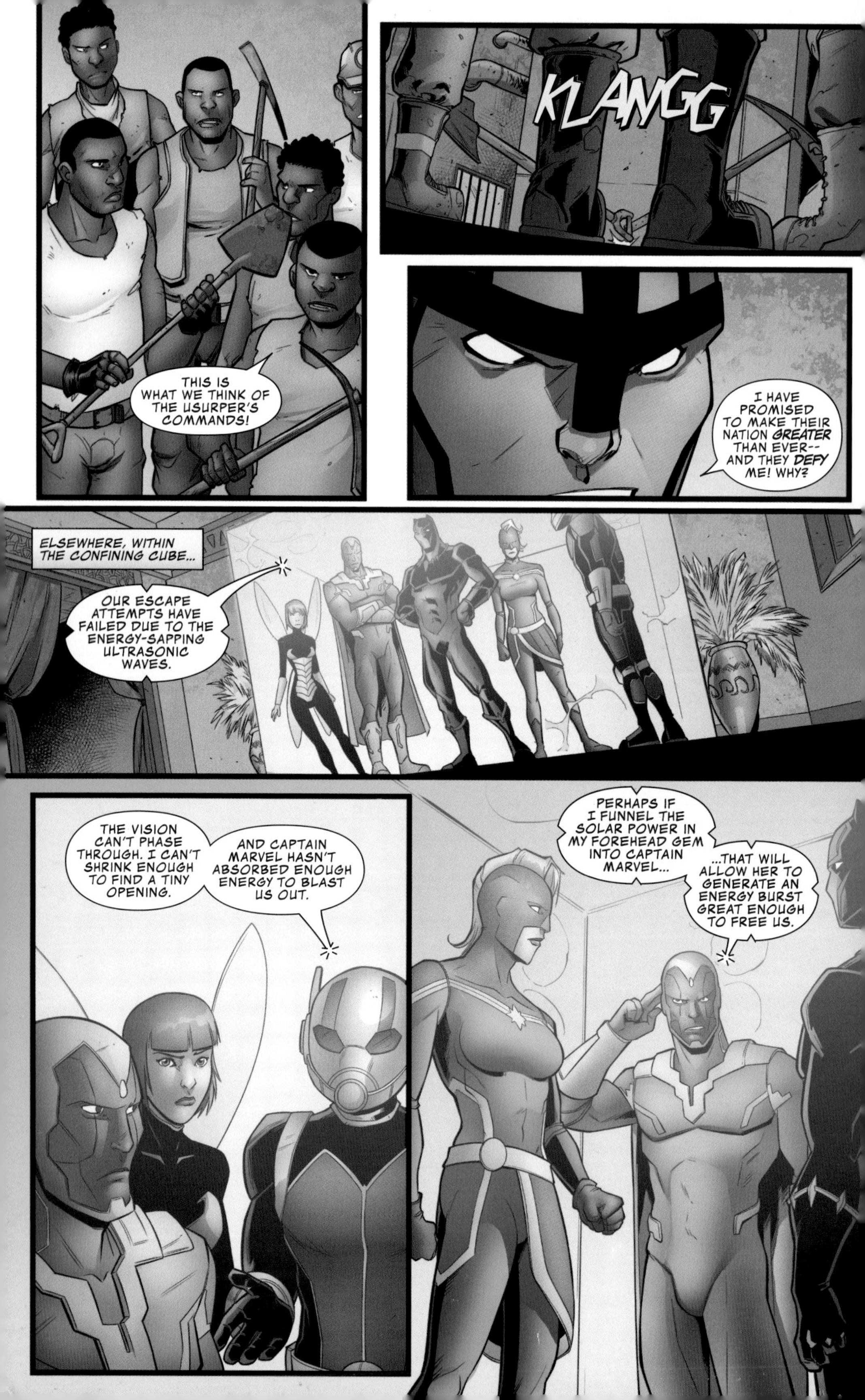
THIS IS WHAT WE THINK OF THE USURPER'S COMMANDS!
KLANGG
I HAVE PROMISED TO MAKE THEIR NATION GREATER THAN EVER-- AND THEY DEFY ME! WHY?
ELSEWHERE, WITHIN THE CONFINING CUBE...
OUR ESCAPE ATTEMPTS HAVE FAILED DUE TO THE ENERGY-SAPPING ULTRASONIC WAVES.
THE VISION CAN'T PHASE THROUGH. I CAN'T SHRINK ENOUGH TO FIND A TINY OPENING.
AND CAPTAIN MARVEL HASN'T ABSORBED ENOUGH ENERGY TO BLAST US OUT.
PERHAPS IF I FUNNEL THE SOLAR POWER IN MY FOREHEAD GEM INTO CAPTAIN MARVEL...
...THAT WILL ALLOW HER TO GENERATE AN ENERGY BURST GREAT ENOUGH TO FREE US.

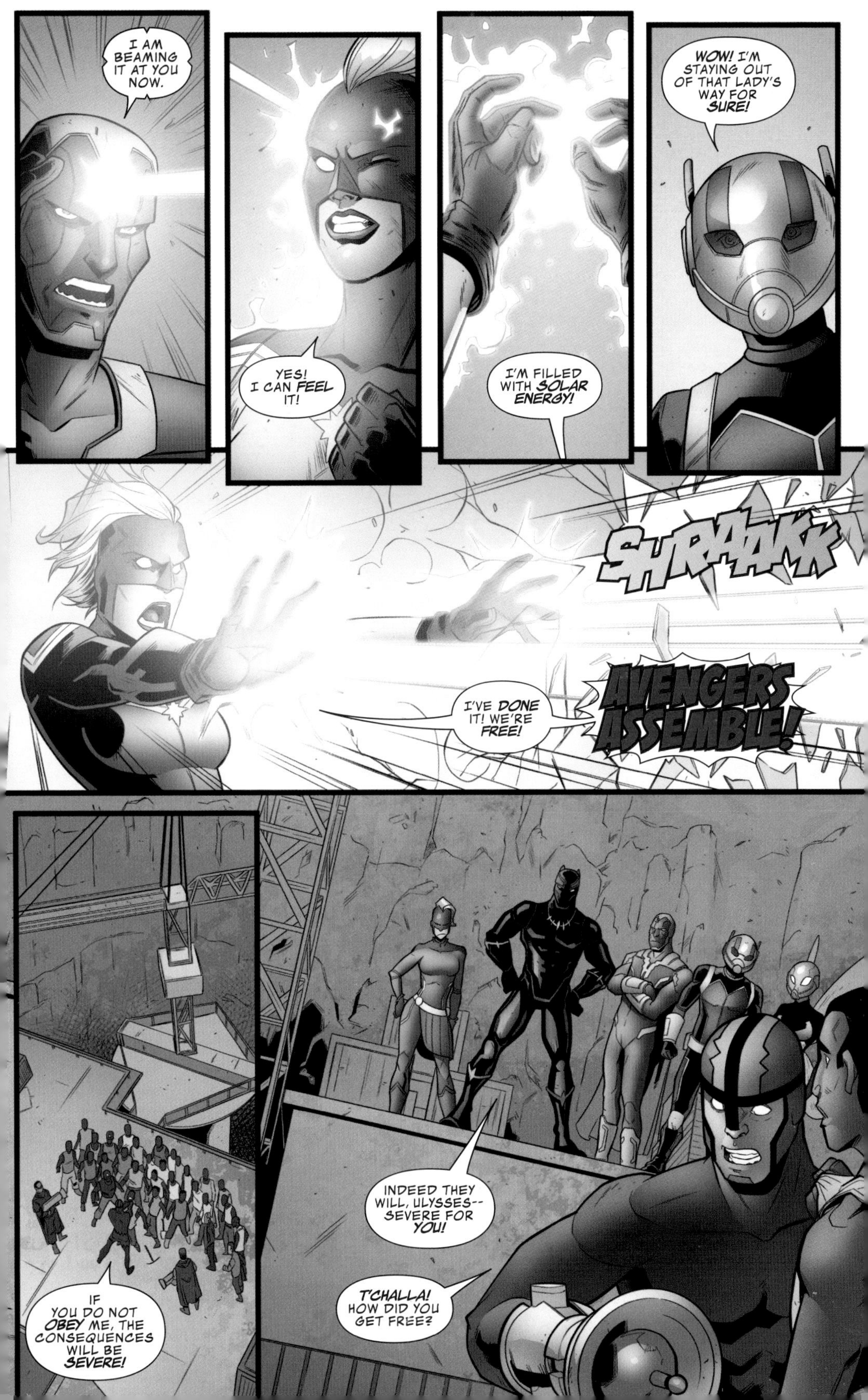
I AM BEAMING IT AT YOU NOW.
YES! I CAN FEEL IT!
I'M FILLED WITH SOLAR ENERGY!
WOW! I'M STAYING OUT OF THAT LADY'S WAY FOR SURE!
SHRAAKK
I'VE DONE IT! WE'RE FREE!
AVENGERS ASSEMBLE!
IF YOU DO NOT OBEY ME, THE CONSEQUENCES WILL BE SEVERE!
INDEED THEY WILL, ULYSSES-- SEVERE FOR YOU!
T'CHALLA! HOW DID YOU GET FREE?

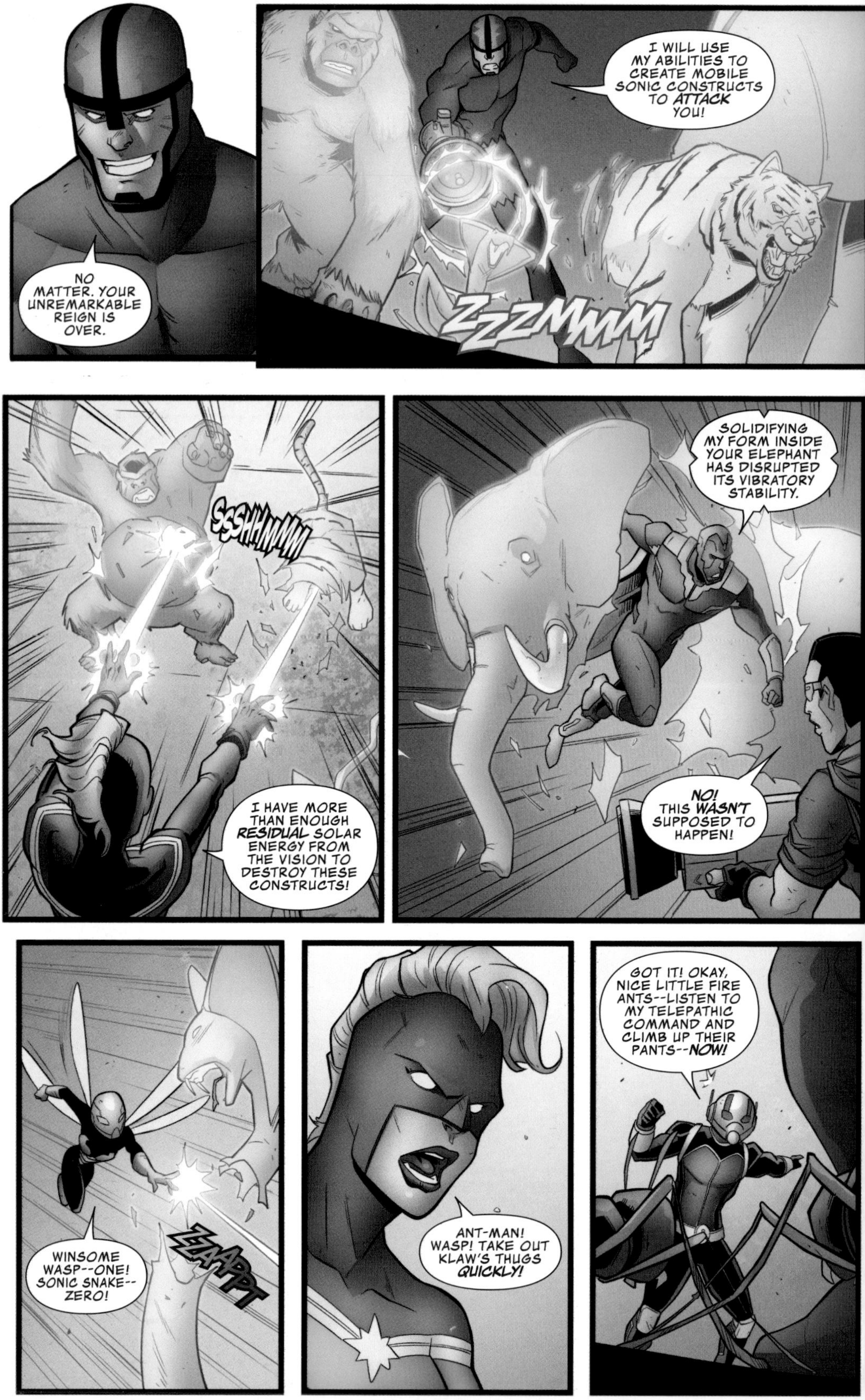
NO MATTER. YOUR UNREMARKABLE REIGN IS OVER.
I WILL USE MY ABILITIES TO CREATE MOBILE SONIC CONSTRUCTS TO ATTACK YOU!
ZZZMMMM!
SSSHHMMM
I HAVE MORE THAN ENOUGH RESIDUAL SOLAR ENERGY FROM THE VISION TO DESTROY THESE CONSTRUCTS!
SOLIDIFYING MY FORM INSIDE YOUR ELEPHANT HAS DISRUPTED ITS VIBRATORY STABILITY.
NO! THIS WASN'T SUPPOSED TO HAPPEN!
WINSOME WASP--ONE! SONIC SNAKE--ZERO!
ZZAPPT
ANT-MAN! WASP! TAKE OUT KLAW'S THUGS QUICKLY!
GOT IT! OKAY, NICE LITTLE FIRE ANTS--LISTEN TO MY TELEPATHIC COMMAND AND CLIMB UP THEIR PANTS--NOW!

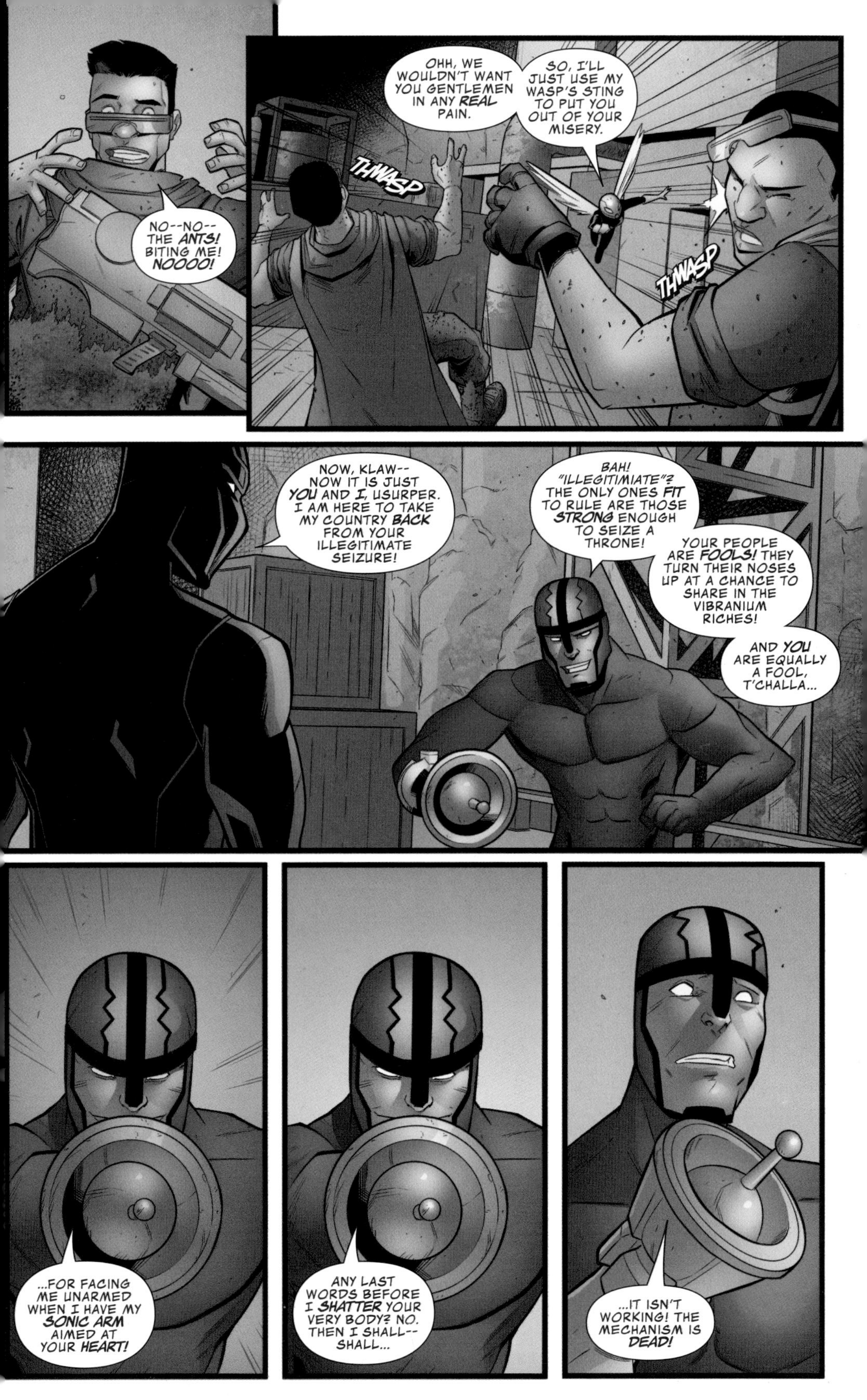
NO--NO--
THE ANTS!
BITING ME!
NOOOO!
OHH, WE WOULDN'T WANT YOU GENTLEMEN IN ANY REAL PAIN.
SO, I'LL JUST USE MY WASP'S STING TO PUT YOU OUT OF YOUR MISERY.
THWASP
THWASP
NOW, KLAW-- NOW IT IS JUST YOU AND I, USURPER. I AM HERE TO TAKE MY COUNTRY BACK FROM YOUR ILLEGITIMATE SEIZURE!
BAH! "ILLEGITIMIATE"? THE ONLY ONES FIT TO RULE ARE THOSE STRONG ENOUGH TO SEIZE A THRONE!
YOUR PEOPLE ARE FOOLS! THEY TURN THEIR NOSES UP AT A CHANCE TO SHARE IN THE VIBRANIUM RICHES!
AND YOU ARE EQUALLY A FOOL, T'CHALLA...
...FOR FACING ME UNARMED WHEN I HAVE MY SONIC ARM AIMED AT YOUR HEART!
ANY LAST WORDS BEFORE I SHATTER YOUR VERY BODY? NO. THEN I SHALL-- SHALL...
...IT ISN'T WORKING! THE MECHANISM IS DEAD!

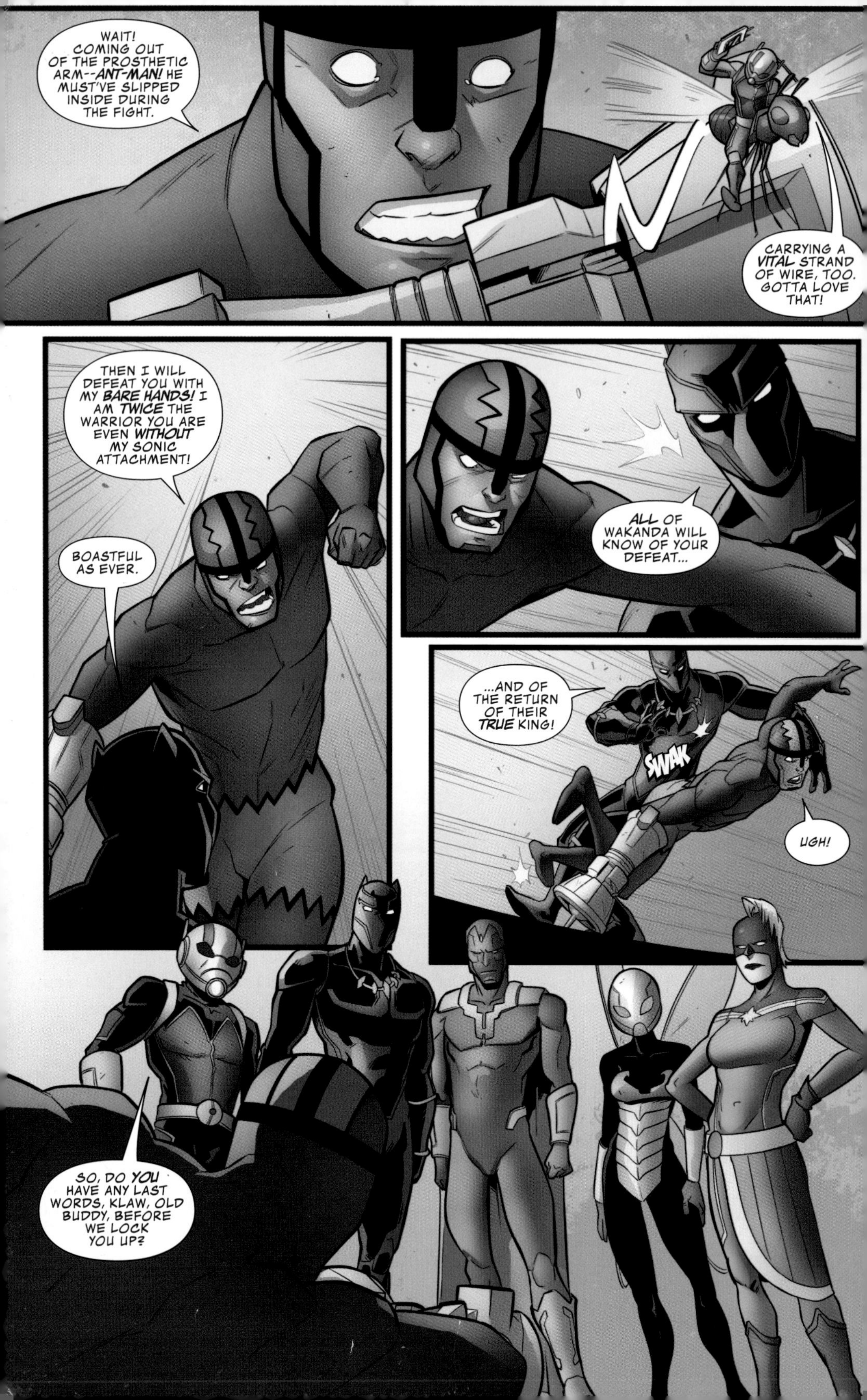
WAIT! COMING OUT OF THE PROSTHETIC ARM--ANT-MAN! HE MUST'VE SLIPPED INSIDE DURING THE FIGHT.
CARRYING A VITAL STRAND OF WIRE, TOO. GOTTA LOVE THAT!
THEN I WILL DEFEAT YOU WITH MY BARE HANDS! I AM TWICE THE WARRIOR YOU ARE EVEN WITHOUT MY SONIC ATTACHMENT!
BOASTFUL AS EVER.
ALL OF WAKANDA WILL KNOW OF YOUR DEFEAT...
...AND OF THE RETURN OF THEIR TRUE KING!
SWAK
UGH!
SO, DO YOU HAVE ANY LAST WORDS, KLAW, OLD BUDDY, BEFORE WE LOCK YOU UP?

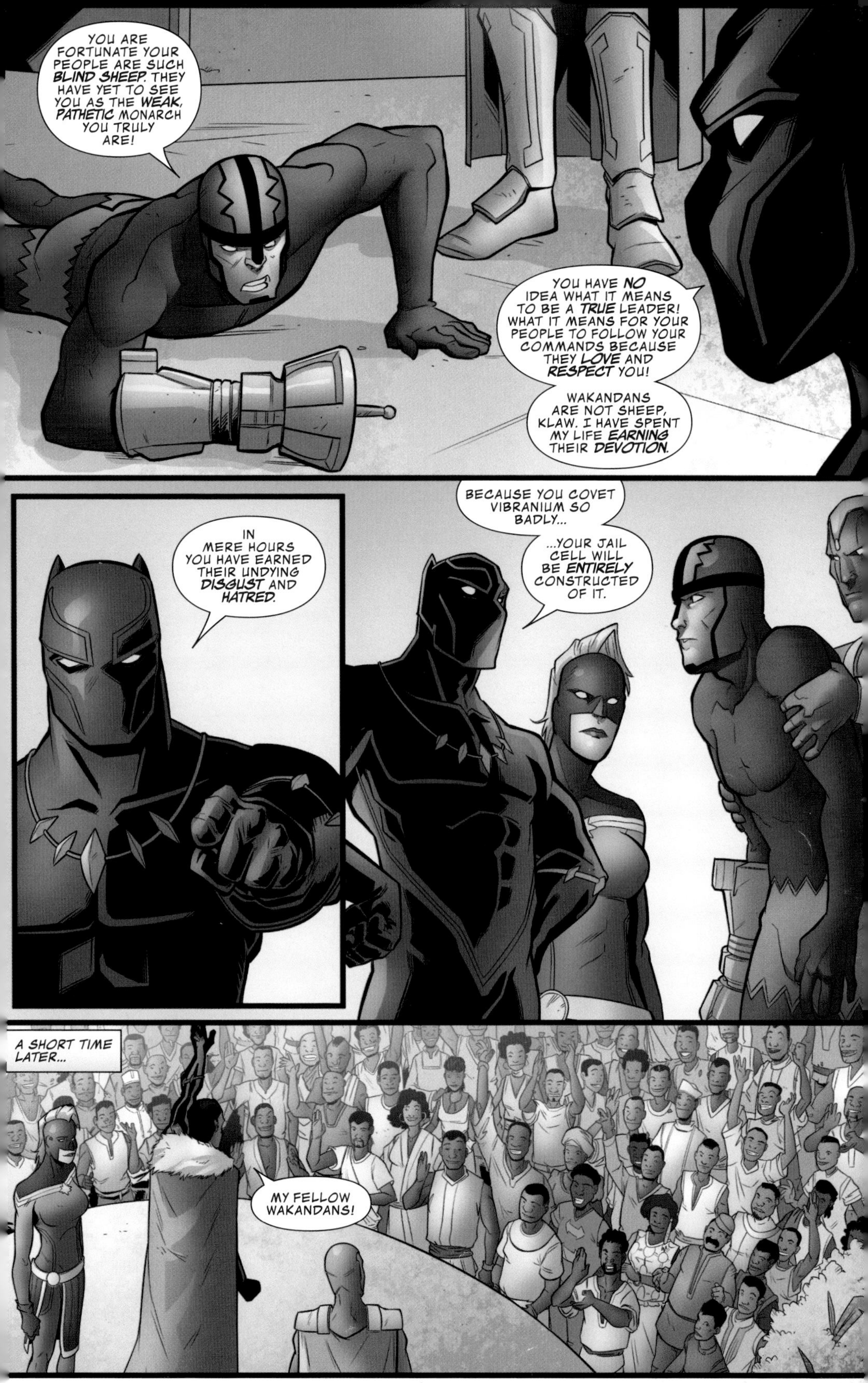
YOU ARE FORTUNATE YOUR PEOPLE ARE SUCH BLIND SHEEP. THEY HAVE YET TO SEE YOU AS THE WEAK, PATHETIC MONARCH YOU TRULY ARE!
YOU HAVE NO IDEA WHAT IT MEANS TO BE A TRUE LEADER! WHAT IT MEANS FOR YOUR PEOPLE TO FOLLOW YOUR COMMANDS BECAUSE THEY LOVE AND RESPECT YOU!
WAKANDANS ARE NOT SHEEP, KLAW. I HAVE SPENT MY LIFE EARNING THEIR DEVOTION.
IN MERE HOURS YOU HAVE EARNED THEIR UNDYING DISGUST AND HATRED.
BECAUSE YOU COVET VIBRANIUM SO BADLY...
...YOUR JAIL CELL WILL BE ENTIRELY CONSTRUCTED OF IT.
A SHORT TIME LATER...
MY FELLOW WAKANDANS!

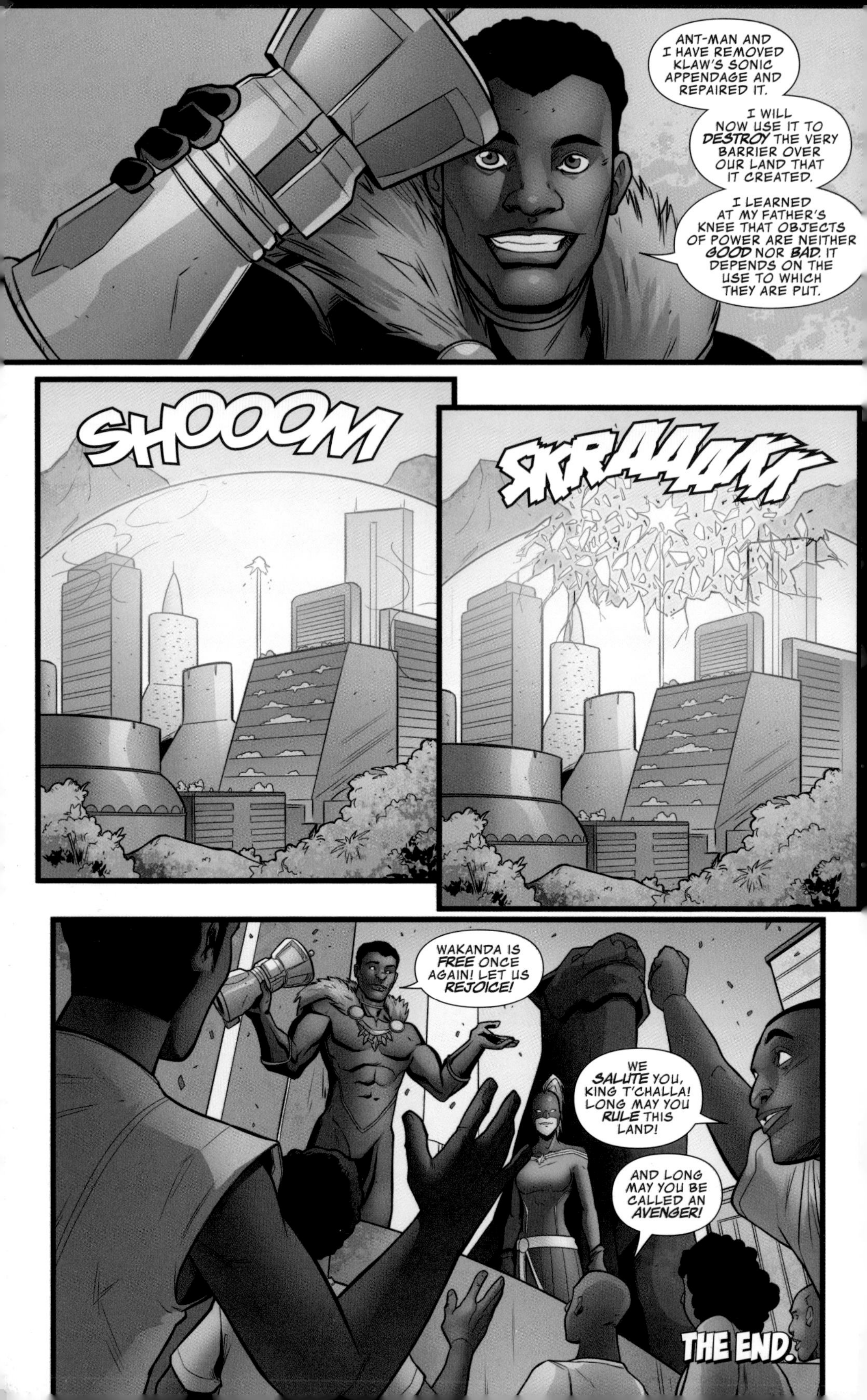

ANT-MAN AND I HAVE REMOVED KLAW'S SONIC APPENDAGE AND REPAIRED IT.
I WILL NOW USE IT TO DESTROY THE VERY BARRIER OVER OUR LAND THAT IT CREATED.
I LEARNED AT MY FATHER'S KNEE THAT OBJECTS OF POWER ARE NEITHER GOOD NOR BAD. IT DEPENDS ON THE USE TO WHICH THEY ARE PUT.
SHOOOM
SKRAAAAK
WAKANDA IS FREE ONCE AGAIN! LET US REJOICE!
WE SALUTE YOU, KING T'CHALLA! LONG MAY YOU RULE THIS LAND!
AND LONG MAY YOU BE CALLED AN AVENGER!
THE END.

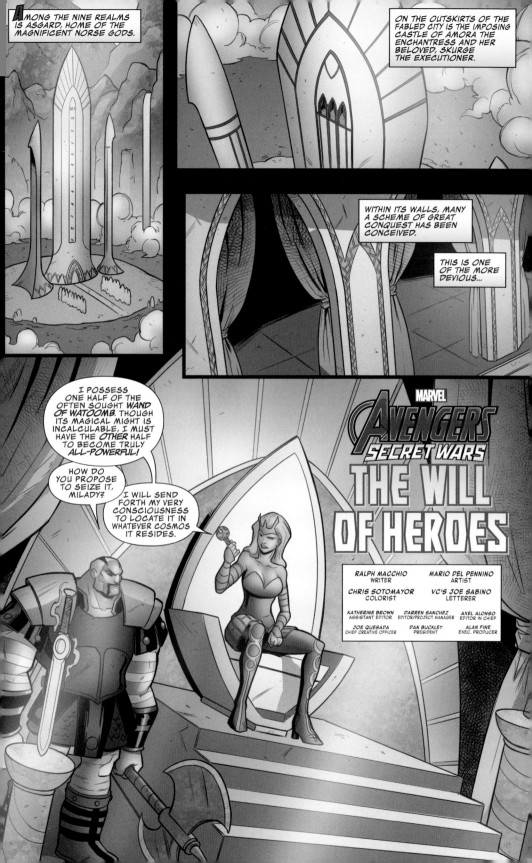

AMONG THE NINE REALMS IS ASGARD, HOME OF THE MAGNIFICENT NORSE GODS.

ON THE OUTSKIRTS OF THE FABLED CITY IS THE IMPOSING CASTLE OF AMORA THE ENCHANTRESS AND HER BELOVED, SKURGE THE EXECUTIONER.

WITHIN ITS WALLS, MANY A SCHEME OF GREAT CONQUEST HAS BEEN CONCEIVED.

THIS IS ONE OF THE MORE DEVIOUS...

I POSSESS ONE HALF OF THE OFTEN SOUGHT *WAND OF WATOOMB.* THOUGH ITS MAGICAL MIGHT IS INCALCULABLE, I MUST HAVE THE *OTHER* HALF TO BECOME TRULY ALL-POWERFUL!

HOW DO YOU PROPOSE TO SEIZE IT, MILADY?

I WILL SEND FORTH MY VERY CONSCIOUSNESS TO LOCATE IT IN WHATEVER COSMOS IT RESIDES.

MARVEL
AVENGERS SECRET WARS
THE WILL OF HEROES

RALPH MACCHIO
WRITER

MARIO DEL PENNINO
ARTIST

CHRIS SOTOMAYOR
COLORIST

VC'S JOE SABINO
LETTERER

KATHERINE BROWN
ASSISTANT EDITOR

DARREN SANCHEZ
EDITOR/PROJECT MANAGER

AXEL ALONSO
EDITOR IN CHIEF

JOE QUESADA
CHIEF CREATIVE OFFICER

DAN BUCKLEY
PRESIDENT

ALAN FINE
EXEC. PRODUCER

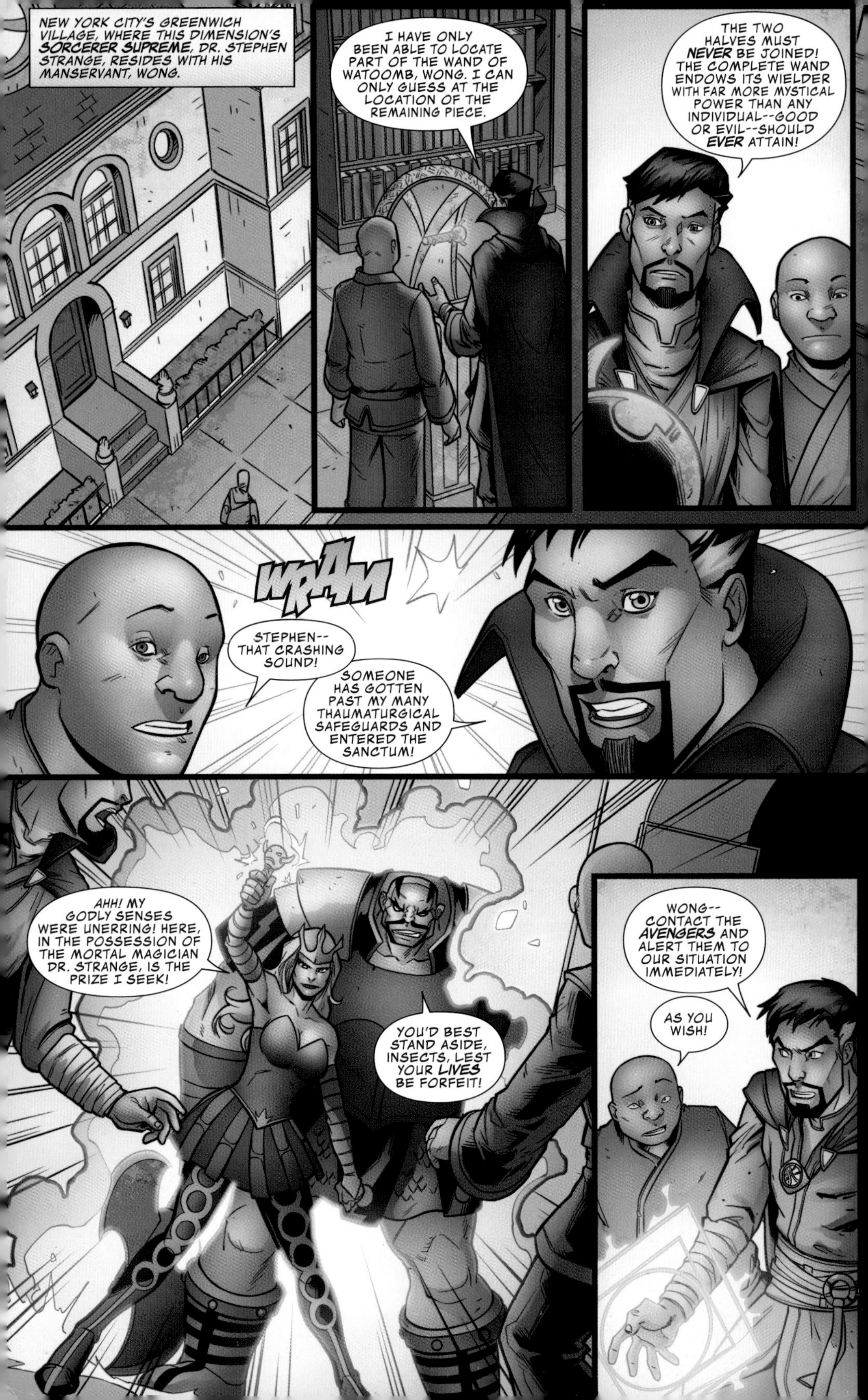

NEW YORK CITY'S GREENWICH VILLAGE, WHERE THIS DIMENSION'S SORCERER SUPREME, DR. STEPHEN STRANGE, RESIDES WITH HIS MANSERVANT, WONG.
I HAVE ONLY BEEN ABLE TO LOCATE PART OF THE WAND OF WATOOMB, WONG. I CAN ONLY GUESS AT THE LOCATION OF THE REMAINING PIECE.
THE TWO HALVES MUST NEVER BE JOINED! THE COMPLETE WAND ENDOWS ITS WIELDER WITH FAR MORE MYSTICAL POWER THAN ANY INDIVIDUAL--GOOD OR EVIL--SHOULD EVER ATTAIN!
WRAAM
STEPHEN-- THAT CRASHING SOUND!
SOMEONE HAS GOTTEN PAST MY MANY THAUMATURGICAL SAFEGUARDS AND ENTERED THE SANCTUM!
AHH! MY GODLY SENSES WERE UNERRING! HERE, IN THE POSSESSION OF THE MORTAL MAGICIAN DR. STRANGE, IS THE PRIZE I SEEK!
YOU'D BEST STAND ASIDE, INSECTS, LEST YOUR LIVES BE FORFEIT!
WONG-- CONTACT THE AVENGERS AND ALERT THEM TO OUR SITUATION IMMEDIATELY!
AS YOU WISH!

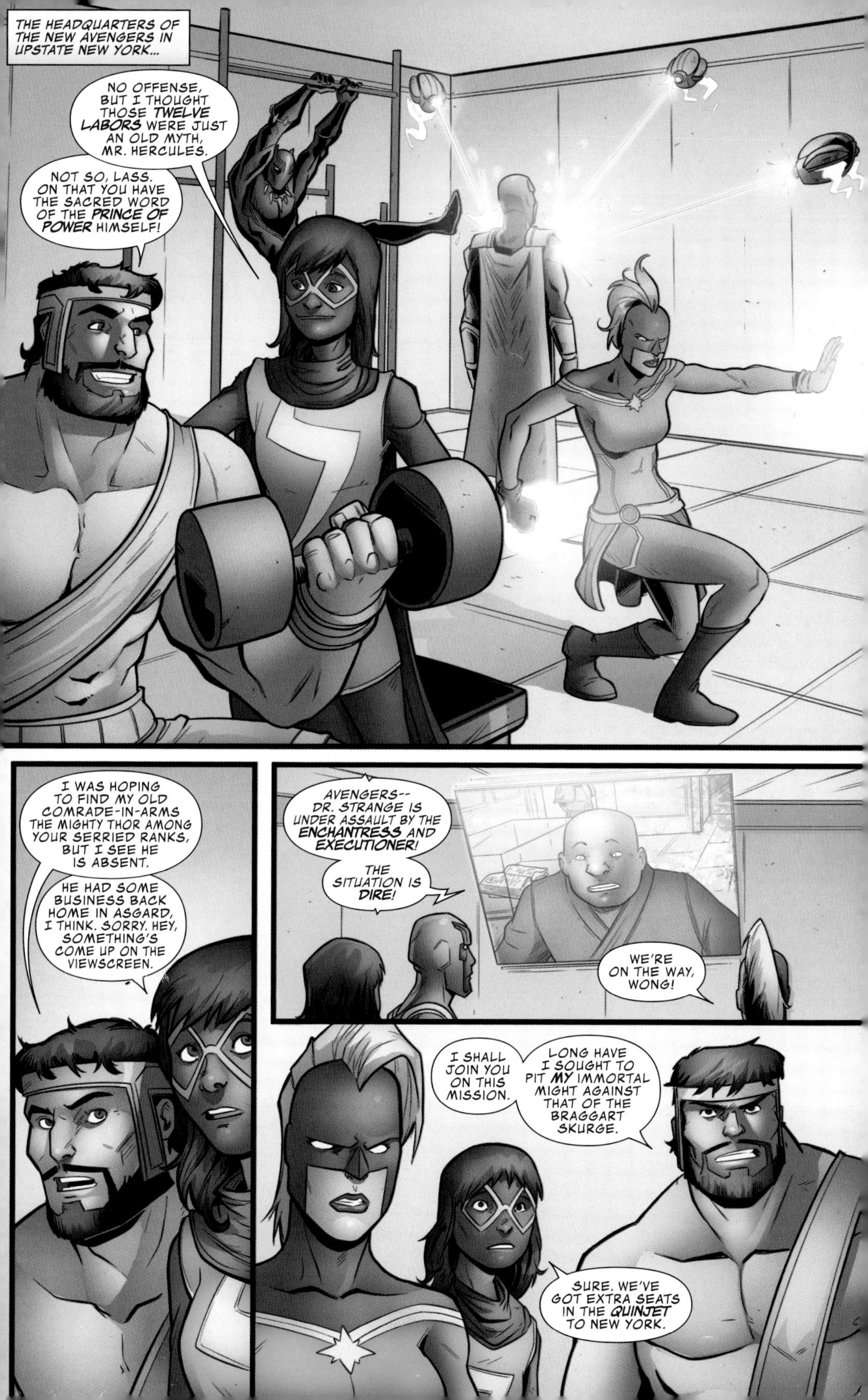
THE HEADQUARTERS OF THE NEW AVENGERS IN UPSTATE NEW YORK...
NO OFFENSE, BUT I THOUGHT THOSE TWELVE LABORS WERE JUST AN OLD MYTH, MR. HERCULES.
NOT SO, LASS. ON THAT YOU HAVE THE SACRED WORD OF THE PRINCE OF POWER HIMSELF!
I WAS HOPING TO FIND MY OLD COMRADE-IN-ARMS THE MIGHTY THOR AMONG YOUR SERRIED RANKS, BUT I SEE HE IS ABSENT.
HE HAD SOME BUSINESS BACK HOME IN ASGARD, I THINK. SORRY. HEY, SOMETHING'S COME UP ON THE VIEWSCREEN.
AVENGERS-- DR. STRANGE IS UNDER ASSAULT BY THE ENCHANTRESS AND EXECUTIONER!
THE SITUATION IS DIRE!
WE'RE ON THE WAY, WONG!
I SHALL JOIN YOU ON THIS MISSION.
LONG HAVE I SOUGHT TO PIT MY IMMORTAL MIGHT AGAINST THAT OF THE BRAGGART SKURGE.
SURE. WE'VE GOT EXTRA SEATS IN THE QUINJET TO NEW YORK.

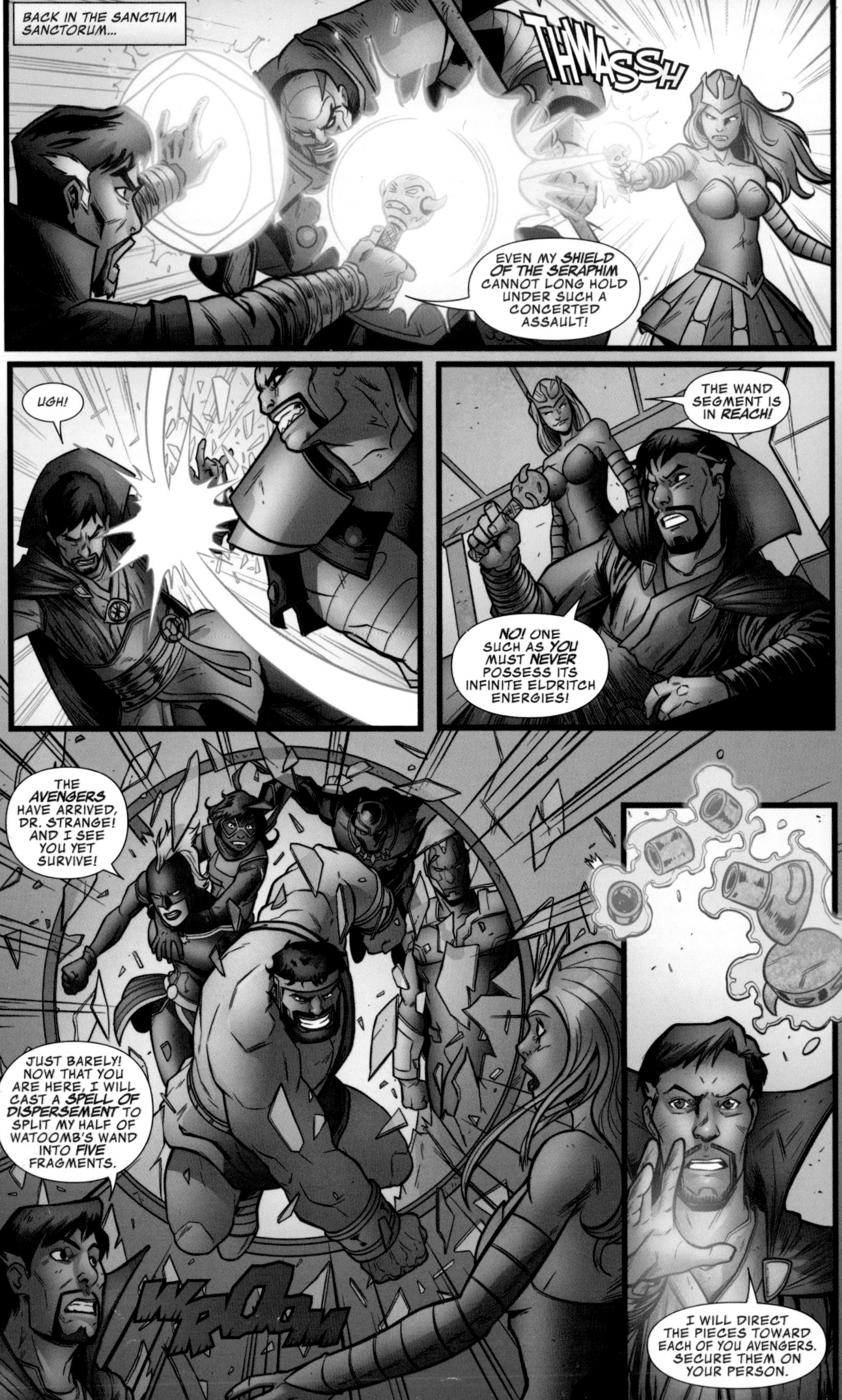

BACK IN THE SANCTUM SANCTORUM...
THWASSH
EVEN MY SHIELD OF THE SERAPHIM CANNOT LONG HOLD UNDER SUCH A CONCERTED ASSAULT!
UGH!
THE WAND SEGMENT IS IN REACH!
NO! ONE SUCH AS YOU MUST NEVER POSSESS ITS INFINITE ELDRITCH ENERGIES!
THE AVENGERS HAVE ARRIVED, DR. STRANGE! AND I SEE YOU YET SURVIVE!
JUST BARELY! NOW THAT YOU ARE HERE, I WILL CAST A SPELL OF DISPERSEMENT TO SPLIT MY HALF OF WATOOMB'S WAND INTO FIVE FRAGMENTS.
I WILL DIRECT THE PIECES TOWARD EACH OF YOU AVENGERS. SECURE THEM ON YOUR PERSON.

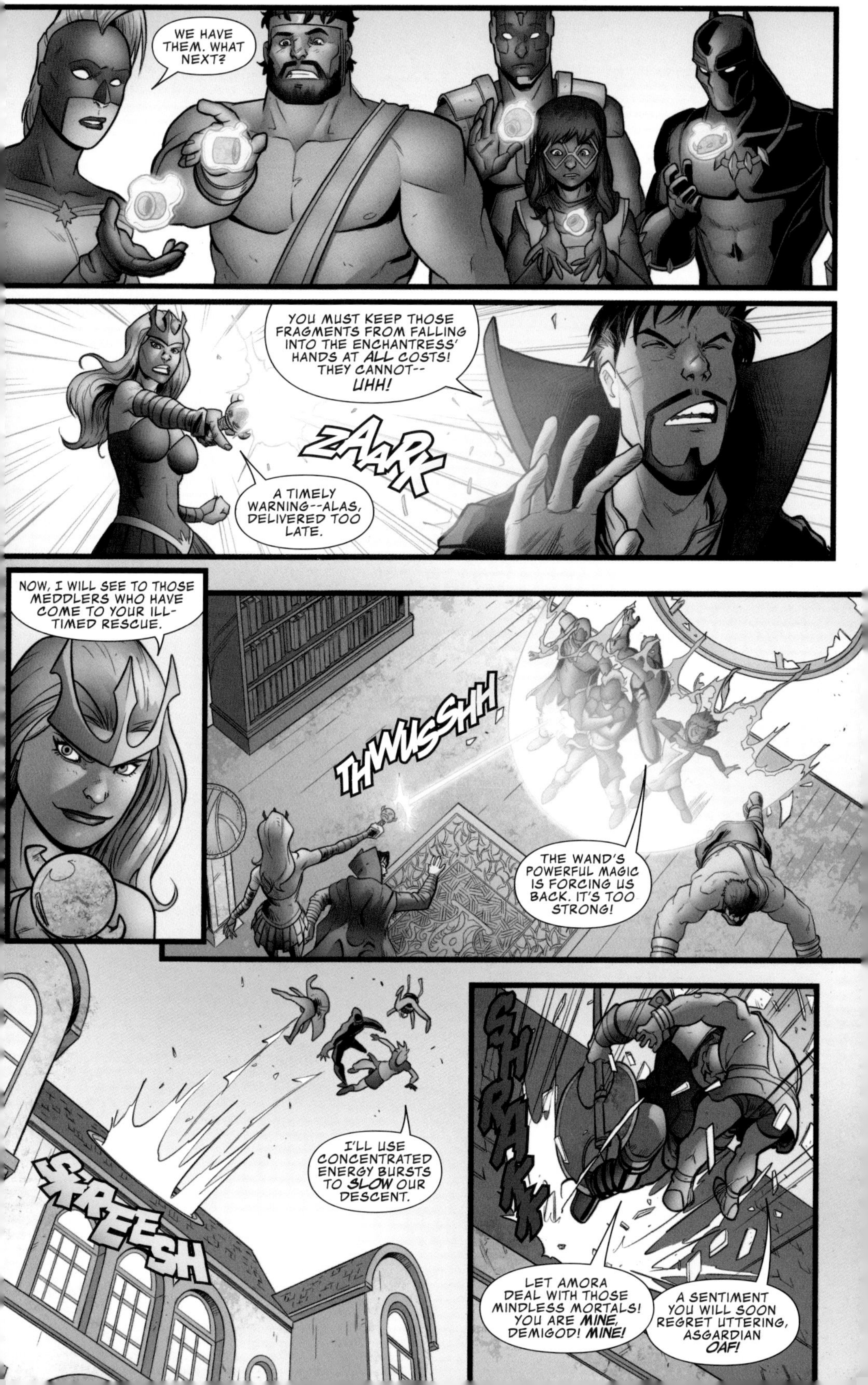
WE HAVE THEM. WHAT NEXT?
YOU MUST KEEP THOSE FRAGMENTS FROM FALLING INTO THE ENCHANTRESS' HANDS AT ALL COSTS! THEY CANNOT-- UHH!
ZAARK
A TIMELY WARNING--ALAS, DELIVERED TOO LATE.
NOW, I WILL SEE TO THOSE MEDDLERS WHO HAVE COME TO YOUR ILL-TIMED RESCUE.
THWUSSHH
THE WAND'S POWERFUL MAGIC IS FORCING US BACK. IT'S TOO STRONG!
I'LL USE CONCENTRATED ENERGY BURSTS TO SLOW OUR DESCENT.
SKREESH
SHRAKK
LET AMORA DEAL WITH THOSE MINDLESS MORTALS! YOU ARE MINE, DEMIGOD! MINE!
A SENTIMENT YOU WILL SOON REGRET UTTERING, ASGARDIAN OAF!

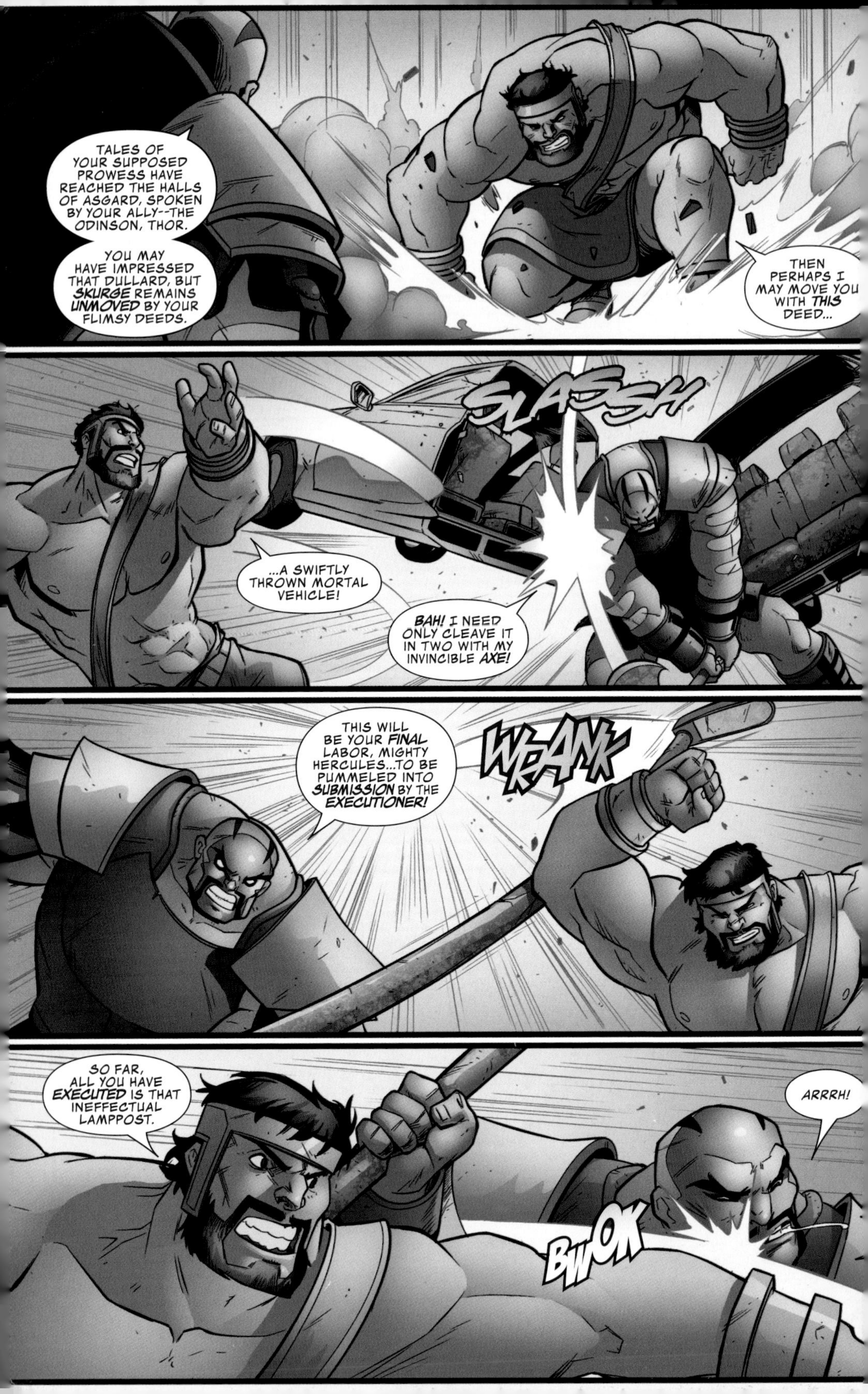
TALES OF YOUR SUPPOSED PROWESS HAVE REACHED THE HALLS OF ASGARD, SPOKEN BY YOUR ALLY--THE ODINSON, THOR.
YOU MAY HAVE IMPRESSED THAT DULLARD, BUT SKURGE REMAINS UNMOVED BY YOUR FLIMSY DEEDS.
THEN PERHAPS I MAY MOVE YOU WITH THIS DEED...
...A SWIFTLY THROWN MORTAL VEHICLE!
SLASSH
BAH! I NEED ONLY CLEAVE IT IN TWO WITH MY INVINCIBLE AXE!
THIS WILL BE YOUR FINAL LABOR, MIGHTY HERCULES...TO BE PUMMELED INTO SUBMISSION BY THE EXECUTIONER!
WRANK
SO FAR, ALL YOU HAVE EXECUTED IS THAT INEFFECTUAL LAMPPOST.
ARRRH!
BWOK

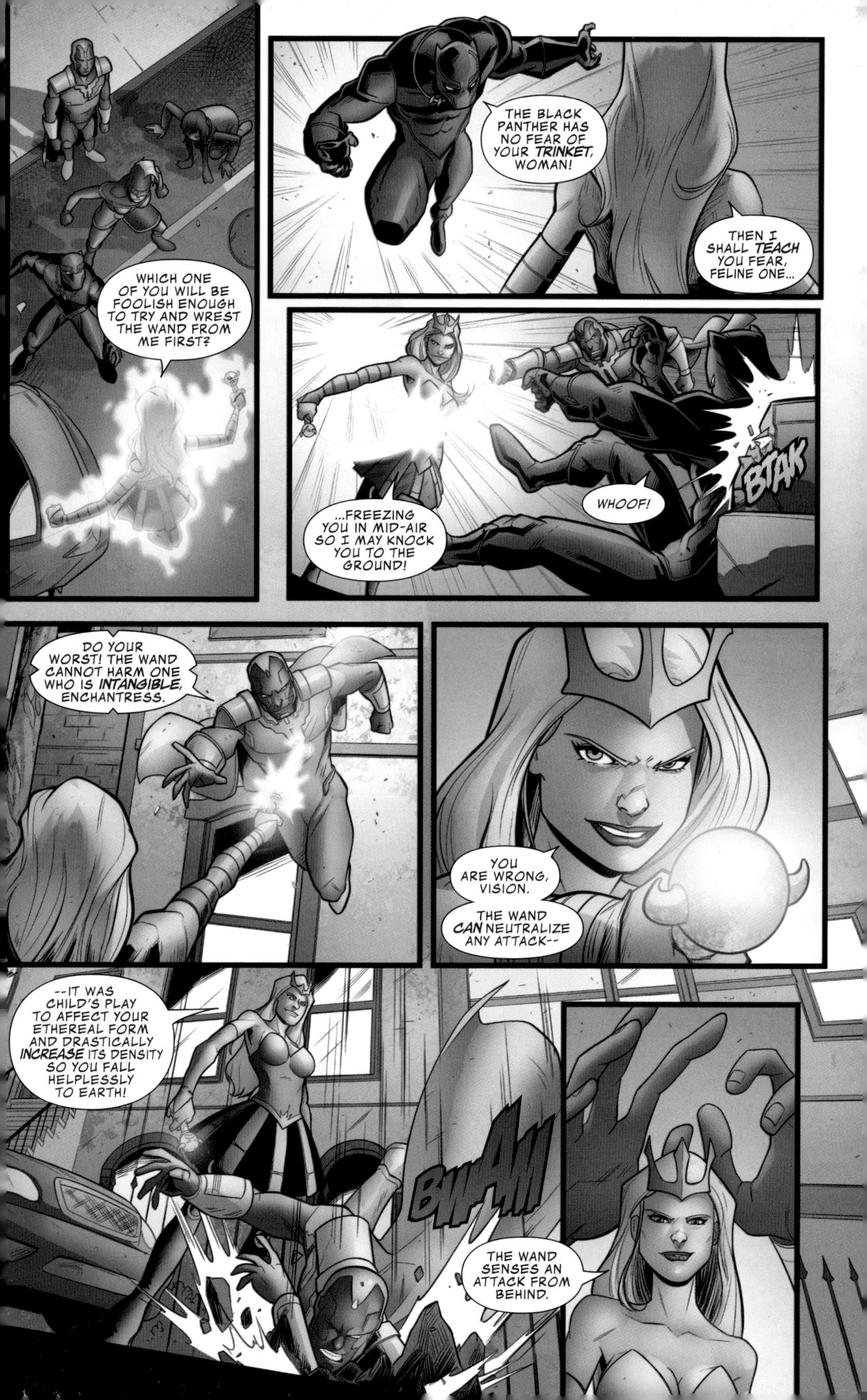
WHICH ONE OF YOU WILL BE FOOLISH ENOUGH TO TRY AND WREST THE WAND FROM ME FIRST?
THE BLACK PANTHER HAS NO FEAR OF YOUR TRINKET, WOMAN!
THEN I SHALL TEACH YOU FEAR, FELINE ONE...
...FREEZING YOU IN MID-AIR SO I MAY KNOCK YOU TO THE GROUND!
WHOOF!
BTAK
DO YOUR WORST! THE WAND CANNOT HARM ONE WHO IS INTANGIBLE, ENCHANTRESS.
YOU ARE WRONG, VISION.
THE WAND CAN NEUTRALIZE ANY ATTACK--
--IT WAS CHILD'S PLAY TO AFFECT YOUR ETHEREAL FORM AND DRASTICALLY INCREASE ITS DENSITY SO YOU FALL HELPLESSLY TO EARTH!
BWAM
THE WAND SENSES AN ATTACK FROM BEHIND.

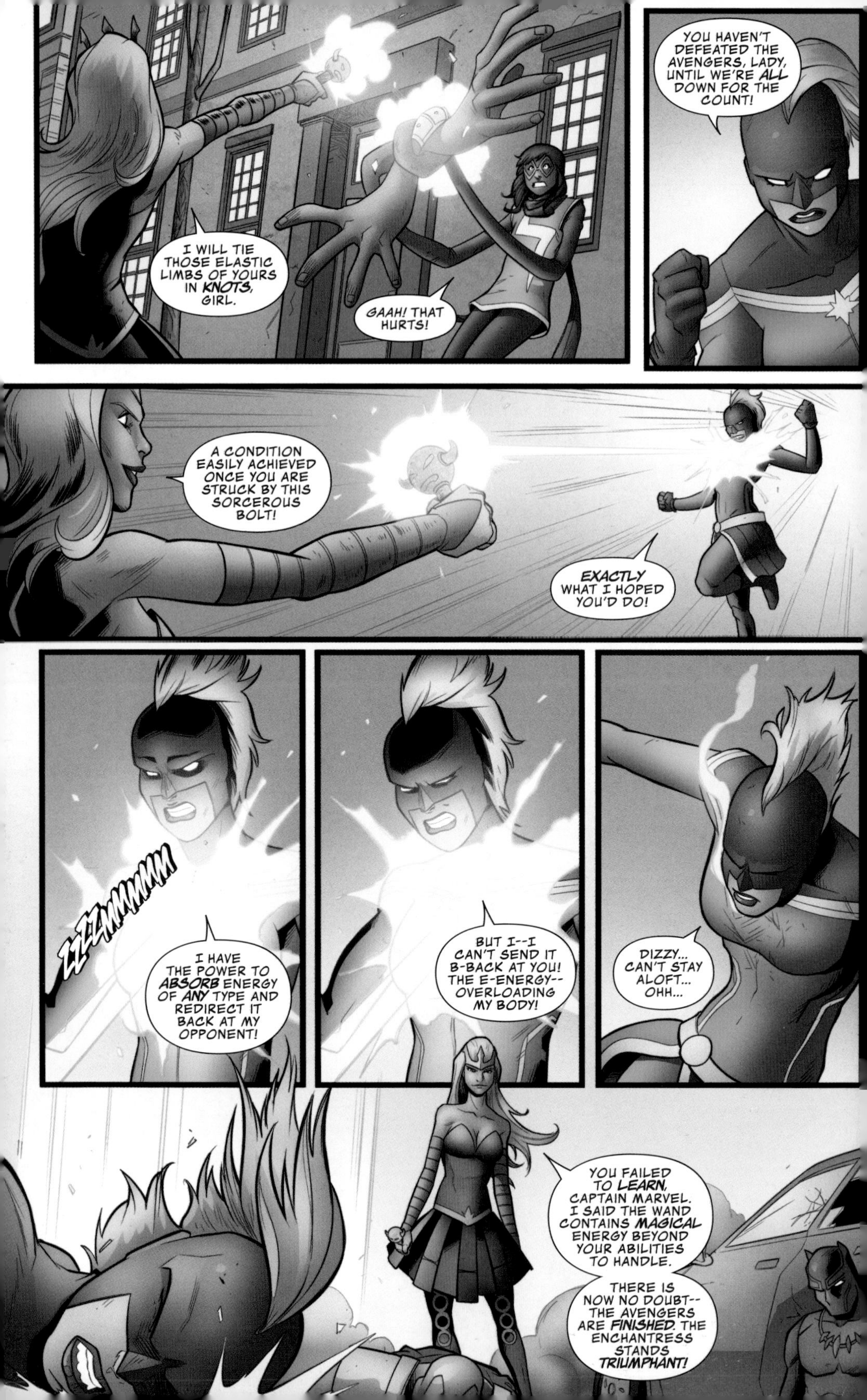
I WILL TIE THOSE ELASTIC LIMBS OF YOURS IN KNOTS, GIRL.
GAAH! THAT HURTS!
YOU HAVEN'T DEFEATED THE AVENGERS, LADY, UNTIL WE'RE ALL DOWN FOR THE COUNT!
A CONDITION EASILY ACHIEVED ONCE YOU ARE STRUCK BY THIS SORCEROUS BOLT!
EXACTLY WHAT I HOPED YOU'D DO!
ZZZZMMMMMM
I HAVE THE POWER TO ABSORB ENERGY OF ANY TYPE AND REDIRECT IT BACK AT MY OPPONENT!
BUT I--I CAN'T SEND IT B-BACK AT YOU! THE E-ENERGY--OVERLOADING MY BODY!
DIZZY... CAN'T STAY ALOFT... OHH...
YOU FAILED TO LEARN, CAPTAIN MARVEL. I SAID THE WAND CONTAINS MAGICAL ENERGY BEYOND YOUR ABILITIES TO HANDLE.
THERE IS NOW NO DOUBT--THE AVENGERS ARE FINISHED. THE ENCHANTRESS STANDS TRIUMPHANT!

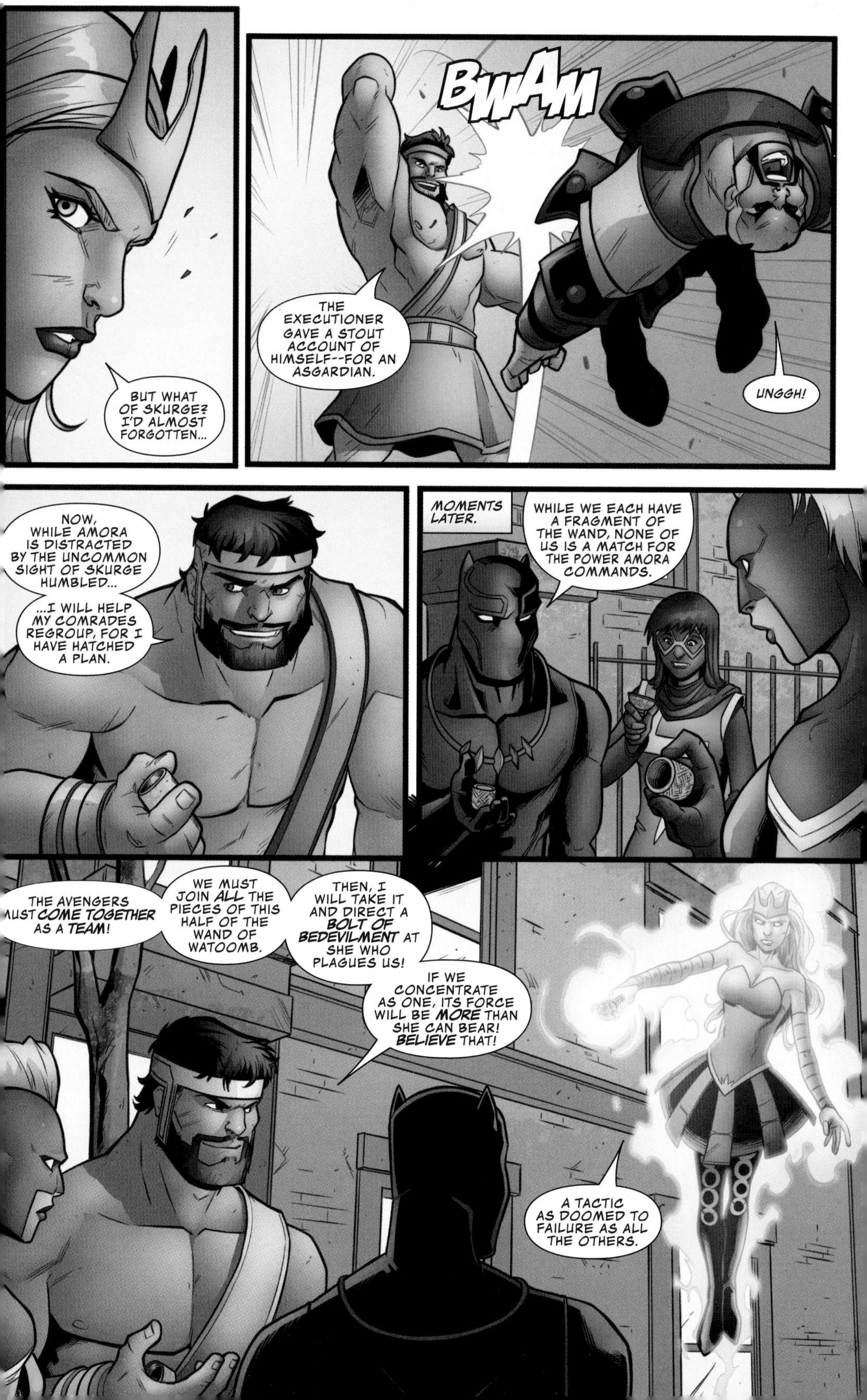
BUT WHAT OF SKURGE? I'D ALMOST FORGOTTEN...
BWAM
THE EXECUTIONER GAVE A STOUT ACCOUNT OF HIMSELF--FOR AN ASGARDIAN.
UNGGH!
NOW, WHILE AMORA IS DISTRACTED BY THE UNCOMMON SIGHT OF SKURGE HUMBLED...
...I WILL HELP MY COMRADES REGROUP, FOR I HAVE HATCHED A PLAN.
MOMENTS LATER.
WHILE WE EACH HAVE A FRAGMENT OF THE WAND, NONE OF US IS A MATCH FOR THE POWER AMORA COMMANDS.
THE AVENGERS MUST COME TOGETHER AS A TEAM!
WE MUST JOIN ALL THE PIECES OF THIS HALF OF THE WAND OF WATOOMB.
THEN, I WILL TAKE IT AND DIRECT A BOLT OF BEDEVILMENT AT SHE WHO PLAGUES US!
IF WE CONCENTRATE AS ONE, ITS FORCE WILL BE MORE THAN SHE CAN BEAR! BELIEVE THAT!
A TACTIC AS DOOMED TO FAILURE AS ALL THE OTHERS.

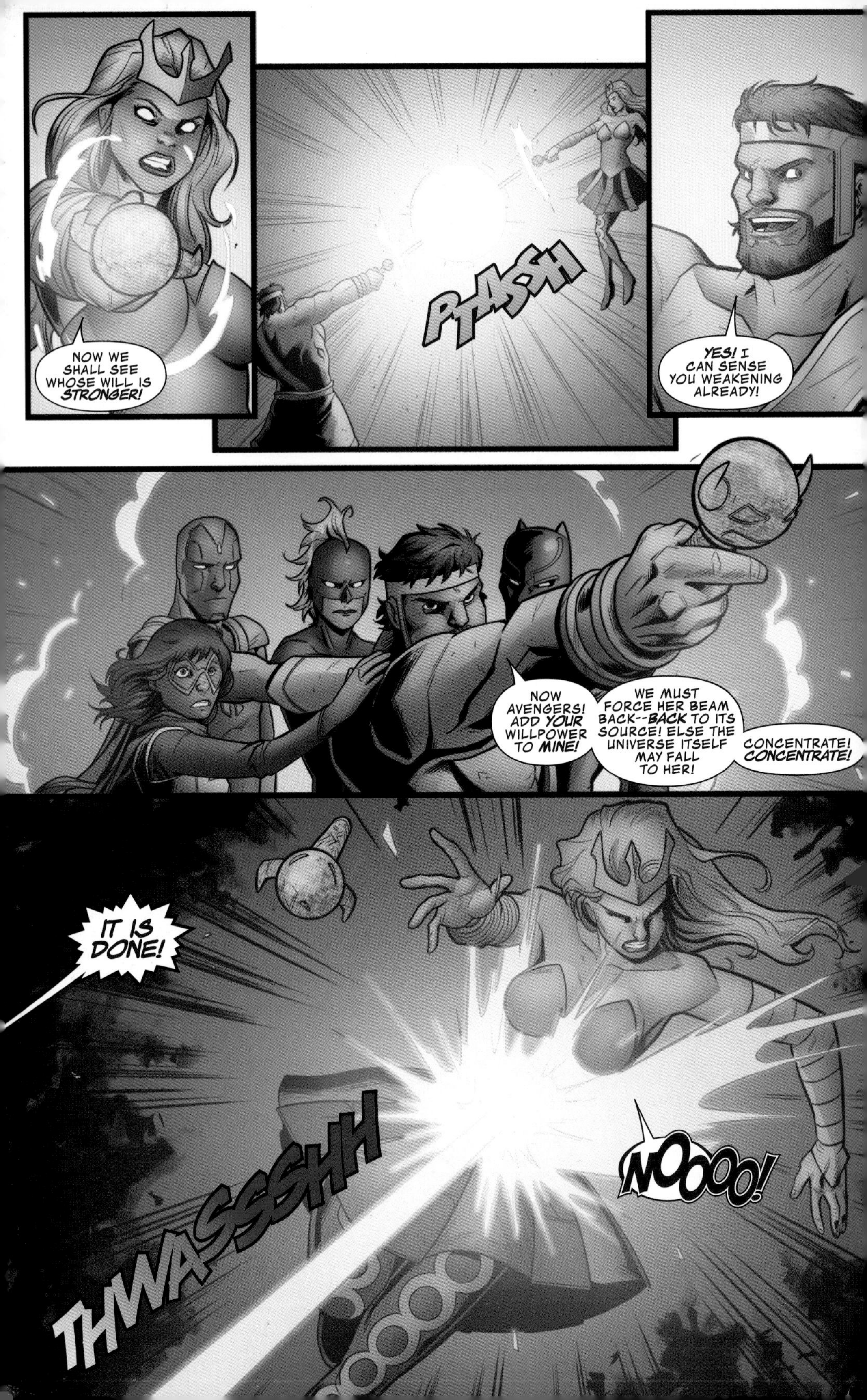
NOW WE SHALL SEE WHOSE WILL IS STRONGER!
PTASH
YES! I CAN SENSE YOU WEAKENING ALREADY!
NOW AVENGERS! ADD YOUR WILLPOWER TO MINE!
WE MUST FORCE HER BEAM BACK--BACK TO ITS SOURCE! ELSE THE UNIVERSE ITSELF MAY FALL TO HER!
CONCENTRATE! CONCENTRATE!
IT IS DONE!
THWASSSHH
NOOOO!

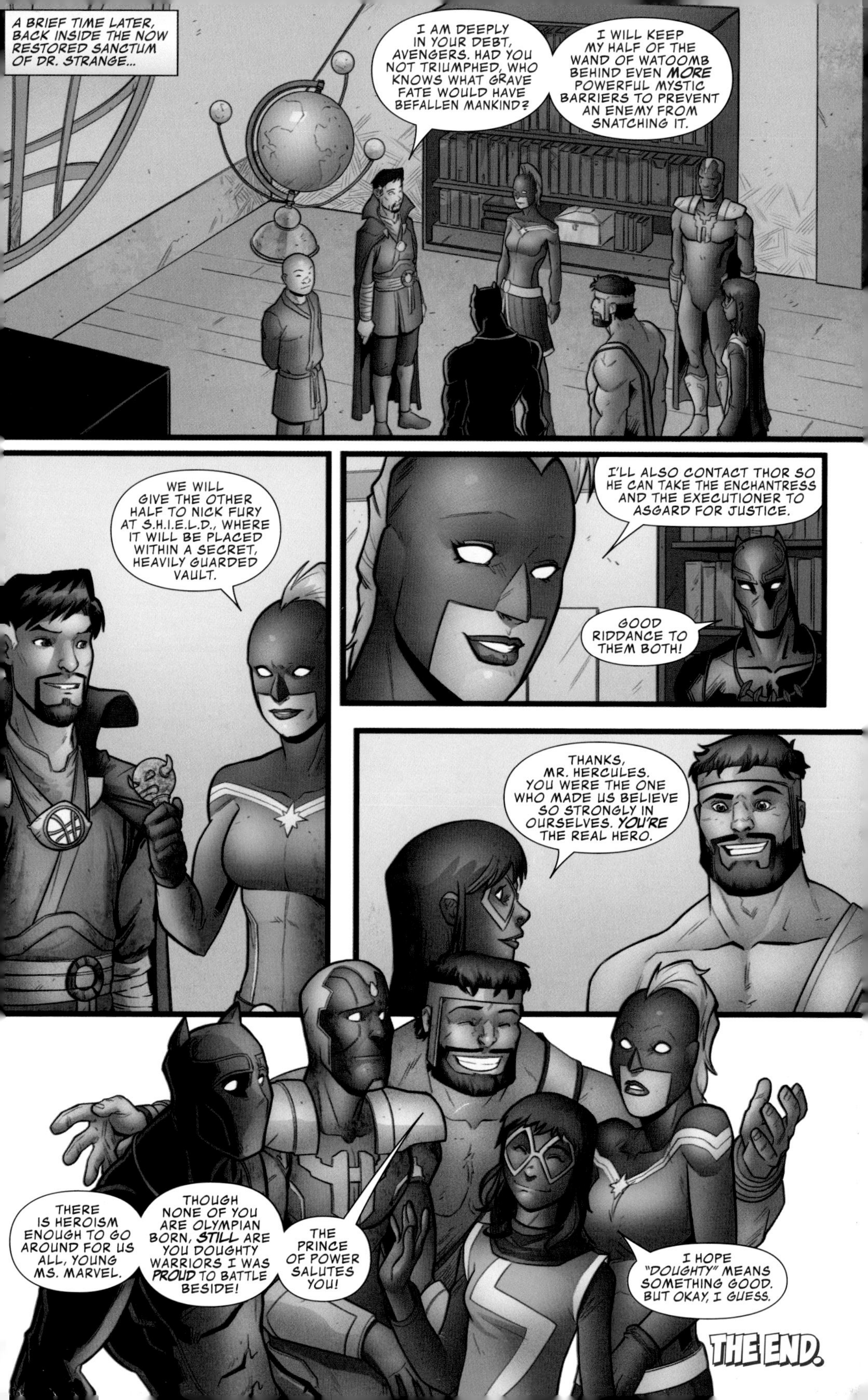

A BRIEF TIME LATER, BACK INSIDE THE NOW RESTORED SANCTUM OF DR. STRANGE...
I AM DEEPLY IN YOUR DEBT, AVENGERS. HAD YOU NOT TRIUMPHED, WHO KNOWS WHAT GRAVE FATE WOULD HAVE BEFALLEN MANKIND?
I WILL KEEP MY HALF OF THE WAND OF WATOOMB BEHIND EVEN MORE POWERFUL MYSTIC BARRIERS TO PREVENT AN ENEMY FROM SNATCHING IT.
WE WILL GIVE THE OTHER HALF TO NICK FURY AT S.H.I.E.L.D., WHERE IT WILL BE PLACED WITHIN A SECRET, HEAVILY GUARDED VAULT.
I'LL ALSO CONTACT THOR SO HE CAN TAKE THE ENCHANTRESS AND THE EXECUTIONER TO ASGARD FOR JUSTICE.
GOOD RIDDANCE TO THEM BOTH!
THANKS, MR. HERCULES. YOU WERE THE ONE WHO MADE US BELIEVE SO STRONGLY IN OURSELVES. YOU'RE THE REAL HERO.
THERE IS HEROISM ENOUGH TO GO AROUND FOR US ALL, YOUNG MS. MARVEL.
THOUGH NONE OF YOU ARE OLYMPIAN BORN, STILL ARE YOU DOUGHTY WARRIORS I WAS PROUD TO BATTLE BESIDE!
THE PRINCE OF POWER SALUTES YOU!
I HOPE "DOUGHTY" MEANS SOMETHING GOOD. BUT OKAY, I GUESS.
THE END.

Here's a special sneak peek of
Marvel Super Hero Adventures: To Wakanda and Beyond!

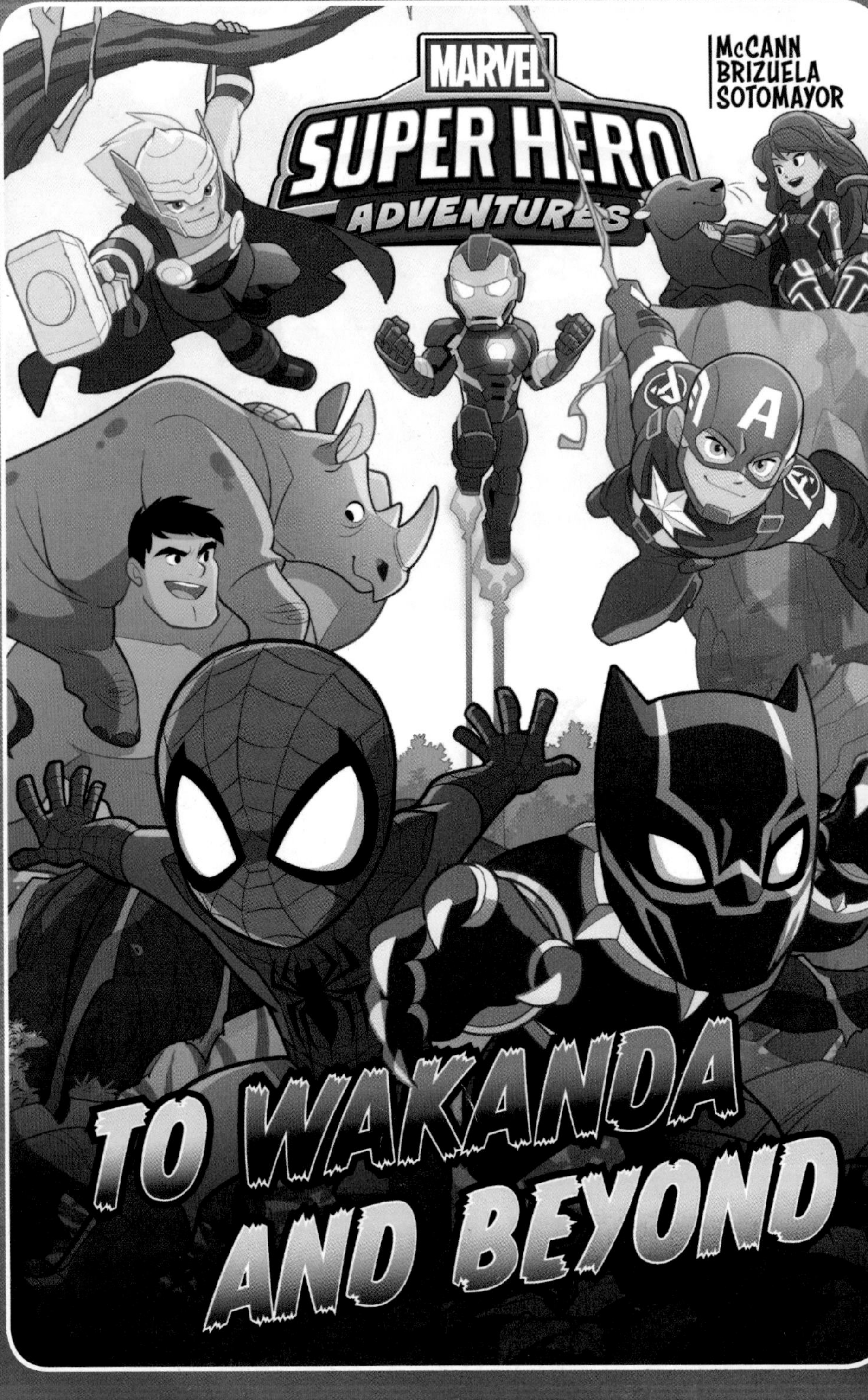
MARVEL
SUPER HERO
ADVENTURES
McCANN
BRIZUELA
SOTOMAYOR
TO WAKANDA
AND BEYOND

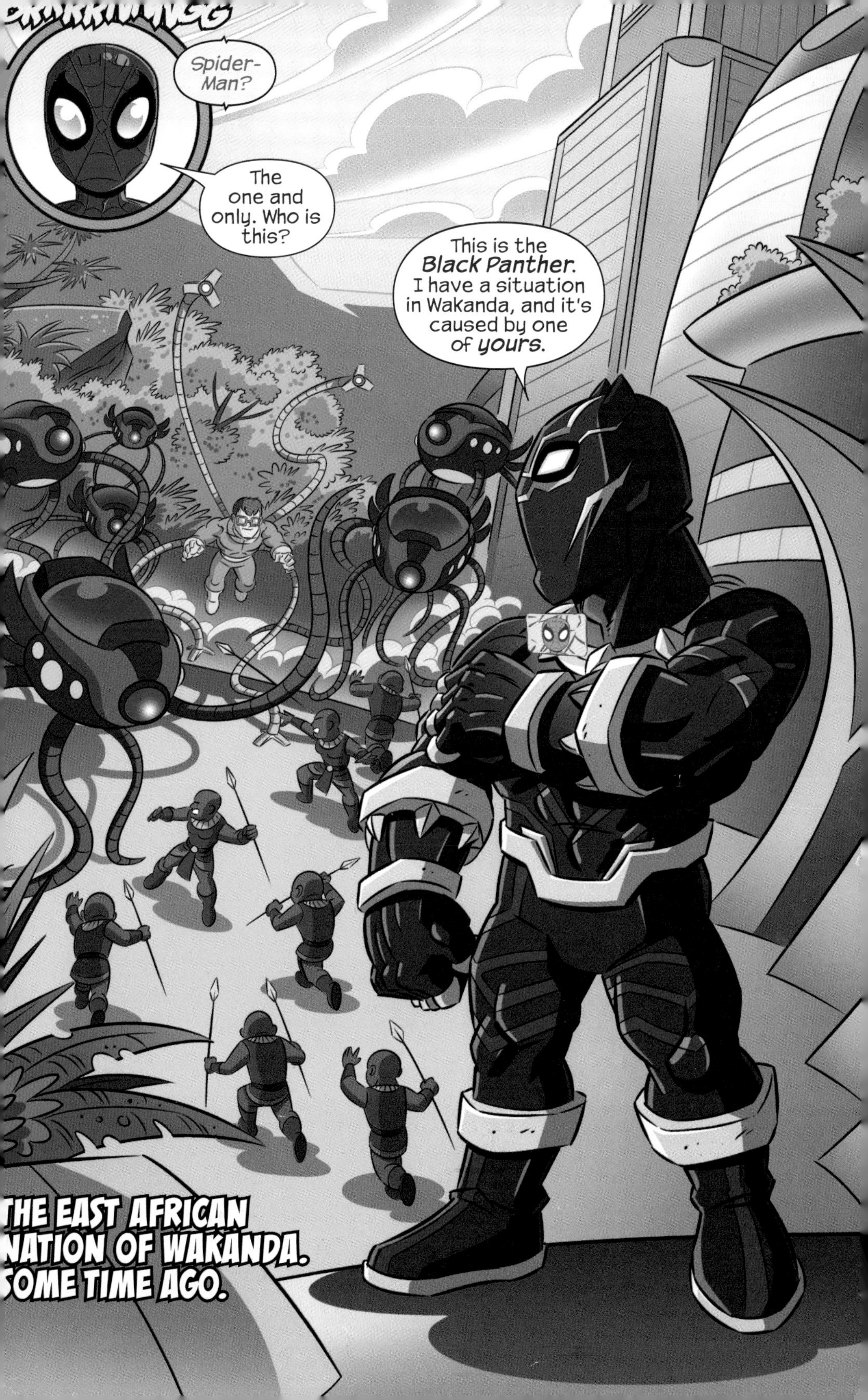
Spider-Man?
The one and only. Who is this?
This is the Black Panther. I have a situation in Wakanda, and it's caused by one of yours.
THE EAST AFRICAN NATION OF WAKANDA. SOME TIME AGO.

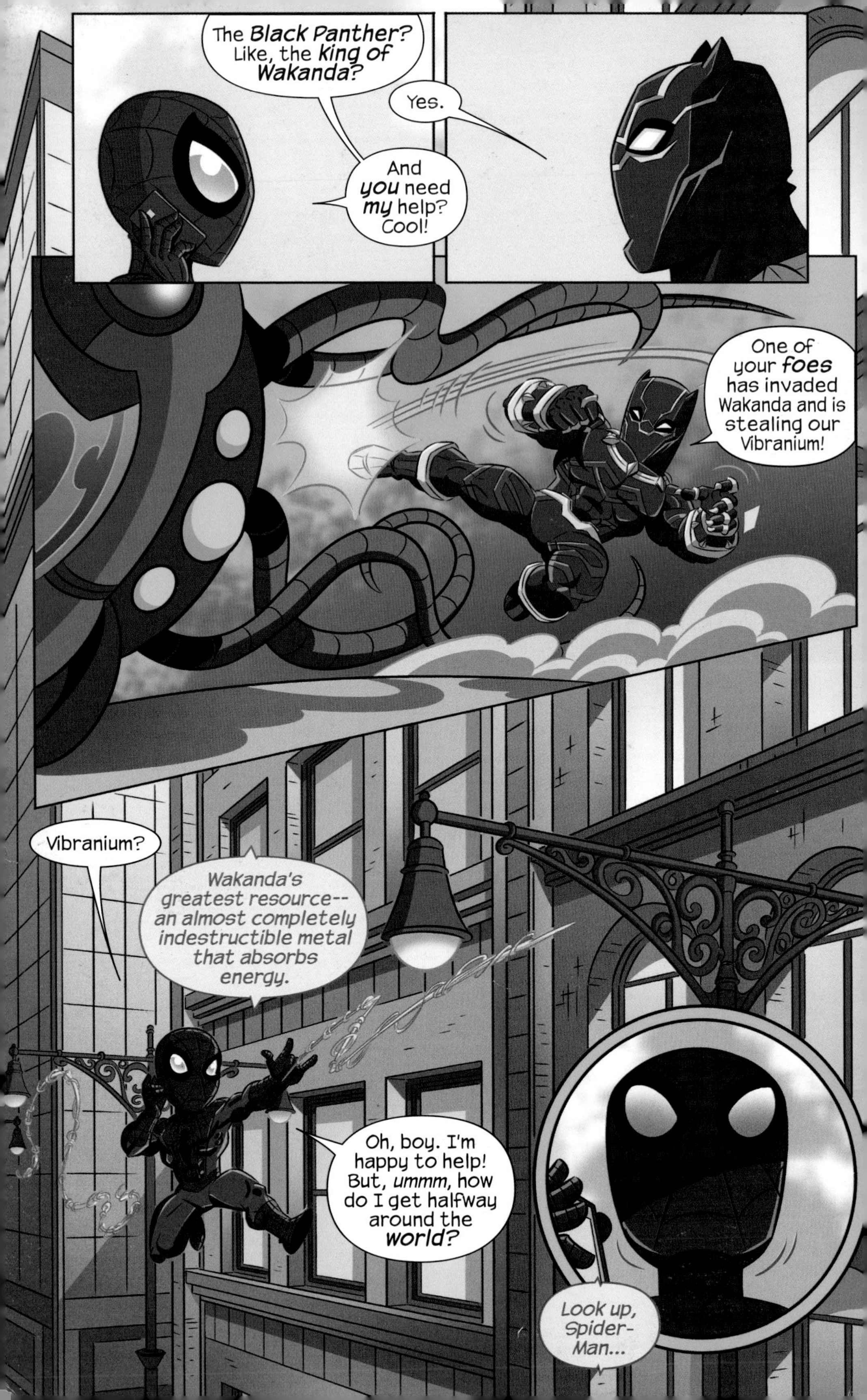
The Black Panther? Like, the king of Wakanda?
Yes.
And you need my help? Cool!
One of your foes has invaded Wakanda and is stealing our Vibranium!
Vibranium?
Wakanda's greatest resource-- an almost completely indestructible metal that absorbs energy.
Oh, boy. I'm happy to help! But, ummm, how do I get halfway around the world?
Look up, Spider-Man...

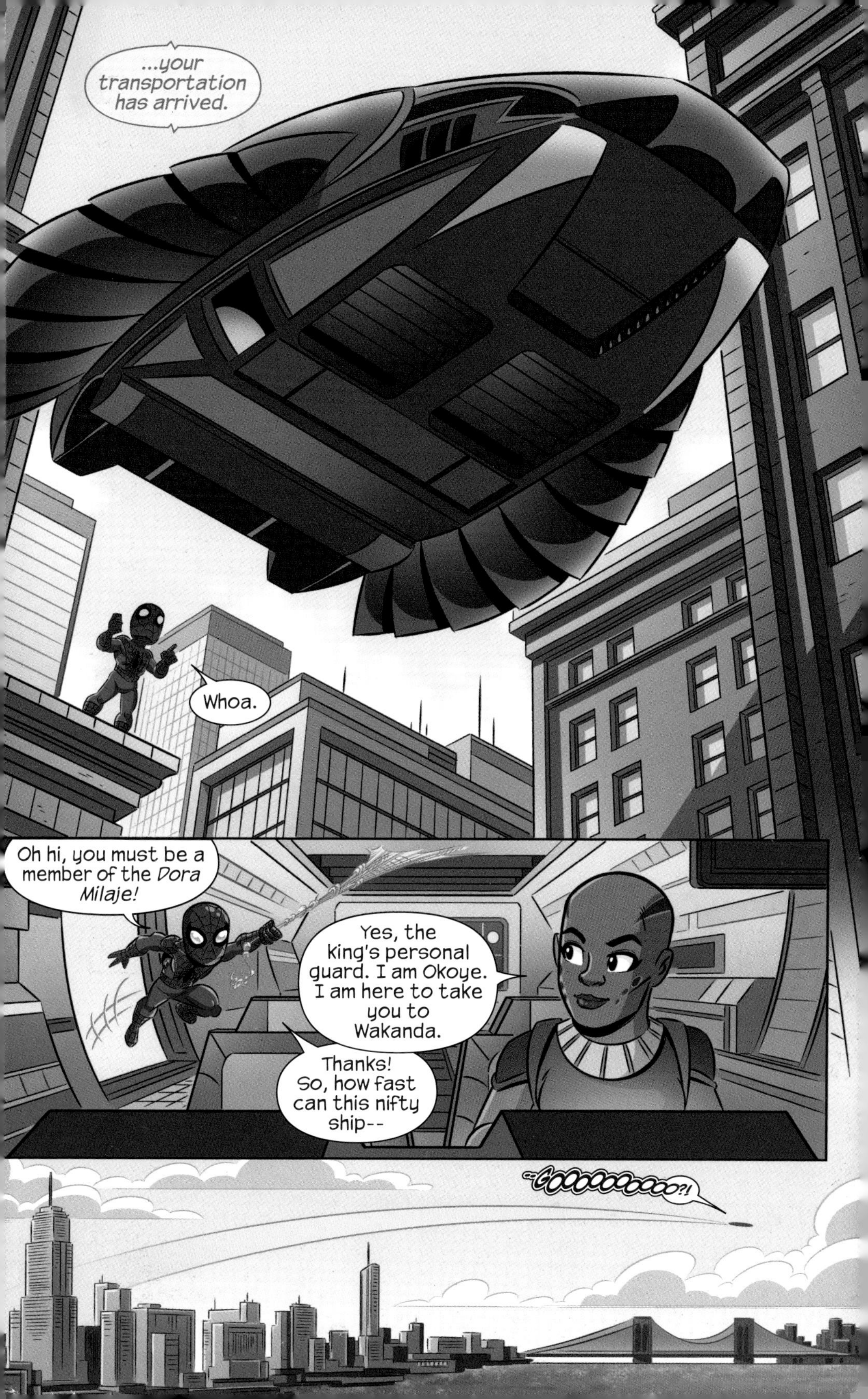
...your transportation has arrived.
Whoa.
Oh hi, you must be a member of the *Dora Milaje!*
Yes, the king's personal guard. I am Okoye. I am here to take you to Wakanda.
Thanks! So, how fast can this nifty ship--
--GOOOOOOOOOO?!

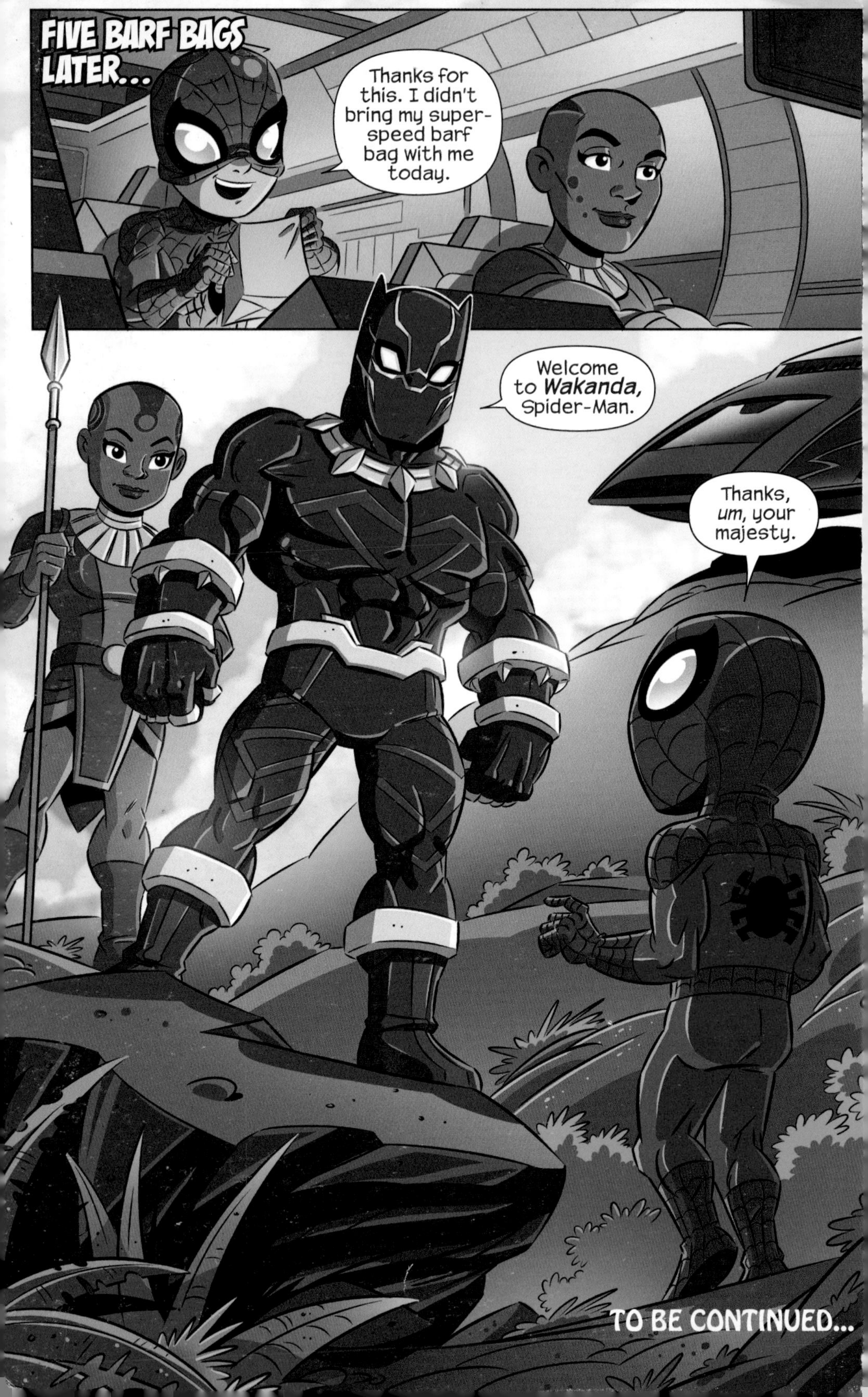
FIVE BARF BAGS LATER...
Thanks for this. I didn't bring my super-speed barf bag with me today.
Welcome to Wakanda, Spider-Man.
Thanks, um, your majesty.
TO BE CONTINUED...